PRAISE FOR ANIA AHLBORN

"…genuinely scary…damn good…"
-Cemetery Dance on *Apart in the Dark*

———

"…good, spooky stuff."
-Jack Ketchum on *Within These Walls*

———

"…creeps under your skin and stays there.
It's insidious…"
-The New York Times on *Within These Walls*

———

"For fans of sleepless nights."
-Portland Monthly Magazine on *Within These Walls*

ANIA AHLBORN

Dark Across the Bay

Born in Ciechanow Poland, Ania has always been drawn to the dark, mysterious, and sometimes morbid side of life. Her earliest childhood memory is of crawling through a hole in the chain link fence that separated her family home from the large wooded cemetery. She'd spend hours among the headstones, breaking up bouquets of silk flowers so that everyone had their equal share.

Ania's first novel, *Seed*, was self-published. It clawed its way up the Amazon charts to the number one horror spot, earning her a multi-book deal and a key to the kingdom of the macabre. Eight years later, her work has been lauded by the likes of Publishers Weekly, New York Daily News, and the New York Times.

She lives in North Carolina with her family.

Dark Across the Bay is her eleventh published work.

WWW.ANIAAHLBORN.COM

ALSO BY ANIA AHLBORN

Seed

The Neighbors

The Shuddering

The Bird Eater

Within These Walls

The Pretty Ones

Brother

I Call Upon Thee

The Devil Crept In

Apart in the Dark

If You See Her

Dark Across the Bay

ANIA AHLBORN

This is a work of fiction. Names, characters, businesses, organizations, places, events, and incidents either are the product of the author's imagination or are used fictitiously. Any resemblance to actual persons, living or dead, events, or locales is entirely coincidental.

FAMILY

AN INTRODUCTION BY JOSH MALERMAN

Every family is an isolated incident. Worthy of investigation.

No matter how good or bad you have it, there's darkness and there's joy. There's confusion and miscommunication. There's someone who isn't speaking their mind and there's someone who's speaking theirs too often. There's someone to blame, there's no one to blame. Good times, bad times, ugly times, too. It's a disaster, it's the greatest thing ever; it's who you are and who you are not. And meanwhile, the biggest problem of all is that the only people qualified to launch the investigation, the only people who have all the evidence, are the family members themselves.

It's a constant conflict of interest...no?

And so...who to trust? Whose motivation is noble and whose is not? Who is acting (sometimes even abysmally) in the name of saving the family, keeping it together, keeping it strong?

Are we all raised by wolves?

Maybe. Yet, there *is* an outside party, there is someone who might tell the family's story from an objective distance. Someone to lay out the facts, the comeuppances, the karma. The one person fitted with wings to give us an aerial view, to show us who got what they deserved, who got screwed, and who made it out alive.

That person is the author. The writer. The seer of such troublesome, and fabulous, dynamics.

Meet...Ania Ahlborn.

And in *Dark Across the Bay,* meet the Parrishes, too.

See, the Parrishes have problems. Enough so that they've booked a few days at a gorgeous solitary house on an island off the coast of Maine. They really need this. But what family doesn't have issues? And who can blame Mom and Dad for thinking complete isolation is the way to cure what ails them? In theory, this is a great plan. In theory, this could work! But in the hands of Ania Ahlborn, chances are, whether it works or not, things are going to get a little bit...

Scary.

None of us writers (should) care about labels, Thriller versus Horror, genre be damned, even if we wear horror with pride. But Ahlborn nailed something with this book, something bigger than the word count: while *Dark Across the Bay* has all the fixings of what the publishing world would deem a "thriller," it still acts as a horror story, i.e., it scares the shit out of you. And more: it's as unsettling and creeping as any ghost story you've read.

Every family is also a ghost story. Did you know?

Specific moments haunt, and sometimes that haunt is welcome, and sometimes it's not. In every family, Dad or Mom invariably do something wrong (often, much more than wrong), whether either is a "good" or "bad" person. And the ghosts of those past events stand in the shadows of the basement every time you need to get the laundry from below. History whistles in the middle of the night. It weighs enough to creak the floorboards out in the hall.

Who can get any sleep with the noise familial history makes?

The Parrishes sure can't. Even when they can. Even when they feel good about the decisions they've made. No matter what they do, they're haunted by decisions they've made before.

And this goes for all four of them. Ezra, the seemingly aloof manchild of a father; Poppy, the piqued mother on a mission; Leo, the grieving yet forward-thinking son; and Lark, the lovestruck, neurotic sister whose biggest fault may simply be that she's still young.

This family loves each other! Don't they? They can work things out! Can't they? Well, it's not so simple, as, in every family, one member's unreasonable self-loathing is another's unreasonable rationalization. Dynamics have a way of grating, highs and lows often bump heads, and it's those moments that become the *incidents*...the *hauntings*...the...

The horrors.

Yes, every family is a horror story, too. Bet you knew that.

And damn, if Ania Ahlborn doesn't know how to unsettle.

I imagine it's in her, in her voice, naturally, as there isn't a moment in the pages that follow that feels inorganic, unlike her, forced. Some writers have that, you know, that way about them, where everything they present suggests the bulk of the iceberg below, in this case: dark waters. Maybe it's Poppy's actual fear of water, yet she booked a weekend on an island. Or maybe it's the feeling that Ezra isn't aloof after all, but intentionally keeping quiet. Possibly it's Leo's future plans, the ticking clock of actual Time he has remaining in close proximity to his family. And maybe, just maybe, it's Lark's being between personas, as most sixteen-year-olds are.

All unsettling. Naturally.

And we, the readers, feel all of this, on every page, in every scene. Ahlborn doesn't relent. But that doesn't mean she bludgeons us to death, either. Herein lies a story told by a truly gifted artist, an author who has long found her voice, and doesn't get caught up in labels, rules, expectations. For this, she's the perfect person to tell the story of the Parrish family. The only.

Ah, family…

For, what is family if not an entity with an unavoidable voice? An organism the defies easy classification? And, even when all the members are asleep, a *thing* that yet dreams?

I'm way excited for you to meet the Parrishes. But more importantly, I'm thrilled for you to experience what I just did: an unforgettable story from Ania Ahlborn.

Some authors have a way of slipping the story under your skin, scaring you, long before the incidents, the hauntings, and the horrors arrive.

Just when everything feels normal, good, safe.

Good luck, I say. And when you're done, maybe hand the story off to a brother, a sister, Mom or Dad. Someone in your family, anyway.

Someone to share the horrors with.

Josh Malerman
Michigan, 2021

DISCOVERY

SEEING THEIR LITTLE ISLAND creep into view made Diedre Allan's stomach twist. It was crazy that they still owned it, crazier still that they had dropped their entire life savings to buy twenty-two acres of stone, sand, and the rustic Shingle-style home that stood among the trees. A long pier jutted into the water, serving as both a boat dock and a spot to relax in a pair of Adirondack chairs. It was quintessential Maine; the perfect place to watch sunsets and the turning of the leaves, to forget the world beyond Raven's Bay.

During family reunions, all of Silas's side would come, but only a few awkward stragglers from Diedre's side would show. Her niece, Gigi, was the one most impressed with the island, having loved the place since she'd been a girl. She and her cousins had spent countless hours within the nooks and crannies hidden inside the walls. They'd knock from within hidden compartments like phantoms unseen, at times frustrating their parents with refusals to reveal themselves for dinner and sleep. Gigi had adored the island home so thoroughly as a girl that, as an adult, she'd booked it for herself as a personal getaway a handful of times. Her love of the house was what had given Diedre the idea of renting it out in the first place. Because after thirty years of living there, a heart attack had sent Diedre and Silas fleeing to mainland Raven's Head, and suddenly the place had no occupants. No breath. No pulse.

Diedre had been curled up in a blanket and sitting on the very dock they approached now when, carrying two steaming mugs of coffee, Silas had collapsed to his knees. Had the Coast Guard not arrived when they had, Silas wouldn't have seen another sunrise.

Silas had taken convincing when it came time to leave. Diedre, however, had been quietly relieved to finally get off that rock. She had always hated the house's seemingly pointless doors, the secret passageways and windowless rooms that had so thoroughly delighted the children. But despite Silas's eventual agreement to move, he wouldn't stand for selling, so she hadn't bothered to suggest it. They'd visit on occasion, watch the leaves on adjacent islands turn red and orange and brilliant hues of gold. But when they were away—which would be for most of the year—they'd line their pockets with rent money. As it turned out, strangers were just as smitten with the island as the children of Diedre and Silas's past.

Renting the place out on AirBnB had been Diedre's idea. *As long as you know there's going to be trouble,* Silas had warned, and he had been right. That was the thing about rental property: you collected the money, but you also had to clean up the mess. Diedre usually had a service do most of the work, but this autumn had been booked up solid until the Allans' own reserved week. The idea of having a cleaning crew flit about the house while they settled in gave Diedre the creeps. She could scrub a couple of toilets, could wipe the counters down with Lysol and wash the sheets.

Steering the boat by its outboard motor, Silas regarded *Easy Livin'* the way a cowboy would an obstinate horse. As the motor cut and *Easy Livin'* cruised up to the dock, Diedre noticed Silas glaring at the pier's tie-off. Part of the dock was singed, blackened with soot as if by lightning strike.

"What in the world?" She squinted at the five or so feet of darkened wood, then shook her head with a sigh. The Allans had discovered their fair share of damage in the past, from scuffed-up floorboards to Sharpie markers decorating the walls of the upstairs hall. The scariest had been the ghosts of dead bonfires, one of which had appeared to have raged so out of control it had set some of the groundcover alight, having crept dangerously close to the spruce trees beyond the beach. It had left Diedre to wonder whether, one day, they would arrive to find the island vacant and the house burned to the ground.

Silas lashed *Easy Livin'* to the pylon as a muffled grumble skirted his lips.

"Goddamn son of a—"

"Cool it, Si," she cut him off. "We don't know what happened yet."

She busied herself with a picnic basket she'd stuffed full of supplies that needed restocking—Lysol and toilet bowl cleaner, garbage disposal tabs and a fresh roll of trash bags; just another convenience traded for the luxury of seclusion.

"They may not be responsible," she said of their most recent tenants. The damage could have been done by any number of the other renters that had used the house in the past handful of weeks. God knew there had been enough of them. The property management company was supposed to alert the Allans to any damage as soon as they discovered it, but there had been incidents that had fallen between the cracks before. Besides, the Parrishes had struck Diedre as a nice family. She had yet to meet them in person but doubted they had anything to do with what was now the focus of Silas's scorn.

"How am I supposed to fix this?" Silas asked, looping the rope around the tie-off as aggressively as one would loop a noose around the neck of an accused.

Placing one hand on the dock, Diedre braced herself, then strong-armed the picnic basket up from around her Bean boots. She hefted up her patchwork skirt to her knees and climbed onto steady ground.

"What in the *hell?*" Silas continued to feed into his aggravation, grabbing hold of a rope lashed to the pylon beneath where he'd moored their own boat. Its end was burnt.

"Did they return the commuter?" Diedre asked.

It had been less than a few hours since the Parrishes had been expected to check out. She hadn't been notified by the AirBnB app that they had done so, but it wasn't the first time renters had forgone the check-out process and simply left. It was annoying, but no harm done. Diedre shrugged it off as she watched her husband prepare for the uncomfortable task of hauling himself out of *Easy Livin'* and onto the dock.

"Here," she said, extending a hand his way, but he waved it off despite his bad knee. His back was also touch-and-go, seizing up on him if he so much as shifted his weight too much to one side. His heart condition was simply the cherry on top of a sundae of suffering. But even a pacemaker couldn't compete with his bullheadedness.

Silas swatted at her hand, and she pulled it back.

"The commuter," she said again. "Is it at the dock?"

The commuter was little more than a dinghy the Allans had purchased after their first few tenants kept calling, kept asking how they were supposed to get off the island to go shopping or have dinner in Raven's Head. She and Silas had considered only renting to folks who provided their own watercraft, but they eventually caved and bought a little boat as an added convenience. Now, after renters were ferried to the island by Gill, they could go back and forth from the house to the mainland whenever they pleased.

Silas groaned as he hefted himself up, then paused to take a breath. "Didn't check with Gill," he said through gritted teeth. "Didn't think I had to."

"You should give him a ring," Diedre said, resting the picnic basket on the swell of one of her hips. "If you can catch a signal, at least." The island wasn't so far out into the bay that there was no cell phone service, but it was notoriously spotty.

"Yeah, yeah," Silas mumbled, securing the tie-off before slowly straightening to stand. A moment later, he was reaching for his flip phone and holding it up to the sky.

"You know that doesn't work out here," she told him, turning away. "Holding it up to heaven doesn't mean God is giving you full bars."

"Maybe one, you merciful bastard?" Silas quipped, then grumbled a few more expletives as she left him to it, holding back a laugh as she moved down the dock.

But her good humor was cut short when, stalking up the stairs of the deck, she spotted the first clue that something was truly amiss. The deck was covered in mud. There was so much of it that it looked purposeful, like an abstract painting dedicated to the island itself. That, however, wasn't what had her frozen in place. No, *that* was left to the door being wide open, those swirls and streaks of dark mud leading all the way inside.

"You've got to be kidding," she whispered to herself. Of all the renters they'd had over the years, they'd experienced their fair share of inconsiderate behavior. Damaged furniture, sticky kitchen floors, clogged toilets, and dirty dishes left piled in the sink. The Sharpie that once decorated the upstairs walls refused to scrub clean; Silas had been left to repaint the board and batten himself. But an open front door? It was a first.

Diedre opened her mouth to yell back to her husband. *Call Gill right now.* But the ominous feeling of the house gave her pause. Renting the place had been *her* idea. If the house had finally been ransacked, then the damage was hers to discover.

She shot a look over her shoulder. Silas was still trying to get a signal, holding the phone over his head, rotating right to left like a rusty weathervane. Seeing him struggling that way only reminded her of just how stubborn he was. It also reminded her that the commuter boat was gone. Certainly, it was back in Raven's Head, which left the question: if the Parrishes had departed the island, why was Diedre suddenly sure there were still people inside?

"Maybe they didn't latch it," she told herself of the door. "Maybe it just blew open." There had been a heavy storm a few nights ago, but today the gilded tree leaves were breathtakingly still.

Stalking up the muddy porch steps, Diedre found herself hesitating after taking the last riser.

"Hello?" She called out, assuring herself that her trepidation was nothing short of ridiculous. Meanwhile, her heart thudded hard within her chest.

She reminded herself that the Parrishes had seemed lovely, that they had come with a recommendation. The woman who had reached out to her on the AirBnB site was over-the-moon excited when Diedre had shuffled a few dates around to accept their request. *Oh, thank goodness,* Poppy Parrish had written. *You have no idea how much my family and I need this.*

And yet, Diedre continued to approach the door with bated breath, sure that someone would come blasting through it at any moment, scaring her half to death.

"Hello?" she repeated, her gaze continuously drifting down to her boots, trying to read the smears of mud that slashed across the deck planks the way one would read tea leaves or Tarot cards. But the mud revealed nothing.

She reached out to touch the door frame, as if placing her palm against the wood would allow her to see all that had transpired over the past few days. But rather than diminishing her hesitation, her pulse quickened instead. Because there, a few feet shy of the door jamb where the mud traversed the doorway, the colors changed from a dry brown to a deep rusted red. The moment she saw that swirl of shifting hue, her nostrils flared against the smell.

The picnic basket tumbled from her hip and onto the ground with a heavy thud. Her hand clamped over her mouth to stifle a scream. Not that one would have escaped her, because all at once she couldn't catch her breath. Not to speak. Not to shout. Not to cry out for Silas to hurry and meet her there on the threshold of what had once been their home.

Diedre hadn't yet met the Parrishes in person, but she immediately knew who they were. Four bodies lying on top of their own distinct ink blot like a true crime Rorschach test. Two of the bodies were so thoroughly covered in blood, it looked as though their top halves had been drowned in rust-colored paint. This one, not abstract; this one, still life.

That was the whole of what she was able to take in before she felt her knees buckle and her head spin. Vertigo threw her off-kilter, and before she could yelp for her husband to hurry, her vision went black as she collapsed to the floor. Because in all of her imaginings—raging bonfires, wild parties, crazed toddlers armed with permanent markers—she'd not once imagined something like this.

Who would have imagined it?

We cannot wait, Poppy Parrish's email had read.
Who would have?
It will be a vacation we'll never forget.

ARRIVAL

POPPY

THE BOAT MADE Poppy nervous enough to call the whole thing off. *Stupid,* she thought. *The house is on an island. How had I expected us to get there?* The logistics of it hadn't crossed her mind, at least not until the moment she found herself staring at the extended hand of a man she'd just met. She'd been excited enough about this trip to not sleep a wink last night, but now she was hesitating, eyeing the older gentleman's crooked fingers—the guy who had introduced himself as Gill.

"She's as steady as the *Titanic,*" Gill assured Poppy and her family. "As long as we don't hit any icebergs, we'll make it there just fine."

Poppy had been smitten by the online listing that had popped up on her Facebook feed. Whether it was an ad or a link someone had posted, she couldn't recall, but it made no difference. The house called to her, assuring her it was kismet. She spent hours poring over the AirBnB site, flipping through the forty-some-odd photos of the property on a loop. She imagined herself in those rooms and on that rambling porch, or sitting out on the dock, bundled in her favorite sweater and watching the glass-like surface of the water while cradling a steaming mug of coffee between her hands. The place looked perfect sitting on the edge of a rocky bluff, nothing but water and spruce trees. The floor-to-ceiling living room windows gave the indoor space a sense of being outside, right on the water. Funny that such a detail had struck her as nothing short of stunning when oceans and lakes made her a nervous wreck.

Hell, maybe she had been kidding herself from the start—perhaps an island retreat was a less-than-sane proposition coming from someone who was uncomfortable around water. But there had been one photo—a pier stretching to infinity across the bay, an incredible sunset performing a perfect ombre fade from deep blue to pink—that had her breath catching in her throat. *Perfect,* Poppy had whispered to herself. *It's just perfect...* Perfect to start fresh. Or maybe to give it all up on a high note. Hell, she didn't know what she expected this trip to achieve. All she knew was that something needed to change. Something needed to shift, for better or worse.

"What about the rest of our bags?" Ezra asked, readjusting his plastic-rimmed glasses and motioning to two suitcases that appeared to be staying behind. One of the bags was Poppy's, which she suddenly found embarrassing. She had stuffed at least five sweaters in there, all for a three-day trip. She should have pushed everyone to pare down. A pair of cozy pajamas, some slippers, one warm sweater. They were going to be out there all by themselves, practically quarantined. There wouldn't be a need for anything else.

Gill nodded toward a docked houseboat just shy of where their current ride bobbed up and down. "That's my place, there," he told them, as though the location of his residence would somehow offer them comfort. "I'll come back for the rest of your bags as soon as I drop you folks off at your destination. You won't even notice those bags aren't on the island before they appear in your rooms. Poof." He made flashes with his hands—a rusty magician trying to dazzle his audience with spectacle rather than skill.

Ezra gave Poppy a look, as if waiting for her to give the go-ahead. But he also looked skeptical, and for a second she was sure he was going to insist he stay behind. That was Ezra's way. He was fiercely protective of the wrong things, busy safeguarding the stuff that didn't matter. Poppy looked away from him, her lips pressed in a tight line. Despite it all, sometimes he still managed to make her heart swell. Ezra with his boyish good looks despite being well into his forties; the guy who had resembled Christian Slater so thoroughly that she'd jokingly told him her name was Heather when they had first met. Those tender moments were rare instances now, but they were ones she remembered well, guaranteeing that when they finally did call it quits it would hurt like hell. She'd sob tears of heartbreak into her hands while he walked away. Unless this trip turned the tide.

When she finally looked back to him, his dubious expression prompted her to act. Her gaze snapped from his face to her children. Leo was watching the exchange with a cocked eyebrow, the bullring in his nose glinting in the late afternoon light, his hair a stylishly disheveled mess, thumbs jutting through the holes he'd worn into the stretched-out sleeves of a thrift store cardigan. Poppy knew what he was thinking. He was wondering if she was going to freeze up, maybe call the whole thing off. Leo had been the first to voice his concern about this whole trip. *Mom, it's in the middle of a bay…*

Lark, on the other hand, was hiding behind her thick-cut black bangs, her nose buried in her phone, her chipped thumbnails tapping against the screen faster than a court stenographer. Poppy couldn't think back to the last time she'd made eye contact with her daughter; it had been that long. Lark was only one of the reasons why Poppy had to suck it up and get on that goddamn boat.

Gill watched Poppy with patient eyes, his hand held aloft in a steadfast offer to come aboard. White shocks of hair stuck out from around the rim of his woolen beanie. He was a quintessential Maine fisherman if she'd ever seen one, and it was exactly what she'd wanted—an authentic New England experience. She hadn't dared mention it, knowing that Ezra would have rolled his eyes, but she'd wanted to visit Maine since she'd been Lark's age. That was around the time she'd read her first Stephen King novel. Twenty years later, she'd read them all.

She eventually gave Gill a weary smile, then took his hand firmly into her own.

"Sounds great, Gill. Thank you," she said, then steeled her nerves and stepped onto the boat with her husband and kids.

Fear hit hard the moment the boat pulled away from the dock. She had to gnash her teeth to keep quiet, sure that if she allowed herself to speak, the first words out of her mouth would be for Gill to turn the boat around. *Just think of why you booked this trip,* she told herself as she clung to the side of the boat. She needed to reconnect with her family, to hopefully bond them all together before their relationships faded like the colors of a sun-bleached photograph. This trip was for Leo, who needed to heal after the hell he'd been through. It was for Lark, who was scaring Poppy with how helpless she'd become to the pull of the device in her hand. And then there was Ezra. *You've never seen Heathers?* she'd asked with an amused sort of scoff. *I'm not sure I'm allowed to date someone so culturally out of touch.* Hell, maybe they still had a shot. They had been great together, once. Genuine. If they could salvage a glimmer of that sincerity, they'd be okay.

She tried to distract herself with all of those thoughts, but found herself preoccupied with simply trying to breathe in the end. And as she sat there, fingers digging into her seat cushion, she couldn't help but wonder if this trip was a mistake. Isolating everyone, carting them off this way, forcing interaction; there had to be a better way to get them all on the same page. But as the Parrishes were whisked to their vacation home, there was a thought Poppy just couldn't shake.

This is either going to work, she thought, *or it's going to tear us apart. It's going to be a disaster or a revelation. There will be no in-between.*

LARK

AS THE BOAT CIRCLED around the side of the island, Morrissey hummed against Lark's eardrums, and when the house came into view, her eyes went wide. It was stunning, like something off an autumnal picture postcard, and it was going to be theirs for a whole three days. It was enough to bang out at least a chapter or two of her current work-in-progress, and the fall scenery was sure to be inspiring, which was good, because inspiration was nothing short of lacking these past few weeks.

She exhaled a breath as the wind pushed her bangs from her eyes, her freshly dyed ponytail whipping behind her like a swallowtail flag. The boat continued its approach and her gaze settled on the pier ahead—gloriously long and perfect for an Instagram shot. The world, however, could keep its pretty melon-colored sunsets. The eerie gloom of a foggy dawn would be Lark's pursuit. Pulling her phone from the exterior pocket of the military surplus backpack at her feet, she deftly navigated to her messaging app. But before Lark could compose a message of how gorgeous the rental was, she blinked at her screen, then furrowed her eyebrows. Had it been a month ago, she would have been texting her best friend, Allison, but that ship had sailed. She would have been texting David, but he was now nothing more than a ghost of her past, a hole in her heart. She shook her head at herself and tossed her phone back into her bag.

Reaching the dock, Lark didn't wait for Gill to finish lashing the boat to the tie-out. She was the first one to climb onto the pier, her 20-eyelet Doc Marten lace-ups hitting the planks, earbuds still firmly in place. There was a smaller, sketchy-looking boat on the opposite side of the dock; definitely not big enough for transporting luggage, but good enough to motor back to Raven's Head to check out the little café she'd spotted when they'd arrived in town. Because coffee was life, and not even an island would keep her from her morning buzz.

"What's this, then?" she heard her father ask during a lull in her music, prompting her to free one of the buds from her ears.

"That, sir, is your chariot for the next few days," Gill explained. "Have you ever piloted a boat before?"

"No," her dad murmured with a bit of a laugh, pushing his fingers through his hair the way he always did when he was out of his depth. Not that there was much for him to be apprehensive about. Her dad could figure out how to do just about anything. Bake a soufflé. Mend a fence. Turn old paperback pages into wallpaper. Often, Lark considered her father unstoppable—a man who could do whatever he put his mind to, so long as he had a few hours with YouTube or Google.

"No worries, Mister Parrish," she heard Gill say. "I'll give you a tutorial before I leave." But that's when Lark stopped paying attention and started wandering down the dock toward the island, leaving her family behind.

"Man," she whispered to herself, retrieving her phone from her bag to snap a quick picture. "I could live here."

"Really?"

She nearly yelped when Leo appeared next to her, his eyes squinting against the wind, his hair slashing across his forehead.

"All the way out here?" Leo asked, then gave her a look, an eyebrow cocked in skepticism. His expression carried a clear message: *bullshit.* "Do you even have a signal?"

Lark pushed her too-long bangs out of her eyes, helpless against the way Leo's inquiry made her heart jump. But she wasn't about to satisfy him by allowing her gaze to dart to her phone. Instead, she played it cool.

"Makes me think of Walt Whitman or something." She shrugged, immediately regretting dropping Whitman into her brother's lap. She always tried so hard with him, wanting to impress her elder sibling with her quirks and off-kilter interests. It never seemed to work, especially not these days. "I mean, it's not Thailand with its sexy beaches and malaria-carrying bugs," she continued, deciding to pull Leo's current obsession into the conversation.

"You're right," Leo said flatly. "It isn't. It's a rock with a house on it. Fucking amazing."

Lark's heart sank, but before she could think of how to respond, of how to keep their dialogue going, Leo moved past her, hefting his own patch-covered backpack onto his right shoulder with a disarming sense of determination.

And in her ears, Morrissey sang:

The more you ignore me…let me in, let me in.

LEO

HE COULD HEAR Lark's boots slapping against the planks of the dock to catch up to him—those boots a new style choice for her, as was all of it. Everything black. Not that Leo was complaining. Six months ago, she'd been sporting Converse All-Stars that matched his like something out of a sibling parody; the little sister emulating her older brother. He had hated Lark picking up the All-Star trend, had bitched about it because who the hell wanted to match shoes with their kid sister? But Lark had abruptly ditched the style choice soon after Julien's accident, and Leo had been too traumatized to ask her why she'd suddenly gone from grunge to goth.

He considered popping the question as soon as she sidled up to him again. *So, what's up with the boots, anyway?* Lark had a thing for brooding, but the all-black thing had been unanticipated, nearly thoughtless. Asking her about the new funeral attire would get her off the subject of Thailand, anyway. Knowing Lark, she'd clam up, hide behind her hair. But before she could come shoulder-to-shoulder with him, their mother called out from the boat that was now a good distance away.

"Lark! The bellman is on vacation!"

Lark exhaled an exasperated sigh behind him, and Leo glanced over his shoulder just in time to see her stomping in the opposite direction. By the time Lark found her way back to the house, their exchange would be dead in the water. Talk of Thailand would lie dormant for another day, which suited him just fine.

Lark was right about the island, though. There was something about it that was drawing him in. The house looked like something out of a movie—iconic coastal style with its wood shingle siding, its big porch and too many windows to count. His mother had no doubt chosen this place because it was overwhelmingly American; a place you'd find pictured in a history book.

And here, a photo of JFK's favorite coastal getaway. He could read his mother like a book. Perhaps all the Americana would sway him from the exotic locale of Thailand's pristine beaches, right? But Thailand was less about the country and more about paying tribute to the person Leo would never see again. He would take his best friend's place among the bustle of Bangkok. It was what Julien would have wanted. It's what felt right, what Leo was determined to do.

But oh, how his mother had flipped.

When Leo had laid a brochure for Krabi and the Hong Islands on the table during a family dinner, his father had said nothing. He had simply sat there, a spooked animal, unsure of what to do. Leo's mother, on the other hand, had never reacted to anything as passionately as she had right then. She just about wailed *I won't allow it,* then slammed her fist against the table hard enough to make the silverware jump. Leo had stared at her, taken aback, then excused himself and disappeared upstairs. He left the brochures behind as a message. He'd already made his decision. No amount of yelling would change his mind. And there had been *plenty* of yelling that night. Mom and Dad screaming at each other. Mom demanding Dad "do something." Dad insisting that it wasn't either of their choices to make. Leo listened to their back-and-forth from behind the stair banister, like a kid sneaking into a rated-R movie, avoiding the usher's flashlight beam.

He had considered going downstairs to speak for himself, but quickly concluded that there was no talking reason to someone who was sitting on the knife's edge of a meltdown, especially if that meltdown was triggered by the idea of losing someone they loved. Hell, he knew that feeling better than anyone, knew how volatile and hysteric it was. He'd been dealing with that very version of himself since the night Julien wrapped the front of his car around a tree.

Leo paused at the base of the house's wide deck stairs and looked up. It was beautiful, but there was also something ominous about the high gables and asymmetrical roofline, about it being all alone out there in the middle of the bay. The wood shingles curled up ever-so-slightly at the ends, no doubt beaten by years of harsh coastal weather. And then there was the fact that, at least from the outside, the place didn't make sense. Usually, you could look at a house and imagine a living room behind one of the windows, a kitchen behind another. This house revealed nothing. There were windows of all shapes and sizes, looking as though they'd been placed by a madman at the height of his lunacy. The roofline seemed to be off somehow. Off-kilter? Off-center? Leo couldn't put his finger on it, but it gave him a sense of vertigo. Perhaps that's why that house was on an island in the middle of nowhere. Maybe it was a black sheep. A troublemaker. But being creeped out by a house was kid stuff, and Leo shook off the unease with a quick climb up the steps.

He wasn't sure why he tried the door. Impatience, maybe. The last dregs of childlike curiosity. There was a numeric keypad above the door's lever handle. He'd gotten an email about the house code via his mom—she'd been forwarding the entire family emails from AirBnB for the past two weeks. One of them had included the security code to the very door Leo was standing in front of, but he'd be damned if he could remember those digits now. That, however, didn't matter, because as soon as his hand hit the doorknob, the front door swung open on soundless hinges, unlocked.

Leo furrowed his eyebrows, then looked over his shoulder and back down the dock. His family was still with Gill and the boat. It was weird, though, the door being open the way it was. *Maybe Gill unlocked it*, he thought. Nobody else would have been out on the island, so why not just leave it open? Hell, the keypad was fancy enough. Leo bet Gill had an app on his phone that let him lock and unlock the door remotely, a lot like the way the Parrishes could control their thermostat.

While the detail of the front door being open only amplified the weird vibe the house gave off, Leo shrugged it off and stepped inside. But the moment he set foot in the entryway, he stopped dead. Because while he'd never been here before, he was hit with a scent so familiar it made his skin crawl; a scent he knew so well, it made him want to turn and run.

LARK

LARK HAD PLACED her earbuds back in her ears long before she'd hefted her top-loading duffel down the dock. Arriving at the house's door, Lark nudged Leo out of way, then dropped her bag onto the kitchen floor with a thud. There was a bank of windows making up the entirety of one of the living room walls. The view was overwhelming, the spectacular sight allowing autumnal light to spill from the living room and into the kitchen like liquid gold. When she spotted the antique writing desk tucked into one of the house's many corners, her heart swelled with possibility, then sank just as fast.

Writing had become difficult since her falling out with Allison. Once upon a time, they would bounce ideas off one another, share unfinished chapters and spend hours texting back and forth about story arcs and character traits. When Lark had talked of finally writing a novel, Allison had encouraged her to leap. But that had been before everything had gone off the rails. Before she'd lost both Allison and David. Before her passion for writing had started to fade.

Still, it was hard not to imagine herself cozied up at that desk—the kind with a roll-top and dozens of tiny drawers where secrets could safely be kept. Perhaps she'd take a seat in that straight-backed wooden chair regardless of it all, stare out across the water and cross her fingers that inspiration would strike.

But with her two greatest champions gone, who would read her words now? Leo? Her mother? Lark quickly put that crazy idea out of her head. Her mom's contempt for all things having to do with Lark's phone was, at times, awe-inspiring. And while Lark understood where the vexation came from—because yes, Lark *did* spend an incredible amount of time on her device—sometimes she couldn't help but think that her mother's hatred had shifted from genuine disdain to mere principle, and that hurt. Mom had never asked exactly how "that writing thing" worked, never cared to understand that, yes, you *could* tap out an entire book on a phone. She didn't know that Lark had thousands of subscribers who read her posts—people who told her they loved her stuff and couldn't wait for more; nor that writers were discovered on that very platform by agents and publishers alike.

It would have been nice to have her mother's support when it came to doing what she loved, but Lark knew that that kind of support was rare. Reality was nothing but annoyed mutterings beneath her mother's breath, and it made Lark wonder if her mom's annoyance had grown bigger than the size of her cell phone; if it had, perhaps, grown wide enough to swallow the entirety of her mother's affection.

But she didn't want to think about that. Not here. Not now. Not when she was faced with the beauty of an incredible coastal home—exposed ceiling beams and gray-painted shiplap as far as the eye could see. The hardwood floor was a deep forest green that matched the spruce trees surrounding the house, and a large stone fireplace stood centered against the living room wall. The bookshelves were stuffed to capacity with hardbound books, most standing upright while the overflow occupied the empty spaces above them, horizontal and stacked high until the shelf above stopped their climb. It reminded her of a dusty bookstore, like that famous Parisian shop, Shakespeare and Company. She was determined to visit it in person one day.

Tugging an earbud out of her ear, she cast a glance over her shoulder at her brother. He was still standing just shy of the open kitchen door.

"God, *look* at this place," she said. "This is great, right?"

Leo shrugged, seemingly ambivalent, which only made Lark breathe out a sigh. He'd been a smartass not that long ago; always one with a witty retort or a wry smile riding easy upon his lips. Lark hadn't seen that side of Leo in a long time, unsure she ever would again. Her brother had been replaced by a shrugging, spiritless shadow. And while she wanted to feel nothing but sympathy for him, his melancholia was starting to aggravate her…which was saying a lot, since Melancholia was Lark's middle name.

"Christ," she said softly. "You're such a fucking ghost." *Just like*

David, she thought a moment later. *Just like him.*

She could tell Leo had heard her, knew by the way he shifted his weight ever-so-slightly despite not moving from where he stood. A moment later she was looking away from him with a frown, feeling guilty about not being more patient. Her irritability was what had gotten her into trouble before, was what had destroyed the relationship she'd been so sure of.

She shook her head and muttered a soft "sorry" beneath her breath, trying to distract herself with her new surroundings. Because Leo still *looked* like the same Leo she'd always known—the messy hair, the bull-ring piercing and raggedy Kurt Cobain look. Lark had half-hoped that Julien's death, which had transformed her brother so thoroughly on the inside, would have changed his outward appearance as well. It would have been easier had she not been able to recognize him, if he had ditched his T-shirts and stonewashed jeans for something a little more oppressive, something a little more like what Lark had adopted for herself.

It had been almost funny how fast she'd gained new readers when she'd decided to ditch the shy girl in a vintage band T-shirt and transform herself into a full-blown gothic gloom queen. *Told you it would work,* Allison had said. *The horror geeks can't resist.* Allison's idea of darkening Lark's persona had been nothing short of a brilliant business move. The perfect launch for Chapter One. Smart. Savvy. A slight departure from the truth, sure, but…

"Lark."

She blinked up at Leo, surprised to hear him speak. She had expected him to have disappeared down some random hall in exploration or a search for seclusion, but he was still standing in that doorway, not having budged an inch.

"Do you smell that?" he asked, and for a minute he looked genuinely addled, as though he wasn't sure it was safe to take another forward step. As if there were a gas leak. Or black mold. Or a body decomposing inside the walls à la Edgar Allan Poe.

Lark pulled a breath in through her nose, trying to pick up the scent Leo was referring to, but all she could smell was saltwater. Maybe a hint of Lysol or hand soap underneath.

"It's faint," he said. "Smells like black licorice."

Lark furrowed her eyebrows at him. She didn't smell it, but even if she had, she liked the scent he was describing. It reminded her of jack-o-lanterns and witchcraft, of black cats and midnight mass.

She shook her head. "I don't—"

But her statement was derailed upon seeing their mother climbing the house's front steps, her voice already calling out to them both.

"Someone needs to run to the store with your dad."

"Why didn't we go before we came out with Gill?" Leo questioned.

"Because my mind was elsewhere and I didn't think of it," their mother confessed. "Lark…"

Lark released an exasperated breath and spun around where she stood, giving the room her trademark glower. "You're sending *me?*"

She could see her mother hesitate, could see her holding back what she really wanted to say. No doubt something about bad attitudes and not ruining their fun-filled family vacation within the first few minutes of their island arrival. But rather than snapping, Mom took what seemed to be a steadying inhale and eventually sighed.

"Lark," she said, "sweetheart…" Terms of endearment. They were only used when Lark's mother needed something, when she was tired and wanted to diffuse conflict. "You know being on the water makes me uncomfortable," she said, then gave Lark an imploring look.

Lark rolled her eyes and looked away. *Yeah,* she thought. *We've heard the story a million times.*

Their mom, her Uncle Bill laying down the throttle of his fancy Bayliner on choppy Atlantic water. Their mother tumbling head-over-feet into the wake the boat left behind in a life jacket two sizes too big for her nine-year-old frame. Mom had been sure she was drowning until Uncle Bill hefted her out of the water by the scruff of her neck. *Then why an island?* Lark wanted to ask, but Leo had already tried that back home. And yet, here they were anyway.

"Besides, don't you want to see Raven's Head?" Mom asked.

Lark turned to face her mother fully, then twisted her face up in an expression only the blind could misinterpret. *Um, not really?*

"Look, I need you to go with your father."

There it was. The "sweetheart" request had expired in two seconds flat. Now it was a full-on demand.

"I'll make a list," Mom murmured, then sauntered deeper into the kitchen.

Lark squeezed her eyes shut and pinched the bridge of her nose. *Don't say anything. Don't say anything. Don't.* She'd just go, get it over with. Maybe she'd talk her father into ducking into that coffee shop. The least she could do was get a latte out of this lousy errand. Then again, if she was going to hit up the café, maybe she could talk Leo into coming as well.

Lark opened her eyes, but the spot where her brother had been standing was now vacant. And for a moment, seeing the empty space he had left felt ominous. A foreshadowing of his departure, or maybe a metaphor for the hollowness she'd feel once he was gone.

Or maybe it was none of those things, maybe it was the house. Because now, as she stood quiet and waiting for her mother's shopping list, she caught a whiff of the scent Leo had mentioned. Black licorice, so faint it could have only been left by a ghost.

EZRA

EZRA STOOD on the dock, watching Gill leave them behind. There was something about being left out there that felt strange, as though Gill had no intention of returning with their bags and the commuter dinghy was nothing but a stage prop.

Staring out across the water, he pulled his glasses from his face, then pushed his fingers through his hair. This vacation was about trying to fix everything he'd broken. Maybe if he tried hard enough, he could make it happen. Hell, he'd already half-way convinced himself that he was here because he was a good husband, a good father no matter his mistakes. It was a matter of wanting something so intensely that the near-impossible actually seemed achievable. But he caught himself snorting as soon as optimism managed to coil itself comfortably around his heart. Yes, he wanted those things, but that wasn't why he was here. This little vacation was a way to get as far away from the mess he'd left back home as he could, and for now, a private island was as close to total seclusion as he could get.

Ezra exhaled a breath, rubbed the lenses of his glasses with the corner of his sweater, then slid them back onto his face in time to see Lark come into view. She lifted a skinny trenchcoated arm above her head and waved from the opposite end of the dock, a threadbare Bauhaus T-shirt flashing beneath the unbuttoned flaps of her coat.

She began speaking long before he could hear her, gesticulating with her arms, clearly unimpressed with whatever scenario had sent her out of the house and back onto the pier.

"What?" Ezra lifted a hand to his ear.

"—the store," was all he heard the second time around.

"Store?" he asked.

"Store!" Lark yelled, then pulled something from the back pocket of a pair of skinny black jeans, waving it in the air. It was a piece of paper, unmistakably one of Poppy's shopping lists. He had yet to set

doorbell. Besides, she hadn't seen her uncle in forever. Last she'd heard, he and her dad had gotten into some sort of argument. The Parrish bi-monthly family cookout had gone by the wayside nearly a year ago.

Not that it mattered. The more she thought it through, the Gill thing didn't seem like that big of a deal. She was just being paranoid. Gill would knock, regardless of what he said. And even if he didn't, he was just doing his job.

Let it go, she told herself, then shoved her earbuds back into place, blocking out her thoughts. Blocking out the world.

LEO

THERE WASN'T A DAY when Leo didn't think back to his time at the hospital. He tried to distract himself with music or movies or art. But some days were worse than others, and today was one of those days. There was something about the stillness of the bay that was exacerbating his thoughts, threatening to drown him in the memory of all those days he'd spent at Julien's side. One hundred ninety-four days to be exact. One hundred ninety-four before it was all for nothing, before Julien was let go.

Leo often wondered what would have happened if his best friend had opened his eyes and rejoined the world. He wondered if Julien would have been able to process the fact that he no longer looked like himself, that he resembled something twisted lurking beneath a childhood bed. And if Julien *did* wake up, if he *could* process it all…how would he have dealt with something like that? *Impossible,* Leo concluded time and time again. *Impossible, so maybe it's better that he's gone.*

It had been an invasion of privacy, but during a moment alone in the ICU, Leo had snapped a photo of Julien in case that horrific wakeup call came to pass, in case Julien ever wanted to know just how bad it had been. Julien's head had been bandaged for an array of reasons. A fractured skull. A broken cheekbone and nose. A dislocated jaw. A craniotomy to get the hemorrhaging under control. All that was left exposed was the left side of his face, which was so bruised with blood it had turned a grotesque purple; so swollen it was shiny, the skin threatening to split if it was stretched even a millimeter more.

When Leo first saw him, he stepped out of the hospital room as quickly as he had stepped in. In an eerily empty hospital hallway, the sound of Julien's ventilator had seemed incredibly loud. And as Leo stood in that hall trying to hold back a wail, all he could think of was the ocean. The vent sounded like the goddamn *ocean*. Like the beaches and reefs Julien had been determined to save because *the world is dying, dude. Who needs college when we all might not have air to breathe in a decade's time?*

Now, Leo found himself squeezing his eyes shut against the lapping of the bay. It was no ocean, but it reminded him of that awful hospital cacophony either way. There was no way to turn it off, no way to completely block it out. Even with Jack White's guitar blasting against his eardrums, Leo swore he could still hear it. The lapping of water. Julien's ventilator. One continuing forever while the other had gone quiet a month before.

Turning up his music even more than it already was, Leo grabbed his sketchpad and readied himself for a millionth failed attempt of getting his mind off of everything, but then he noticed the boat. That crusty guy, Gill, was motoring toward the pier with his parents' bags, which reminded him…this was supposed to be a vacation. *Cheer up, dude.* He could hear Julien laugh the words, could see his face light up with that typically relaxed and easy smile, never one to let the world get him down. That thread of humor had once laced all of Julien's sentiments, all except the last couple of sentences Leo would ever hear him speak—a voicemail Julien had left maybe five minutes before the crash.

Hey, Julien had said in a breathless sort of way, no humor to be heard. *We need to talk. You aren't going to believe this shit.*

POPPY

DESPITE THERE NOT being food, there was plenty of Lipton in the cabinet over the stove. Poppy had initially sighed at the lack of selection—not a single bag of Twinings to be found—but eventually grabbed a plain white mug and fixed herself a cup. *When in Rome.*

It was barely in the 50's today. Clouds gathering in the distance. There was a stormfront closing in. It was weather that couldn't have been predicted when Poppy had booked the place a few weeks before, but a little rain wouldn't have stopped her from committing to this getaway regardless. She imagined it beating against all those panes of glass, anticipated the sound and smell as a comfort rather than a worry. Rain was, after all, one of the only things that seemed to quell the anxiety that constantly lurked beneath her skin.

Steaming mug in hand, Poppy stopped and recalibrated herself between the den and a hall that led back to the laundry room. The stairs had two landings, yet both led to roughly the same spot on the first floor. Despite the house's quirky charm, there was something slightly unsettling about it. Perhaps it was the size. She'd expected something smaller, more quaint. When they had pulled up to the dock, it had looked half its actual size, but that was because most of the home sprawled away from the rocky beach and into the spruce trees behind it. Because of its awkward placement, some rooms had ample light while others were tombs. Then there was the layout—almost nonsensical how some rooms fed into other rooms while others seemed to loop in on themselves. And while those odd rooms were jarring, the doors that decorated the walls were far worse. There were doors to closets and bathrooms and random tucked-away hidey holes big enough for a single box of Christmas decorations, some fishing gear, or a few spare winter parkas. There were doors that opened up to hidden bookshelves overstuffed with paperbacks, like passageways to secret libraries that never intended on being found. And then there was the attic, so big it just about took her breath away.

Having crept up the fold-down staircase and popped her head up among an endless array of treasures, she gave in to her curiosity and spent an hour snooping. Her fingers drifted across the chrome of vintage kitchen appliances as she peeked at what looked to be genuine crystal glassware left atop an open moving box.

It was only when she stumbled upon what looked to be a makeshift campsite that she furrowed her eyebrows in genuine curiosity. She remembered an area like it in her own childhood attic, complete with sleeping bag and colorful holiday lights strung up between the roof beams. Poppy had spent endless hours hidden away, reading trashy bodice-ripper romance novels she'd pilfered from her grandmother's weird Avon collection. Sometimes she'd write in her journal which, now that she thought about it, shot her through with a pang of guilt. Because here she was, not the least bit supportive of Lark's hobby when she herself had flirted with fiction for years.

Maybe it was the adult in her—the parent that wanted to see their child find success rather than struggle on a starving artist's paycheck. Poppy and Ezra had raised two artists between them, and while Teenaged Poppy would have rejoiced at the prospect, Poppy the Parent was scared for them both. Because if Leo really did go to Thailand, how was he planning on making any money? How would he buy food? What if he ended up living on the street in a Bangkok slum? What if he found himself desperate in the hands of some wealthy businessman, some guy who—

Stop it.

Poppy forced those worst-case scenarios out of her head. She was overreacting. It wasn't like she couldn't just hand the kid some money and say *here, at least stay off the street. Eat something. Please, whatever you do, just don't die.*

Pulling in a breath, she recentered herself, then allowed her attention to fall back to the somewhat utilitarian hideaway with its Coleman LED campsite lantern, pile of cheap flannel blankets, and crumpled plastic water bottles. There was some strange-looking electronic gear there—a black box with an array of stubby plastic antennas jutting up from one side. Poppy squinted at it, remembering the old computer router Ezra had battled whenever they had problems getting online. No doubt it was little more than another hunk of junk, tossed into the abyss of the attic along with all the other stuff.

She was just about to peek into another cardboard box when she heard the distant whine of a boat motor. Pivoting on the soles of her shoes and away from the attic's vast array of junk, she only hesitated at the attic ladder, realizing it was far more difficult to descend with a mug of now lukewarm tea than it was to climb up. But she eventually made it, folded the ladder up into the ceiling, and retraced her steps back to the kitchen to take their bags off Gill's hands. But when she finally reached the ground floor, Gill was nowhere to be found. And when she peered out the living room windows, there was no boat lashed to the pier, not even a ripple in the water to suggest that he had come and gone.

She blinked at the isolation that surrounded her beyond that glass, feeling simultaneously nervous and at ease. This place cost a pretty penny—money she knew would cut deep into their savings. But it was also the perfect place to regroup. Forget the fact that she'd wanted to stay somewhere like this since she'd first watched *Misery* in her early teens. Never mind that an absurd part of her was crossing her fingers that they'd run into the Master of Horror himself if they just hung around Raven's Head for long enough. It was ludicrous, really. And yet, here she was anyway.

But where was Gill?

Deciding it was, perhaps, a passing boat and not Gill after all, she turned and made her way to the master bedroom. A nap would be nice before Lark and Ezra returned with groceries and Poppy found herself standing in a stranger's kitchen, wondering what to feed everyone.

Reaching the room, she slipped out of her shoes and grabbed a throw blanket off an armchair. It was only then that she stopped short, her gaze fixed on the foot of the bed. There were the bags, as though they had been sitting in that very spot the entire time. Except they hadn't.

Gill. He had slipped into the house unannounced and undetected.

How he had managed it, she couldn't fathom. Yet, here she was. Alone.

LARK

LARK NOTICED THE WOMAN at the end of the cereal aisle as soon as she dropped Leo's box of Cocoa Puffs into her cart. She had to do a double take, swearing she was looking at Helena Bonham Carter on a spectacularly bad day. It was the hair—a rat's nest of box dye black so dark it glowed indigo beneath the grocery store's florescent lights. Not that she was in the position to judge. No doubt she was just as much an anomaly in a place like Raven's Head as this woman was. It wasn't hard to pick up the local flavor. Couples wearing flannel and Bean boots, eyes turned upward toward the leaves while paper cups of coffee wafted steam skyward. Salty local guys like Gill. And then there was Lark…and this woman, Helena, with her explosion of shellac-stiff hair sticking up every which way. Helena in her fur-lined winter coat and Jackie O sunglasses, looking like a Russian spy.

Perhaps Lark had been staring and that's why the woman turned her head. Maybe Lark had zoned out, trying to place whether the woman was genuinely that off-the-wall or whether she was a celebrity in disguise. That may have been why the woman regarded her with a hard stare from behind those dark lenses, a curt smile pulled tight across her blood-red mouth.

The moment Lark realized she'd been caught, her heart somersaulted into her throat and she looked away with a wince, the buzzing of her nerves not at all matching the upbeat Smiths' tune skipping across her ears.

"Shit," she whispered to herself, afraid to open her eyes again, worried that Helena would still be there, waiting for some sort of explanation.

Weren't you ever taught it's rude to stare?

Lark forced her eyes open and glowered at the pack of English muffins her father couldn't live without. She could feel the woman's eyes crawling across the back of her neck. Catching her bottom lip between her teeth, Lark eventually peeked away from the Smucker's Strawberry Preserves in her cart, still sensing that the woman was lingering there in the aisle, as if waiting for Lark to look her way again.

God, what does she want?

Or maybe it wasn't that lightning-struck Helena wanted Lark to look at her, but that she was busy staring at Lark. After all, Lark was just as out-of-place in the cereal aisle of this little tourist town, what with her trench coat and knee-high boots. Lark shifted her weight from one foot to the other, suddenly uncomfortable in her own skin, aggravated with herself that she had decided to embrace this persona so fully instead of just keeping it online. She could have easily posed as the all-black-wearing goth while posting on the boards, could have stuck with her Converse All-Stars look in her daily life. But David had complicated things. She had met him as her alter ego, had fallen for him hard. He'd mused about how mysterious she was, how intriguing. And that, right there, had sealed the deal. Lark Parrish was no longer who she used to be. She was now a moody, broody, mysterious writer trying to catch some attention, determined to make it big in the literary world.

But Raven's Head was about as far away from the literary world as Lark could get, and whoever the woman was, she was thoroughly creeping her out. Hell, it wouldn't have been all that weird for Lark to accuse *her* of staring. *Take a picture, lady. Jesus Christ.*

Glaring at the crumpled paper in her right hand, Lark unfolded her mother's shopping list, shuddering when she felt the dark-haired woman move closer as if to start a conversation. Lark held her breath and yanked her phone out of her pocket, her headphone wire pulling tight and nearly jerking her earbuds free. She sensed Helena slow her steps, as though the appearance of Lark's phone had made her reconsider her approach. A moment later, the woman passed, gliding down the aisle with the soft click of boot heels.

"I mean, really," Lark whispered to herself. "People are so *weird.*"

She hit the PREVIOUS button on her music app and cranked Morrisey's voice up loud enough to soothe her frazzled nerves, then looked back to her mother's carefully scripted list, exhaling the breath she'd swallowed down deep. Finally glancing back up, she discovered the woman long gone. The encounter had been so thoroughly odd, it would have been something she had immediately messaged David about. But that was then. Now, Lark found herself staring at her cell phone while a sense of emptiness tendrilled across the curve of her heart. She frowned as she scrolled past Allison's name. Stopping on David's number, she reflexively tapped it, pausing for a long moment to consider whether she should make another attempt. She hadn't tried to contact him in over a week. Maybe, this time, it had been long enough of a silence; enough time for him to have reconsidered. Perhaps the mention of Helena and how completely bizarre the grocery store run-in had been would be enough to spur a response, even if it was sarcastic. Or maybe she was kidding herself. *He never gave a shit,* she told herself. *Allison was right. He's not the guy you thought he was.*

Shaking her head to herself, she backed out of David's profile and sighed, choosing to text her brother instead.

MARLA SINGER LIVES HERE.

Looking up from her phone, she cast a glance toward the registers. It was then that she saw Helena approach a guy leaning against a Red Box rental machine. Lark couldn't make out his face—he had the brim of a khaki military cap pulled down over his eyes—but she could tell he was younger than his eccentric counterpart. And while he didn't stand out the way Dark Helena did, there was something off about him as well; something that assured Lark neither one of them belonged in that small coastal town.

Lark squinted, trying to get a good look at them both, but the woman turned away and ducked out of the store. And the guy? He slid a pair of aviators onto his face, further obscuring his identity, but he paused before following the woman out. Tipping his chin upward, he made Lark's nerves fizzle like popping candy. She could swear he was staring at her from across the bank of checkouts and conveyor belts, making direct eye contact from behind those shades.

I see you, Lark Parrish, the pause seemed to say. *I see you whether you like it or not.*

REMEMBRANCE

LEO

THAT PHANTOM LICORICE SCENT was so faint, Leo could only smell it if he stood perfectly still, but it continued to linger. He spent what seemed like hours searching the house for its origin, pressing his face into throw pillows, taking deep whiffs of the bed sheets. The more he sought out the smell the stronger it seemed to become, but no matter how hard he tried, he couldn't place it. Eventually, he was smelling his own clothes, his hands—was it him? Whatever its source, it was enough to put him on edge, to make him jumpy, to twist his stomach into a sickening knot.

Distraction came in the form of Lark and their father hefting shopping bags up the pier and toward the house. He met them in the kitchen, where both Lark and their mother began to unpack the paper sacks.

"Hey," Lark said, giving him a curious look. "Did you get my text?"

"Yeah, sorry," Leo said, approaching the bags of groceries. He remembered a Fight Club reference, but he'd been too preoccupied with his hunt for that unnerving smell to reply. And now, with all the food being unloaded onto the countertop, his stomach unwound itself enough for his appetite to come on strong. Leo picked through his father's typical impulse buys, grabbed an apple, and turned away from the kitchen, his attention fixed on the view of the bay.

"It's only three days, guys," Mom said. "Think you bought enough?"

Leo watched his mother's reflection in the window's glass. She waved a dismissive hand, then told them to "just put it anywhere. Not like we're going to be here long enough to need to organize it all."

There was a rustle of a paper bag, then "Really, Ezra? Twinkies?"

Leo stopped chewing, a mouth full of masticated Honeycrisp lying dormant between his cheek and gums. He turned back to the kitchen counter, and there it was: a box of Hostess snack cakes, Twinkie the Kid holding court over those golden delights. Leo swallowed, that half-chewed bite of apple going down hard.

"What?" Leo's father turned away from putting something in the fridge, then gave his wife a curious look while pushing his glasses up his nose. "Those aren't mine." He held his hands up in surrender. *Scout's honor.*

But they were right there, winking at Leo like an inside joke. *Hey,* they said. *Remember us? Remember how once upon a time Julien loved Twinkies so much that he dressed up as Twinkie the Kid for Halloween?*

"Uhuh." Mom didn't sound convinced, because everyone knew Dad had a serious sweet tooth. Not so long ago, he could eat an entire row of Oreos in a single sitting. Those Twinkies, though…they were more than a random grab from the junk food aisle.

"I swear," Dad continued, still showing his hands as if to prove he didn't have anything to hide. "You know I cut that stuff out a while back. Though, if they're already here…" He reached for the box and tore open the top. "Vacation, right? Leo, you want one?"

Leo most certainly did not want one, but before he had a chance to respond, a Twinkie was arcing through the air. Instinctively, he caught it, but not before a sleeper wave of nausea crashed against his diaphragm and threatened to drop him to his knees.

"I don't—" Leo swallowed against the sudden dryness at the back of his throat. "—don't want it," he finished in a mere whisper, his attention stuck on the thin cellophane wrapper, on the bright yellow pastry in the palm of his hand.

"So, *nobody* bought them?" Mom shook her head, not getting it. "How does that work? Lark?"

"It wasn't me," Lark said.

Leo narrowed his eyes as he watched his sister. There was something off about her demeanor. She was eyeing those Twinkies with suspicion, same as Leo. But she also looked a little spooked, like maybe she was having déjà vu. And then there was her silence. Lark talked too much, especially when she was nervous. The fact that she wasn't talking a mile a minute was a sure sign that something was wrong.

"Hey, what does it matter?" Dad asked with a shrug. "Maybe it was a joke. Small town kids throwing random crap into a tourist's cart."

"Sure," Mom said, unimpressed, busying herself with the groceries once again. "I suppose anything's possible, especially if someone is distracted."

Leo felt his sister tense from across the room. She had pulled her phone out of her back pocket as if to check something, or maybe text someone, but was now hurriedly putting it away.

"That's something I want to talk to everyone about," Mom said. "These few days are important to me, okay?"

Lark and Leo exchanged a glance. *Here we go.*

"We all need it to center ourselves, to regroup after everything that's happened over these past few months. Part of this adventure is getting back to being a family, to reconnect to ourselves and to each other."

Lark rolled her eyes. If their mother had noticed, she was pretending not to have seen. Dad shifted his weight from one foot to the other. He had just as big a cell phone habit as everyone else.

"The only way to do that is to keep the phones to a minimum," Mom told them.

"Wait." Lark immediately jumped at that. "What does that mean, exactly? Like, what's a minimum?"

"If you're with the family, no phones," Mom said. "We focus on each other, not on screens. We play board games. We do puzzles. We talk. I'm sick of seeing the tops of your heads and not your faces."

Lark looked to Leo as if seeking support, because had their mom finally lost her damn mind? Board games? Like *Monopoly*? Or, worse yet, *Trivial Pursuit*? Her once spooked expression was now nothing short of panic. *Say something,* her face read. But Leo kept quiet. He wasn't fazed by their mother's request. Ever since Julien's passing, all Leo did was stare at his phone. He'd scroll through Reddit for hours or glare at stupid inspirational quotes on Facebook.

Every day is a new beginning! said one.

I am the master of my fate; the captain of my soul! read another.

Those stupid quotes aggravated the hell out of him. *I'm wasting my life on this,* he thought. *A voluntary lobotomy…* He'd considered deleting all his social media accounts. What good were they, anyway? He was leaving. Ditching this life. Flying the coop. Shit, he'd deleted his girlfriend. Deleted his friends one-by-one over the last seven months. And then Ms. Bellamy had deleted Julien, so what did it matter? No phone, no problem. Who was he going to talk to anyway?

Mom wanted to play *Monopoly*. She wanted to put together a kitten jigsaw puzzle and sing kumbaya around the goddamn fire. *Shit,* Leo thought, *bring it on.* Maybe some Brady Bunch bullshit was what he needed to finally get his head on straight.

And then, as if to say *not so fast,* Leo felt his phone vibrate against his leg.

"Mom, hold on." Lark exhaled a calculated breath. Leo could already hear it in the steadiness of her tone. This was now a hostage negotiation. Lark was trying to talk their mother down. "I need my phone to write," she explained. "I can't just stop. That isn't the way this works, okay? I'm in the middle of a chapter and I was looking forward to this being kind of inspirational, you know? I mean…"

Mom frowned at her.

"Are you serious?" Lark asked, gawking back at her. "This isn't fair." She looked back to Leo. *Help me, please!*

Leo blinked at the Twinkie in his hand, then fixed his attention on their mother. "Mom…"

"Fine." Mom cut them off. "You can have it for writing," she said, giving Lark a pointed look. "But no *Plants vs. Zombies.* No *Angry Birds.*" She shot Dad a hard stare. "No social media. If I have to ask anyone to put their phone away even once, it's curtains for everyone. You get me? Three days isn't that long, guys."

Lark twisted her face up in a sour expression, eventually relenting with an exasperated sigh.

Mom turned to Leo.

"Yeah. Okay," Leo said, throwing the Twinkie onto the kitchen island, then wiping his hand against the leg of his pants, his fingers inching toward his front pocket. Despite their mother's anti-technology diatribe, the buzz he'd felt against his leg left him itching to see what had come through. Was it an email? A text? Amelia had sent him a handful of messages after their breakup, most of which were heartfelt and tearful. Mostly, she was making sure he was okay, which only served as a reminder of why he'd fallen in love with her in the first place. Amelia had been a steadfast cheerleader in Julien's fight to survive. She'd been supportive of Leo's determination to be at his best friend's side. And what had she gotten for her unwavering understanding? A hard lesson in just how debilitating grief could be.

"Lark?" Mom was waiting for her to agree to the deal.

"This isn't fair," Lark argued. "If Leo or Dad screw up, *I* have to pay for it?"

Leo smirked.

Lark didn't like that. She shot him a glare.

"And what's *that* supposed to mean?" she demanded.

Leo shrugged. "Just that if anyone is going to screw up…" he said, leaving his sentence unfinished, sure that she could read him loud and clear.

"Okay, enough," Mom said. "Three days. That's all I want, okay? For God's sake, it's not that much. If I have to ask *anyone* to put their phone away, they're all going into the bay."

"Fine," Leo murmured.

"Fine," Lark hissed back at him, then turned to look at their mom. "You're right. This is going to be the best vacation ever." And then she stormed out of the house and down the porch steps toward the dock.

Mom pressed a hand to her forehead, then exhaled a sigh. Only a few hours in and her plan for the perfect getaway was falling apart.

"And what are we supposed to do with these?" she asked, almost flabbergasted by the Twinkies on the counter, minus one, which Dad had inhaled in less than three bites.

It was then that Leo stepped forward, swept the loose Twinkie and box of snack-cakes up, and deposited them into the trash. Because if he didn't see another Twinkie for the rest of his life, it would be too fucking soon.

LARK

"FUCK!" LARK YELLED out across the bay, the toes of her boots hanging a millimeter off the edge of the pier.

This was supposed to be a vacation, not some test of will. If her mother thought banishing phones was a smart attempt at bonding, she was out of her mind. Puzzles and small talk? It was proof of just how out-of-touch her mom truly was. When Leo had announced his plans to take off to Thailand, Lark had sympathized with her mother's anger. She didn't want Leo to go either. But maybe Leo was right in wanting to flee, and maybe she'd do it, too. Dublin. Edinburgh. Glasgow. Hell, *anywhere* would be better than home.

Angrily swiping at her eyes, Lark glared across the water, wondering if anyone back at the house would notice if she jumped in and started swimming away. Wondered if they'd notice if she started to drown, her arms frantically slapping the water, her head just barely above water, gasping for air. Wondered if they'd notice, and if they did, whether they'd give a damn.

"Stupid," she murmured beneath her breath, then took a few backward steps and let herself fall into one of the Adirondack chairs at the end of the dock. "Because it's better to sit around in silence and feel awkward, right?" she grumbled, pulling her coat tight across her chest. "Because it's better to force everyone into having a good time than to be content on their own. Jesus, let's play games. Let's play charades! I'll go first." She smirked, then made like she was looping a noose around her neck, tightening it, and choking out a gasp. "Oh, and maybe if someone had been paying attention to the shopping cart, we wouldn't have ended up with an unwanted box of Twinkies. Because Dad doesn't throw enough random shit into the cart in the first place. Even if I *had* noticed them, how the hell would I have known?" She grimaced, then dug her phone out of her back pocket. She unlocked her screen only to stare at it, because there was no one to text. Maybe it was time to call a truce with Allison. *You were right, okay? I'm sorry. Let's just forget it, forget him. The whole thing was dumb.* Or perhaps trying David again was a better, more hopeful idea. The Twinkie thing was a perfect segue from silence to conversation, after all.

She exhaled a sigh and shook her head, leaning back in her seat. God, that lightning-struck Helena person at the grocery store. What the hell was *that* all about? Something about the whole encounter left a bad taste in her mouth, because that woman had lingered. She was still lingering, lurking at the back of Lark's mind now. Lark hadn't surveyed the contents of the grocery cart because she'd been frazzled. Dark Helena could have easily dropped that box into Lark's cart.

No, she thought, *not could have. Did.*

Was she supposed to admit that to the family? *There was this weird woman, and she kind of freaked me out, and I was nervous, and...*

But it was the item in question that really got her.

What's your favorite food? Lark had asked David during one of their hours-long messaging marathons.

It's embarrassing, David had replied. *But...Twinkies. I've loved them since I was a kid.*

It wasn't a detail one easily forgot. Sure, it could have been a coincidence, but she seriously doubted it. Which left the question: who was this Dark Helena? Was David behind this whole thing? Was it possible that the guy in the aviators was—

"No way," she whispered. "There's no damn way." Because that was crazy. She and David were done. Over. He'd been the one who had ditched *her*. The idea of him following her all the way out to Maine was nuts. And how would he have done it, anyway? He didn't have her home address, let alone the address of the vacation house.

She peered at the sleeping screen of her phone, then pressed the power button again, suddenly determined to shoot David a message. Something nondescript. Something to help her figure out where he was, or whether any of this could possibly be real.

And it was right then that a message came through, the notification popping up on her home screen from a number she didn't recognize.

HELLO, LARK, it read, causing her heart to somersault within her chest.

WELCOME TO RAVEN'S HEAD. ENJOY YOUR STAY.

LEO

LYING ON THE BED in his selected room, the last thing Leo wanted was to think about where he was, who he was with, or why he was there. He just wanted to get some sleep. Maybe, if he was lucky, he'd sleep for three whole days.

With his arm folded across his eyes and his headphones blasting in his ears, it was almost enough to transport him to better times; to days when Julien hadn't been a ghost forever haunting him, to when Amelia had been his obsession, his muse. He remembered the endless hours they'd spent locked in her room, recalled all the early hour Netflix binges they'd staged just to be together. Then there was the time when, sitting in Leo's car after a concert, Amelia told him she loved him. Hell, he tried to remember all the words she had yelled at him during their breakup—anything to get his mind far from where it was. But he always ended up in the same place. Sorrow pulsing heavy at the pit of his stomach. A thudding heart black with grief.

He could see the fluorescent-lit hospital hallway. His nostrils flared against the sharp scent of rubbing alcohol. His pulse was replaced by the steady beep of a heart monitor, so loud it drowned out all else. All thoughts. All hope.

In Leo's mind, the hall was infinitely long, fading to a pinprick as it stretched around the earth and back. There was but one blemish upon its pristine white walls: a single open door. Behind it, a room. The source of the heart monitor blip.

He fought against his dream-self's inclination to take the first forward step. *Don't go in there,* he told himself. *Stay where you are, even if you have to stay forever.* But no matter how hard he pushed to keep his feet cemented to the floor, the Leo inside his head couldn't resist. *Stop,* he'd yell. *Stop!* This time, surprisingly, he succeeded in halting his own steps. But it was only for the slightest of hesitations, not nearly enough to keep himself from following the incessant beep that was now a siren-like blare. And as he approached the hospital bed, he realized that it wasn't Julien that was lying motionless and bandaged upon stark white sheets. Despite the swelling and blood-bruised skin, he stared at his own broken face. Unrecognizable, yet still him, as much dead as alive.

He jerked at the sight. His arm pulled away from his eyes to reveal a room not his own. It had turned a deep glowing blue as moonlight spilled in through the window overlooking the bay. Nightfall had come fast. Pulling his earbuds free by the cord, he took a swipe at his eyes, then sat up and stared out beyond the glass. Being able to see nearly everything that surrounded the house was cool during the day, but it felt different now. The evening brought with it the promise of a kind of darkness that wriggled beneath the skin; the kind that made every knock and every creak both dreadful and suspicious.

Disconcerted by being in a strange room within a strange house, he clicked on the nightstand lamp, then slid off the mattress and approached a window. Tugging a curtain panel into place, he nearly smirked at himself, realizing that he was eager to keep the writhing dark beyond the glass at a distance. But why? Could it do something to him? Twist him up more than he already was? He pulled the panel sideways, not remembering curtains in any of the communal spaces downstairs. The living room, the den, all those areas were left to experience the full impact of what a private island really was. Secluded. Exposed. Swallowed whole by the night.

Turning away from the curtain he had pulled across the glass, he was on his way to the second drape when a loud thump sent his heart skittering up his throat. Something had fallen behind him, though, when he veered around, he saw nothing out of place.

He stood motionless for a long while, as though whatever had crashed to the ground would eventually make itself known; perhaps roll out from under the bed or…*or what? Fly across the room?*

Exhaling the breath he hadn't realized he'd been holding, he took a reluctant step toward the bed, unsure of why he was so nervous. *What're you going to see?* he asked himself. *A memento left by Julien's ghost?*

And if it *was* the phantom of his best friend, was he back to reveal the secret he'd died with? Was he there to tell Leo what had happened that night? Would Julien appear the way he'd looked in life, or would his face and half his body be unrecognizable, smashed beyond repair?

"Don't be stupid," he whispered to himself, those words buffering his nerves enough for him to take a few forward steps toward where the sound had come from. His eyes scanned the floor, searching for God only knew what. There was stuff on the walls, just as there was stuff on *all* the walls of the house, but it all checked out. All the framed photos were where they were supposed to be. The round galvanized wall mirror still hung from a thick rope above the headboard, undisturbed. The nautical map of Maine's various bays and waterways remained steadfast. But it wasn't as though he'd imagined the hard thump that had come directly from behind his bed, which only left one other option. Something had fallen on the opposite side of the wall outside of his room.

Furrowing his eyebrows, he moved to the bedroom door, tugged it open and peeked his head into the hall. His room was at the end of the upstairs hallway, purposefully selected so that no one had to walk past his door. When he looked toward where he was sure the thud had come from, there was nothing but an exterior wall. Nothing…except for a small door tucked against the corner. It was an access door; one of many throughout the house. He hadn't paid those little doors any mind, except the one he was staring at now, and this one was suddenly giving him the creeps.

Shooting a glance down the hall, he began to reason the noise away. Maybe it had been Lark. She seemed enamored with all the crap nailed to the walls. Maybe she'd knocked something down. But he knew his sister, and had something gone tumbling to the floor under Lark's watch, she'd still be in the hall trying to put it right. The hall was, however, empty. No Lark, and no explanation for where the noise had come from.

Steadying his nerves, Leo ducked out of his room and approached the access door. Again, there were a lot of these. He'd spotted one in the kitchen, one in the living room beside the fireplace. But something about the one just outside his room made the hairs on his neck stand on end. It felt out of place, like something out of *House of Leaves.* Except, this was an AirBnB, not a portal to another dimension. Exhaling a breath, Leo tried the small door. It opened easily, its hinges silent, as though freshly oiled. Squinting into the darkness, he patted his back pocket, then cursed beneath his breath. His phone was back on the bed along with his headphones and sketchbook, which meant he had no way of illuminating whatever may have been lurking within that vertical crawl space. Maybe there was an animal living inside the wall—a bird, or chipmunks, or maybe bats. The mere idea of it had him closing that door fast, his skin crawling at the idea of something flying out of there, straight at his face.

Sucking in a breath, he shuddered, then closed his eyes and centered himself. It was a tactic he'd picked up during his six-month hospital residence. Every so often, shit got too heavy. Sometimes, he needed a better way to cope beyond shoving his nose into his phone, or drawing, or reading the battered Stieg Larsson paperbacks he'd found at the back of a hallway closet the previous winter. He'd Googled ways to handle panic disorders and anxiety attacks, had scoured the internet for ways to help himself without having to resort to pills or booze or, God forbid, asking his parents to find him a shrink. His mom had anxiety, so he knew it ran in his blood. If he didn't figure out how to keep it quelled, there was no point to Thailand. He'd be a wreck there, same as he was here. *And if you can't handle a bump in the night,* the voice inside his head whispered, *then you're more far-gone than you think.*

Lifting his hands to his face, he rubbed his eyes and turned away from the access door. "It was a bird," he reassured himself. "Or fucking bats." Again, his skin prickled at the possibility, because those damn things had rabies, right? He'd have to look it up. The internet would know.

He moved back to his open bedroom door, and it was then that he saw something that left him both breathless and baffled. The drapes he'd pulled into place were pushed away from the glass, allowing the night to creep in. Pushed open, as if to assure him that there was no hiding from the darkness. And that scent of licorice was back, so strong that it reversed the flow of his blood. So strong it was almost as though he was smelling it from the inside out, as though the scent was inside him. Leaching out from within his very bones.

LARK

LARK SAT PROPPED UP against the bed's rustic headboard, her screen lighting up the already dim room with its bright blue glow. She'd been staring at her phone for what felt like hours, her attention fixed on David's old text messages, diverging to the new message that had come in a few hours before. There was no way she was going to be able to sleep after her nerves had been so thoroughly frazzled, and certainly not in a strange new place.

She tried to shift gears and get some writing done, but her mind was a million miles removed from where it needed to be; still distracted by Dark Helena, by the way that aviator-wearing guy had stared across the length of Ouellette's and straight at her. *I see you, Lark Parrish. Welcome to Raven's Head.*

Squeezing her eyes shut, she tried to convince herself that the guy in the retro shades hadn't been looking at her at all, that it had just been an illusion. But, for once, she refused to give in to her own naivety. *Yeah, and there's a chance that woman isn't behind the Twinkies, too.* Yeah, no. Dark Helena had definitely been the one to drop that box of snack cakes into Lark's cart, which meant she knew David. *Somehow,* she knew him. And somehow, she'd found Lark in Raven's Head, over a thousand miles away from home.

And how did that happen, Lark?

She navigated to her home screen, then tapped the Instagram icon. Allison's profile sported a glowing green dot next to it, which meant Lark's wayward friend was online. *How could they have possibly found you?* Lark could hear her asking. *How is that possible, Lark? You wouldn't have just flat-out* told *them, right?*

The truth of it was, finding Lark would have been a cakewalk. She talked to anyone who sent her a direct message, because the mere sentiment of someone liking her writing was enough to make her slip. She opened up way too quickly, trusted blindly, made friends way too fast. She'd collected nearly a dozen of those "friends" over the years; folks she connected with but never met in person, never spoke to on the phone. They were people who were there when it was trivial banter, but vanished as soon as things got heavy. It's what had happened with David. She'd fallen too hard, too fast. It was why Lark and Allison weren't speaking anymore.

Allison had admonished Lark's relationship with David, the mystery man. *You have no idea who he is. He won't talk to you in person, won't send you photographs. And now you're asking him to meet you at a hotel?* Sure, it was nuts, but love had no logic. It had no fear. Lark felt alone so often, felt overlooked by her father, misunderstood by her mom. Her online friends weren't really friends and she and Leo didn't hang out anymore; they certainly weren't the type of siblings to have heart-to-hearts. She was alone, having nothing but the digital faces of social media to comfort her when she needed it most. They were people that always failed her, no matter how much they praised her work.

But then she met David and everything changed.

You have no idea who he is, Allison had hissed, but it didn't matter by then. Lark knew it was crazy, but she was in love.

But now, this…

Welcome to Raven's Head.

She bit her bottom lip, then clicked Allison's profile picture and began to type.

Al, something weird is going on. I'm freaked out. Please, can we talk?

But, no. *No.* Screw that. Lark deleted the message, then looked up from her phone into the shadows of an unfamiliar room. She wouldn't give Allison the satisfaction. Besides, Lark didn't know if Allison was right or not. Yeah, there were the Twinkies, but…

But what? she wondered. But it was a coincidence? No way.

Just forget it, she told herself. *Let it go. Go to sleep.* If David really was behind the Twinkie thing, so what? Not like he could get to her out on Raven's Bay. If she really did have a stalker, they were back on the mainland fifteen minutes away. *And besides,* she thought, *it's not a stalker. You're not that important. Why would he even bother?*

Atticus was why.

Lark chewed a thumbnail as she stared at Atticus's profile picture—the quintessential brooding boyfriend, like Edward Scissorhands without the razorblades and cookie heart. Maybe she'd made him too perfect to be convincing. Maybe David had caught on, maybe he knew…

"And what would it matter if he did?" she asked aloud, then shoved the sheets off her legs. "Like it would matter, right? Like he'd suddenly give a shit? Wake up, idiot. He stood you up, cut you off." Tossing her phone onto the comforter, she padded across the floor in a pair of thick socks, heading toward the bedroom door. "You could make up a million boyfriends and it wouldn't make a difference."

She frowned at herself, those last few words warbling with emotion. Enough of this, damnit. She was going to bed, going to put this nonsense out of her head. But she needed to pee first, so she pulled open her door and skulked down a hallway lined with books, decorated with various bits of weird maritime memorabilia.

There were endless photographs of fishing boats and fishermen holding up massive catches—some so big that they had to be hoisted up by pulleys and ropes. There were small bookshelves built into every nook and cranny the homeowner was able to find. One was little more than a windowsill that stuck out a bit further than usual, the books that lined the window packed so tight Lark doubted she could dislodge one if she tried. There was an old wooden oar attached to the wall, high up, painted white with a turquoise tip. An antique brass wall bell hung on the wall, mounted to a wooden plaque. She had to restrain herself from ringing it as she passed. She paused to peer at an ancient-looking ship in a bottle, confounded as to how it could have ever been placed inside the glass.

It was then, standing in the hall just outside the bathroom door and studying the ship's tiny sails, that she felt the sensation of not being alone. Bent forward with her eyes fixed on the curve of antique glass, her breath caught in her throat when the energy in the hallway took a shift. *It's Leo.* Logic always tried to outrun panic, but it didn't *feel* like him. This energy…it was strange. Heavy, as if laden by animosity, nefarious and rotten. With every muscle in her body having gone stiff, Lark's eyes widened as the bottle's dulled reflection mirrored the movement of a shadow she couldn't see; couldn't, because it was behind her and Lark was too petrified to move.

Haunted was the first word that came to mind, igniting bright like a fourth of July sparkler. *This house is haunted, and there's no one to help us when the spirits come.*

But again, logic kicked in, simultaneously reassuring and reproachful. *It's not haunted, stupid.* But wouldn't it have been perfect if it was? *But it's not,* the voice of reason told her. *It's not, Lark. Just turn around and you'll see.*

"I'm going to turn around now," she whispered, warning whatever or *whoever* may have been looming behind her of her intent. "If you're real, just go away," she said softly. "I'm going to turn around, and when I do you won't be there anymore."

Closing her eyes tight, she counted to three.

One.

She clenched her teeth.

Two.

Her fingers curled into fists.

Three.

She pulled in a sharp breath and performed a quick pivot, staring down the length of the hall. There was, of course, no one there. But there was one thing. A scent.

And it smelled like licorice.

Like exactly what Leo had described.

LEO

SOMETIMES, IT FELT like his grief would never get better, as though he'd be stuck in a perpetual cycle of sorrow until it was his turn to die.

It had been a horrific chain of events, a type of heartbreak that had only gotten exponentially worse with the passing of time. Leo often thought about the fact that, if anyone had gotten the sweet end of the deal, it had been Julien. Sure, he was in a coma. He had to have blood drained from his skull to keep him from teetering into the great abyss. But he had gotten to sleep through it all, lying around for half a year while the people around him felt the agony he couldn't. Every day, the sense of impending doom intensified, so the day Julien's mother had decided everyone had been tortured enough should have come as a relief. At least with Julien dead and buried, there was no chance that he was suffering; no possibility of him opening his eyes and screaming himself blind at the sight of his own mangled face. But for Leo, the relief had yet to come.

After Julien's ventilator had gone silent, the emptiness in Leo's life amplified. People were quick to offer condolences, to ask if there was anything they could do, tossing out that ever-popular line of *if you need anything...* They were empty promises of comfort; promises that would have been tarnished by hesitation, if not flat-out refusal, had Leo called any of his well-meaning friends out on the extended favor. Not that it mattered. He hardly registered their pity, their voices but a muffled whisper within the empty chasm that had become Leo's heart.

He had managed to maintain at least a semblance of his relationship with Amelia while Julien had still been alive. When he died, Leo was hit with such an all-encompassing sense of exhaustion, he couldn't be bothered to care about anything or anyone for even a second more. Julien's mother had unhooked her son from life support, but Leo was the one who flatlined, terminating his and Amelia's relationship without so much as a second thought. Amelia had cried, but she hadn't argued. She was smart, knowing that there wouldn't have been a point to debate, what with Thailand on the horizon. As far as Leo was concerned, he was doing her a favor. It would have been selfish to string her along. She's waited for him for so long already. The last thing he wanted was to leave her with a lie, a farewell kiss before boarding a transatlantic flight, a promise of return when return was the last thing he'd consider, at least for a long, long time.

Besides, that six months had taken a lot out of them. Their bond had become brittle, ready to crumble. But it wasn't just with Amelia. Every relationship Leo had went sour with a keening ache. The only connection he had managed to make was with Felix, Julien's older brother, and that had ended as abruptly as it had begun.

Sometimes, he missed being at the hospital, missed reminiscing with Felix about the stupid things Julien used to say or do. Leo knew better than anyone that there were major problems in Julien and Felix's relationship. Hell, only months before Julien's accident, there had been noise about Felix getting in trouble with the law. Julien's mother had been scrambling to put together bail money so she could spring Felix out of jail...again. And yet, when the shit hit the fan, Felix showed up. Despite the awful circumstances and the pain he knew Felix had caused Julien in the past, Leo bonded with the guy. Together, they had hoped for the best. Felix became a surrogate best friend; a vessel for the overwhelming sorrow that threatened to pull him under like a rip tide. But when Julien's vent went quiet, Felix vanished, as though astral projecting his way out of Leo's life.

Or maybe Felix had never been there at all, Leo thought. *Maybe you made him up as you slipped into madness. Maybe that's why you keep smelling that scent...the one nobody else seems to smell.*

Theories circled his brain like a wake of vultures as he stood motionless in his temporary room, his attention not once wavering from the drapes he was sure he'd pulled into place before he had stepped into the hall. If there was a possibility that Felix hadn't been real, there was a chance he hadn't pulled the drapes over those windows. Maybe he'd imagined it. Dreamt it. Hallucinated the whole thing.

"Christ."

Drawing a hand down his face, Leo exhaled a breath and forced his eyes away from the bedroom windows, sure that if he stared at them for much longer he'd force himself over the brink. He needed a distraction. A strong cup of coffee and some Netflix, if this place even had it.

Grabbing his phone and his sketchpad, he slipped out of his room. But navigating an unfamiliar house in the dark was easier said than done. He avoided the dead end of the hall along with its access door and made a beeline for the stairs. Pausing on the landing where the stairs split in two, he found himself unsure of which path to take, eventually settling on right rather than left. And then there were all those damn windows downstairs. No drapes, the night full-on. The sensation of being enveloped in darkness was overwhelming. He kept his footsteps swift, his eyes forward.

Finally finding himself the kitchen, he flipped on the overhead light, then winced against the glare. The track lighting didn't make the pitch darkness outside the windows any less disconcerting. Now, rather than feeling as though he was standing outside without any protection, he was inside a painfully bright room, unable to see past the gleam of the glass.

He tugged open the refrigerator door and stared at shelves. They were empty compared with the chaos of their fridge back home. Fine, coffee it was. He moved to the cupboards and began to pull them open, one after the other, searching for a mug.

That was when he sensed movement just beyond his periphery. His head whipped around to look over his shoulder. He listened for any sound that would suggest he wasn't the only one up.

"Lark?"

Once upon a time, he and his sister used to run into each other during dead-of-night kitchen raids. They'd make popcorn and watch movies until neither one of them could keep their eyes open. Maybe it was her now, same as it had been upstairs when he'd heard the bang in the hall. *Except she hadn't been there, remember?* Yeah, but it had been her regardless. Maybe she'd bumped something, and it had thumped to the floor after she'd returned to her room. Hell, maybe something had fallen off one of those cramped walls all on its own. Who knew what the owners had used to hang all that kitsch. Once, Leo used a scrawny Command hook to hang a framed poster in his room. A few days later, the thing came crashing down in the dead of night, glass shattering. Leo had just about died of a goddamn heart attack.

"Lark, is that you?"

No response.

The master bedroom was downstairs somewhere, though Leo hadn't been interested enough to pinpoint its location. He had no idea whether the room was just off the kitchen or clear across the house. But like Lark, his dad was notorious for staying up all night, too. Maybe Dad had the same idea as Leo: Netflix into the small hours of the morning. Or, perhaps he was vegging out on the couch, sling-shotting cartoon birds into wooden structures, playing his games in another room so as to not get busted for breaking cell phone rules.

"Dad?" Leo spoke into the quiet of the house. Waited. Listened.

Finally, he heard it. The soft rustle of fabric. Someone was shuffling around, keeping to the dark.

Furrowing his eyebrows, Leo stepped toward the sound, toward a dark living room with the bay moonlit and glowing beyond the glass. And there in the furthest corner, he saw a silhouette. A woman.

Leo blinked. "Mom?" Again, no response. The silence seemed to deepen instead.

Goosebumps rose along the backs of his arms.

Something was off. Not right.

There was a goddamn woman standing there in the darkness. His mother or Lark. Either that or his suspicions were correct and he really was losing his mind.

"Jesus, *Lark?*"

Still nothing, which only brought on an overwhelming sense of panic. If it wasn't his mother or sister, who the fuck was it? His hand slapped the wall beside him, blindly searching for a light switch he was sure had to be there somewhere. Unable to locate it by feel alone, he tore his eyes from the shadow in the corner, desperate for light, intent on waking the whole house if he had to. And if he couldn't find the switch, what then? Would he start yelling? Could he yell even if he wanted to? That panic was tightening around his throat, squeezing like a wrathful fist.

Finally, he spotted the switch and lunged for it, his fingers jabbing the wall. The lights blinked on. Leo's gaze darted back to the corner of the room. He wasn't sure who he was expecting to see, but he expected to see *someone*.

Except, there was no one.

"What?" He shook his head, refusing to believe it, so convinced that he'd seen what he'd seen that he flipped the light off again, waiting for the silhouette to reappear as soon as the darkness was invited in.

But it didn't appear.

Leo's breath hitched in his throat.

I'm going crazy.

He turned the lights on, then off again.

He did it over and over, creating a strobe-like effect, imagining that if someone was watching from another island, from their boat, it would have looked like Morse Code. *I'm losing it. Please send help.* But the shadow was gone.

"Oh my god." Leo pressed a hand over his face, wondering if this was it, if Thailand was out and a psychiatric evaluation was in. Because what else? "What else?" he asked the empty room. *What else?*

Flipping the light off again, he turned away from the room, moved through the kitchen, and pointed himself back up that stairwell. Screw coffee. All he wanted was to crawl into bed and pull the sheets over his face, to sink into the mattress and not wake until it was time to leave.

But the moment he reached the stairwell, he came to a dead stop. Like a hard slap to the face, it nearly took his breath away. That scent. Licorice. The stairwell reeked of it.

For a moment, he was sure he was about to have a panic attack. He nearly screamed, because that scent was strong enough to defy tricks of the mind. It took him back to the hospital. Back to the infinite hallway.

No, not his imagination. What he was smelling was as real as Julien's headstone. As real as the lapping bay outside the windows. As real as the hard thud of his own pulse against his ears. Like the endless and incessant beep of a heart monitor that had yet to cease.

But before he succumbed to that staggering sense of dread, he was knocked out of his downward spiral by a sound coming from overhead.

A single, loud clang. Like a church bell ringing to drive out the demons. A ghost calling a sailor back to port.

A bell, like the one hanging on the upstairs hallway wall.

ARISE

EZRA

THE ALARM CLOCK beside the bed read 9:15 AM. For once, he'd slept in, but from the look of the empty spot next to him, Poppy had not. And yet, despite waking in a strange place, he knew exactly where his wife was. He could smell bacon, pancakes, the heavenly aroma of freshly brewed coffee; could hear the clatter of pans on the stove. She was digging deep, pretending that everything was the way it should have been, fixing what was broken with orange juice and fresh-cut fruit. Ezra wanted to dismiss her desperate optimism as nothing more than naivety, but he couldn't. He was guilty of the same fantasy, willing away the things he wanted gone. If he just *believed* his problems were over, maybe they really would be.

He had to get back to being a dad to his kids. Had to reconnect with Poppy before it was too late. Getting there, however, would take a lot of wishful thinking. Desperate optimism, like what Poppy was serving out there in the kitchen, pretending a stack of pancakes would make everything alright.

But first, Ezra had to teach himself to forget *her*; Poppy's shadow, the woman who had been lurking just beyond his wife's shoulder for so long. Every night, Ezra would go to bed promising to erase her from his thoughts, and every morning he'd wake up with her on his mind. *Gemma.* The way things had ended between them left him feeling hollow and haunted. She was a phantom, refusing to let him get on with his life, to move beyond the past. Not that he truly ever could.

Sitting up in bed, he pulled his hands down his face with a deep exhale, then gave the master bedroom a once-over from where he sat. The place was three times the size of their room back home, and the massive windows that made up the entirety of one wall only made it feel that much bigger. He was no interior decorator, but it was busy.

Themed, like a Disneyland ride. He squinted at the fishing nets hanging on the walls, furrowed his eyebrows at the clock that looked like the wheel of a ship. For how expensive the place was per night, he had expected it to be a little more Hamptons, a bit less theme park. But whatever. It's what Poppy had wanted, so here they were. Besides, this was officially the first full day of their vacation—no travel, no getting settled. As cliché as it was, he thought it anyway. *This is the first day of the rest of your life.* And he was determined to make it count. He had two days to get things back on track, to recenter himself. *Two days,* he thought. *If you can't get your head on straight by then, you may as well stay here forever.*

POPPY

SHE MADE BREAKFAST but decided not to wake anyone to eat it. An early wakeup call was no way to start a vacation, after all. Besides, it was clear that *someone* had been up 'til all hours. She didn't remember hearing Ezra shuffling around, but he was suspect number one. Leo had thrown those Twinkies into the trash, but now that box of snack cakes was back on the kitchen island, dead center, as if being presented as an item up for bid on *The Price is Right*.

It wasn't out of character for Ezra. He'd grown up in a house where throwing out good food was a deadly sin. The Parrishes had, up until a few generations past, survived as peanut farmers out in rural South Carolina. Torrential rains had cost his grandparents their entire crop in 1945. They'd been forced to sell everything, and the scar of losing it all practically overnight never quite healed. Paired with his teacher's salary and his secret envy of his brother Luca's success, Ezra had a miserly side.

He'd been forced to reckon with that particular idiosyncrasy after the kids had come along. When it came to toddlers, wasting food was a parental rite of passage. Ezra had a tough go of it with Leo, but by the time Lark was pushing two years old, dumping entire plates of food into the disposal didn't seem to faze him. But it hadn't come naturally. It had taken Poppy years, reassuring him that his teaching job was enough, that he was a good provider, that she loved him no matter what figure appeared on his paycheck. Once Lark started kindergarten, Poppy's part-time real estate gig helped to pad their accounts.

But Ezra still had his moments. One didn't just shrug off such deeply ingrained familial trauma, didn't forget such tough history. It was why Poppy didn't fuss when Ezra refused to leave restaurants without a doggy bag, taking even the smallest bits of leftovers home because *hey, that can be my lunch*. And here it was again, that box of Twinkies left out on display as if to say, *look, maybe nobody chose to buy this stuff, but we paid for it, so now it's ours.*

Poppy quirked a smile at the thought of him digging the box out of the garbage. Perhaps to anyone else, Ezra's Scrooge-like side would be a turn-off, but she'd always found it somewhat endearing, and that was good; a nice reminder of why she'd fallen for him, if only to keep her from giving up.

Ezra was the first to rise.

"Morning," she said upon his arrival, if only to get things started on the right foot.

"Smells great," Ezra said. "You should have woken me. I could have helped."

Poppy smiled at the suggestion, but she turned away from him to busy herself with the silverware, avoiding small talk. Recently, Ezra had been all about helping out, which was new. At the start of their marriage, he'd always been considerate, loading dishes into the washer after dinner, making coffee in the morning. But as time went on, those sweet little gestures had faded. Dishes were left in the sink. The timer on the coffee pot was never set the night before. Ezra began to leave the house earlier for work, began to come home later, an excuse at the ready. They had grown distant, hardly spoke to each other much anymore. And then, one day, Poppy had decided that Ezra was having an affair. She had no proof, only a feeling. The evidence was lacking, but for her, after all those years together, the feeling was enough.

"It's fine," she told him, still looking away. "It's nice to sleep in. Looks like you were up late, anyway." She turned back to the stove, grabbed a mug from one of the overhead cabinets, then poured him a cup of coffee.

"Up late?"

She didn't regard his confusion, hadn't in a long time. The way his voice went up an octave when he was confounded, the way his face twisted into a countenance of bewilderment—she hated it. It was the very act he'd been using on her for years, that whole innocent *I don't know what you're talking about* schtick. But she let it go the way she always did, because it was easier to keep the peace than fight a hundred-years war. Deciding not to mention the Twinkies, she motioned toward the pots and pans still on the stove.

"Help yourself," she said, placed his mug of coffee on the counter, then busied herself with the bacon. Listening to him move behind her, she took a few sidesteps to give him some room.

"Plates?" he asked, opening one cabinet after the other in that bumbling way of his—a way that had once been cute, but now just made her want to yell.

"Second one from the fridge," she said, pivoting in the opposite direction, thinking that maybe she would wake the kids after all, if only to nip this awkward interaction with Ezra in the bud. But before she could duck out of the kitchen and seek out the kids' chosen upstairs rooms, Ezra stopped her with another one of his baffled little quips.

"Huh. *That's* weird."

Poppy finally turned to look at him, then blinked at what Ezra was referring to.

There was a Post-It stuck to the inside of the cabinet door. On it, in black Sharpie, two words: *Welcome, Parrishes.* And directly beneath it, a crooked smiley face, its skewed features enough to make Poppy's skin crawl.

LEO

LEO CONSIDERED STAYING in his room. He was still frazzled and edgy, still balancing on the knife's edge of a full-blown freak out. He hadn't slept, his gaze fixed on the still-open window curtains, his brain stuck downstairs in the living room, stuck on the shadow that was but wasn't there.

He'd been listening to someone bang around the kitchen for a better part of an hour now, imagining his mother down there, trying to make the most of this family time. He wanted to stay locked away, not bother with any of the family bullshit his mother was so desperately banking on. But wounding her wasn't part of the plan—not when it came to Thailand, and not when it came to this trip. He felt like he was losing his footing, as though the ground beneath him had shifted, tilting at an impossible angle. Perhaps losing his grip was inevitable, but over the past handful of hours, Leo had decided that if he had to spiral into psychosis, he'd rather do it abroad than at home. He was leaving and nothing would change his mind, not even last night. But he also knew his departure would tear his mom apart. The least he could do was make her happy now.

"Hey," he said, announcing his arrival as he stepped into the kitchen.

His mother turned away from the stove and gave him a smile, but it looked strained, as though she was still recovering from a good scare.

"Good morning, sweetheart," she said.

Leo's gaze shifted to his father, who also looked odd, uncomfortable in his own skin. Or maybe Leo was just tired and seeing things; just a trick of the light, like that fucking silhouette the night before.

"Morning, kiddo," Dad said. "Sleep okay?" The question was heavy with insinuation, suggesting that Leo looked as tired as he felt.

"Um, yeah," Leo murmured, then rubbed his face with his hands.

"Is there coffee?" He moved further into the room and around his father, who was seated at the kitchen island and busy with a short stack. When the full length of the island came into view, he stopped dead.

Like a kid tripping over his own feet, his heart stuttered, stalling for a single breathless moment, then hammering against his ribcage double-time.

"Sure," Mom said. "You want your usual café au lait?"

Leo didn't respond. He couldn't. Because there, on the island, was that goddamn box of Twinkies he had thrown away.

"Honey?"

His gaze fixed itself on that box, his mind suddenly doing backflips beneath the curve of his skull. Because what *was* this? What the hell was happening? What the fuck was going on?

"Sweetheart?"

"Huh?" Leo blinked at his mother.

Mom offered him an unsure sort of smile. "Everything okay?"

She was looking at him in that concerned way of hers, the same way she'd been staring at him for half a year now. But her looks in the past handful of weeks had been more intense, like she was waiting for him to swallow a fistful of pills or leap off a bridge.

"Yeah," Leo said, forcing his gaze away from those snack cakes and back to his mom. It was fine. Everything was fine. "Yeah, I'm fine," he said. *You're fine.* "Coffee." He croaked the word. "I'll get it."

He didn't want his mom waiting on him like some over-attentive Denny's waitress. He could get his own coffee, his own breakfast. It would give him something to do, something to focus on other than what sat dead-center on that kitchen island like some cruel joke.

Turning to the fridge to fish out the milk, he hesitated for a second time as he found himself staring into a crookedly drawn smiley face.

"The AirBnB hosts left that for us," Mom said. "They're sweet, aren't they?"

There was a pause. No one spoke.

"That guy," Dad finally chimed in, pushing the fingers of his left hand through his hair before adjusting his glasses. His right remained poised above his plate, fork at the ready. "Gill, was it?"

"What about him?" Mom asked, but she didn't look Dad's way. Tension, same as it ever was. It was one of the many things Leo wouldn't miss about home.

"I don't know." Dad shrugged, then took a bite of bacon. "He seemed creepy, I guess."

"There was nothing creepy about him," Mom rebutted. "He was cordial and friendly…"

"Yeah." Lark's voice cut into the conversation.

Leo glanced over his shoulder to spot his sister standing at the mouth of the kitchen. Lark looked like she crawled out of the wrong end of a sleeping bag—her hair a black tangle atop her head, yesterday's eyeliner not quite wiped clean. If anyone looked more worn out than Leo felt, it was her.

"So friendly that he told us he'd sneak in here when no one was looking," she told the room, her attention settling upon Leo's face. Her expression said it all: she knew he'd experienced something the evening before. She knew he'd heard the ringing of that bell.

LARK

MAYBE NOBODY ELSE remembered Gill asserting that he was going to duck in and out of their rental house like a thief in the night, but Lark certainly did. And after what had happened last night, she halfway believed that her father was right. Gill *was* creepy.

She'd convinced herself that what she'd sensed in the hallway had been little more than a hallucination, but then the hollow ring of a bell had stopped her heart cold. She hadn't dared look out into the hall again, but it was enough to assure her that no, she wasn't imagining things. *Someone* had been standing in the hall, and they'd rung the brass bell on the wall to assure her that they were there, that they were watching.

"What?" Mom looked exasperated, as though Lark's reminder was absurd.

"Dad?" Lark glanced at her father. "Remember?"

Her father nodded once, then readjusted his glasses for the millionth time.

Lark's mother scoffed. "You two are something else," she said, then turned back to the stove. Dad gave Lark a shrug before going back to his breakfast. Neither parent asked why Lark would bring up such a random detail, or why she had dark circles beneath her eyes. No doubt Mom concluded Lark's phone was to blame, and in a way it was. As it turned out, when you're too freaked out to sleep, scrolling through social media accounts was a decent way to pass the time.

Lark was left to peer at Leo, who looked like warmed-over death. The last time he'd looked so tired he'd spent the evening texting Amelia—he and Amelia hashing it out after their one-sided breakup. And while breakups were never fun, Lark had been jealous anyway. At least Leo had an ex that was communicative. Lark, on the other hand, was left with little more than a memory of a person who had once been part of her life but had never quite been real.

ANIA AHLBORN

Leo was watching her with a strange sort of suspicion now. *What the hell is up with you?* his expression read. Lark gave him a look of her own: *I should ask you the same thing.* And then, *we need to talk.*

Now? Leo mouthed.

She widened her eyes at him, day-old eyeliner still needing to be soaped away—*yes, now.* She pivoted on the balls of her socked feet and moved into the living room. Pulling her black cardigan tight across her chest, Lark stepped through the sliding-glass door onto the wrap-around porch, thankful for the sobering autumn chill.

Waiting for Leo to appear, she sucked in a deep breath of cold coastal air. It was windier than yesterday, the air carrying with it a distinct scent of petrichor. There was a hint of fog drifting across the bay, reminiscent of the puffs of breath she could see coiling past her lips. Such a gloomy morning begged for a photo for her Instagram account, complete with an intriguing caption. *Finding inspiration in the most incredible place.* But after last night, Lark was in no mood for doing backbends in the name of digital relevance. Hell, just yesterday she had argued how important being able to write during this getaway was, but she couldn't have cared less about her book now.

Still, she couldn't quite shake the idea that what she'd sensed in the hallway the night before was crazy. There hadn't been anyone there to acknowledge what she'd felt, and she'd been thoroughly creeped out by the whole grocery store thing. It was altogether possible that Dark Helena had clawed her way into Lark's brain and waited for the perfect moment to make a few neurons misfire, producing a sensation that had *seemed* real but had been anything but.

"Except, what about the bell?" Lark whispered.

Leo stepped up to the railing next to her, his sudden appearance making her jump. What was it with this place, with people sneaking around on silent feet? She tried to hide her reaction by tightening her arms across her chest and lifting her shoulders to her ears, playing off her nerves as little more than a response to the chill in the air, but Leo was quick on the uptake.

"Jumpy much? What's up?" he asked.

78

"Nothing," she said. "I don't know." She shrugged again. "What's up with you?"

"What do you mean?" He squinted across the water, refusing to make eye contact.

"You look like shit," Lark murmured. "No offense."

"Yeah," he said. "And you're as subtle as a punch in the mouth, no offense. Speaking of." Leo shot her a sidelong glance, then looked away just as quickly.

"Speaking of what? I *know* I look like shit, Leo," Lark countered. "It may come as a shock, but I've got a little self-awareness."

"Huh."

That grunt of a response rubbed her the wrong way, but the fact that she was annoyed with her brother was an improvement over the emptiness she'd felt lingering between them for the past few months. Annoyance meant connection. It meant that they'd spoken for long enough to aggravate each other, and that was a lot further than they'd gotten in a while.

"What's with all of this, anyway?" he asked, nodding at her, his attention lingering on the smears of eyeliner beneath her lashes.

"What do you mean?" she asked, narrowing her eyes at him; but she knew what he was alluding to. The box-dyed hair. The black everything. Four months ago, she had been a strawberry blonde. *You'll never get back to your natural color again,* Mom had said the morning she set eyes on what Lark had accomplished in the bathroom the night before. *You think this is you now, but wait a while. You'll miss who you once were.*

"The Beetlejuice thing," Leo said. "Who're you trying to fool?"

"Oh, you're one to talk, Cobain," she said, regarding the bull ring through his nose, his tattered cardigan. Rolling her eyes, she looked across the water, trying to pinpoint just how far out she could see. *Everyone,* she wanted to reply to Leo's question. *Anyone.* But, no. She wouldn't go down that conversational path. What she wanted was to talk about last night, to tell him about what she'd sensed, what she was now starting to doubt she'd actually seen in the curve of that antique bottle's glass. She wanted to tell him about that goddamn bell. Within the silence of the house, it had been blaringly loud. *What if he'd heard it, too?* But, if he *had* heard it, he would have brought it up. Besides, nothing had happened. Nobody had broken into her room and held her captive. She hadn't even heard footsteps, and God knew she'd listened for them all night long. Maybe Leo had rung that bell himself, thinking it was nothing but a prop. And because it *had* rung and possibly woken the entire house, he'd ducked into his room and stayed there like a guilty kid avoiding blame.

"Do you think we could get out of here?" she finally asked, giving Leo a sidelong glance.

"What, like off the island?" he asked, raising a skeptical eyebrow. Lark shrugged. "On that shitty little boat?" Leo continued, nodding down the pier toward the commuter docked there.

"Sure, why not? I went on it with Dad yesterday. It was fine." She smirked, looked toward the water again. "And that's saying something, since he crashed it into the side of the dock. So…"

"He crashed it?" Leo's mouth quirked up in amusement.

"Of course he did." She shrugged again. "But it's still in one piece. It can't be *that* shitty, right?"

"I guess." Leo hesitated, then spoke again. "I'm tired."

"So am I," Lark countered. "All the better reason to get some real coffee instead of this drip crap. I need an espresso," she said. "Jesus, I need a double, and from the look of you, you need it twice as bad as I do."

Leo exhaled a sigh, then looked over his shoulder back toward the house. "Mom will flip."

"So what?" Lark muttered beneath her breath.

All at once, she wanted to grab her brother by the arm and beg him to reconsider. *Please don't leave me here by myself with them.* Because there he was, poised to blow out of the country while Lark was left to deal with whatever fallout it caused. Their mom always complained that she could feel oncoming rain in her bones. Well, maybe that sort of premonition was an inherited trait, because Lark could sense the storm of Leo's departure rolling in like a hurricane. The fallout would be cataclysmic, bringing on the apocalypse. *I don't want you to go,* she wanted to tell him. *If you do, I'll be more alone than I already am.*

"There's a coffee place just across the street from the pier," she told him, last night suddenly not feeling all that significant. What did feel important was spending time with Leo. She wasn't foolish enough to believe she had the power to change his mind about Thailand, but she could at least give it her best shot.

"I'll make something up," she told him. "Like, that I forgot to get something at the grocery store yesterday. Whatever. I doubt she'll care that much, anyway."

"I beg to differ," Leo countered, but Lark wasn't deterred.

"Let's just go, okay?" she asked, giving him an imploring look. *Please?*

There was a long beat of hesitation on his part. He was considering his options, weighing the pros and cons. "Yeah," he finally said, then pivoted away from her gaze, trying to hide his expression. "Let's get off this fucking rock," he said beneath his breath. Another glance back toward the house left him looking haunted, and that's when Lark knew.

The bell. It hadn't been him.

He'd heard it, too.

POPPY

"JUST BE CAREFUL."

Poppy wanted to protest, but she bit her tongue and acquiesced instead. If her kids wanted to spend time together, it would be wrong of her to try to interfere. Sure, she would have liked for them to have stayed on the island. She didn't see why they had to boat off to Raven's Head to hang out. But on the other hand, who was she kidding? The island was beautiful, but there wasn't a damn thing to do but stare at the water. It was just another thing that had seemed like a great idea but, in retrospect, was a failure on her part.

Stupid, she thought to herself as she watched both Lark and Leo duck out of the kitchen and back to their rightful rooms. *What did you think would happen?* she wondered, twisting a gingham-checked dish towel so tight in her hands that it may as well have been a rope. At least the kids were compelled to go off together rather than avoiding each other, but it still stung—her kids turning away from her, stretching their fingers toward the outside world rather than reaching inward toward their mother. *We're not babies anymore.* She wished they would have asked her to tag along—a third wheel but still cool enough to hang out. After all, she liked coffee too. But the mere idea of it had her rolling her eyes at herself and turning back to the dirty kitchen, trying to control the quiver of her bottom lip. Not like she could go with them even if they *had* invited her. There was a pile of dishes half a mile high stacked in the sink that weren't going to wash themselves. That, and going to Raven's Head involved voyaging out on that tiny deathtrap of a boat.

"Well," Ezra said after a moment, his voice slashing through the quiet. "That's good news, right?"

"What is?" Poppy asked as she stared into the sink, saline burning the backs of her eyes. Was she really going to cry? Crumple into a heap and melt down on the first day of their "perfect" vacation? She snorted at the thought, but it only made her want to cry more. *This is so stupid,* she told herself. *Why did we come here? What did I think I'd achieve?*

"Leo," Ezra said, their son's name giving rise to goosebumps along the backs of her arms. "Looks like he's finally pulling out of his funk."

Poppy squeezed her eyes shut. Yes, perhaps he *was* pulling out of his depression. She only wished that he'd let her help him break the surface of that dark water; wished that she could be part of his healing, that he'd let her in. It seemed, however, that he was determined to go it alone, holding her moment of hesitation back at the house against her—that moment where all she'd done was stare at him while he'd beaten his fists against the back of their front door. It only assured her that regardless of what she tried, she wouldn't change his mind about his trip abroad. He'd leave, and she wouldn't know how to go on.

She'd still have Lark, of course, but who was she kidding? Most days, she and Lark hardly exchanged two words between them. That, and Lark wasn't far behind her brother, poised to fly the coop. Even as a child, Lark would wander off in malls and parks and grocery stores, as if double-daring herself to get snatched up or lost for good. But Leo…Poppy's baby boy; Leo with his sweet smile, with the way he'd curl up in her lap and have her read him the same book over and over, his little face lighting up every time they came to his favorite part. Leo, her first born. Her revelation. The answer to the question so many asked but never got the answer to. *What's the point of living? Why are we here?* Poppy had discovered the answer while sitting in a dark nursery, rocking her son to sleep. She'd come to understand the meaning of life in his laughter, in his tears. But now, without him, without them both, her purpose in life would be gone.

"Lark, too," Ezra said, sidling up to her in front of the sink.

"Lark?" Poppy shook her head, mostly to try to clear the tears from her eyes.

"Yeah," Ezra said. "She's been in a weird place too, right? I mean…" Watching his reflection in the window ahead of them, Poppy saw him raise his eyebrows in a way that read, *you* have *noticed, right?* Of course she had. Lark's sadness had been just as apparent, if not more so than Leo's. Hers had taken on a life of its own, what with the trench coat and combat boots. It seemed to her that, while Leo had focused his sorrow inward, Lark had done the opposite. She had become a breathing representation of her own melancholy.

"Can I help with the dishes?" Ezra asked, jarring her out of her thoughts. Poppy shuddered as she held her breath, willing herself not to burst into tears.

"Poppy?" She winced when he placed a hand on her shoulder. "Let me help," he insisted.

She hesitated, wanting to tell him to leave her to it. *Just go. I want to be alone.* But that was the opposite of what this trip was supposed to be, and if she couldn't embrace the reasons behind being trapped on that island herself, how could she expect anyone else to? *Let him help,* she thought. *This is about the both of you, too.* They could do the morning dishes together, maybe get cozy out on the front porch with their mugs of coffee. They wouldn't be fancy lattes like the kids would be sipping at some cute coffee shop, but it would be good nonetheless. Hell, with the kids off the island for the day, maybe she'd throw off the bowlines and take Ezra into the bedroom. Perhaps that's what they needed to heal.

"Thanks," Poppy said softly. "That would be nice."

She had to try. Had to push. Had to step out of her comfort zone and figure out how to save things between her and Ezra. Because if she couldn't fix their relationship, where would that leave her when both kids were gone?

Vanished, she assumed. *Erased from the world.*

LARK

THE BOAT RIDE to Raven's Head was far more silent than Lark would have liked. With Leo having loosened up back at the house, it had given her hope that, perhaps, he'd open up during their commute. He could have talked to her, could have tried to at least assure her that she'd be okay on her own. But he didn't, and Lark's heart was left to twist beneath the layers of clothes she'd pulled on to stay warm.

She squinted into the wind, the sky looking far darker than it had when they had left the dock only minutes before. Last night had been disconcerting, and while she was still trying to piece together what, exactly, had occurred in that hallway, a single detail kept nagging at her thoughts: that scent. Leo had asked if she had picked up on something similar when she'd first stepped inside. At the time, she was convinced she hadn't smelled a thing. What that meant now, however, was that the scent—left behind as if by a ghost—hadn't been a figment of an overactive imagination. And while Leo was choosing to stick to his silence, it was assurance that she wasn't alone in this. Someone else had smelled that scent. Had seen that shadow. Had heard that bell. Whatever had happened last night, it had been real.

Except, Lark didn't *want* it to be real. Her mind rebelled against the idea, because how terrifying would it be if someone really *had* been lingering behind her in a house not her own? She looked down to her hands when the Raven's Head port came into view, her pulse quickening at the thought of getting off the boat and wandering through those small-town streets. Dark Helena was out there somewhere, as was the guy who had stared her down from the other side of a grocery store, stared so hard it was almost as though he had wanted her to see him.

She wrung her cell in her hands, suddenly bemused by her connection to that device. Of all the people she knew online, there wasn't a single one she could turn to when things got hard. Yet, she couldn't shake its digital pull. She had to assume this was the lesson her mother was trying to impart. A life on the internet wasn't nearly as powerful as a life lived in real time. Profile pictures were nothing compared to real smiling faces. Social media friends bailed when life got heavy. But David *had* been real. For months, he'd been her everything.

But he's gone now, she thought. *…and you don't need him. Just tell Leo the story. Tell him what happened. Tell him about what you suspect…*

No way. She squeezed her eyes shut at the mere idea of it. Confess that she'd fallen in love with a stranger she'd not once set actual eyes upon, whose voice she'd never heard? That conversation would inevitably lead to Atticus Moore, a boy who didn't exist. To Raven's Head and the mysterious case of the grocery store cart and the fact that, despite not wanting to believe it, there was a very real chance David had followed her to Maine. Because she'd encouraged it. She'd goaded him. She'd planted the seed, and now she was scared by what she may have grown.

Bring it up and all fingers will point back to you, she told herself. Because that was the whole point, wasn't it? She'd made up Atticus to make David jealous. So, if he *had* followed her, if it really was David…

"Oh, shit…"

Before Lark could react to her brother's expletive, the boat thudded against the port-lashed tires. It was an encore performance. Neither one of the Parrish men knew how to pilot a watercraft. Watching her brother struggle to moor the boat, Lark's phone buzzed in the palm of her hand. But before she could check whatever message or notification had come in, she was startled by the appearance of a familiar pair of duck boots upon the pier.

"Miss Parrish." Gill nodded at her, as if tipping an invisible hat her way. "Welcome back to town."

As though having held a penny beneath her tongue the entire ride over, Lark suddenly had a bad taste in her mouth. Gill's appearance on the dock struck her as both unsettling and odd. Maybe it *had* been Gill sneaking around the house the night before. Perhaps he was here now just to see her reaction, to get a read on whether she'd identified the previous evening's trespasser. Hell, Gill had access to the house, owned a boat, and had more than likely traveled to and from that secluded island a hundred thousand times. Who else could it have been? But what Lark had felt the evening before didn't match up to the man who loomed above her now. Gill's aura was rough, saltwater-rusted by life on the bay. It was easy to point the finger at a guy like him, but what had lingered behind her the previous night hadn't been rough, but smooth as a skipping stone, polished by the tide's rhythmic in-and-out.

Gill extended a hand, offering to help her out of the boat the same as he had offered to help Lark's mother step onto his vessel the day before. Lark shot a look over to her brother, but Leo was still struggling to tie a frayed rope to a wooden pylon. A moment later, she was sliding her hand into Gill's sandpaper palm and he was pulling her to her feet.

"Brave of you to come out today," Gill said to them both, then pointed a finger upward as if toward God. "There's a wicked storm fixing to come through. Moving fast. It's going to be a good one."

Lark blinked at the news, then looked back to Leo. Had he known they were going to encounter rough weather on the way back? Probably not. The sky hadn't been nearly as dark when they had set off. They should have checked the weather. God, what the hell were they supposed to do if it started to pour?

"Not to worry," Gill said, noticing Lark's sudden tension. "Probably won't be too bad at first. Should give you a good head-start if you keep your eyes peeled. And if the water gets too rough, you're both welcome to sit out the storm at my place." He motioned to a ragged-looking houseboat on the other side of the dock, and Lark was left to wonder what it was like inside. Tons of nautical kitsch? Yeah, probably. Smelling of licorice? Not a chance.

"Thanks," she said, then ducked her head into her shoulders while giving the man a pensive smile. The wind was becoming brisker. The chill coming off the bay was no longer autumn-pleasant, but saw-toothed and cold.

"Or just ask your friend with the speed boat to take you," Gill suggested. "He'll have you back to the island in half the time."

Lark stared at the man before her, suddenly oblivious to the cold, unable to tear her eyes away from Gill's sun-hardened face, from the deep crow's feet around his bright blue eyes. Her stomach pitched, and for a moment she wasn't sure whether the pier had unmoored itself and was bobbing on top of the water, or whether she was experiencing an overwhelming sense of vertigo. Either way, she reached out and caught Gill by the arm.

"Woah, there," he said, helping steady her with a hand square against the flat of her back. "Don't got your sea legs quite yet, do ya'?"

"Guess not," she said, her words weak, her throat parched. *Your friend with the speed boat...* She wanted to toss the comment aside, to write Gill off as not knowing what he was talking about. She had no friend with a speed boat. He must have her mistaken with somebody else.

"Them folks aren't staying out on the island with you, are they?" Gill asked. "I gotta say, I'd be put in a pretty tight spot with Mr. and Mrs. Allen if they were."

Lark could hear Gill talking, but she couldn't understand the words coming out of his mouth. *Who* was staying on the island? She turned away from him, her gaze scanning the port, unsure of what she was looking for, but looking nevertheless.

"There's an extra charge for visitors, see..."

Gill was still talking. Lark wanted to ask him to be quiet, to please stop with the banter before it made her physically ill. She couldn't remember the last time she'd crashed to her knees in front of a toilet and puked her guts out, but the sensation of overwhelming nausea was never new when it attacked. That squirming queasiness was wriggling deep within her guts now. Her stomach clenched and she pivoted on the soles of her Docs and back toward their crappy little boat, coming chest-to-chest with her brother.

"We're just here for coffee," Leo told Gill. "But thanks for the warning."

Leo's fingers coiled tightly around Lark's arm. He turned her toward town, pushing her forward exactly the way their father used to when they were kids. *Let's go.* Lark immediately fell into step, too sick with nerves to protest. She could hardly catch her breath as that nausea threatened to clamber up her windpipe, the briny scent of saltwater and fish making her queasiness ten times worse.

It was only when they had put Gill far behind them that Leo slowed his steps and turned his attention toward her with narrowed eyes.

"What's that guy talking about?" he asked. "What friend with a boat?"

Lark shook her head, both to insist she had no answers as well as to try to shake off the sick feeling that was turning her green. She couldn't see it for herself, but she could feel how pale she had gone as a result of Gill's one-sided talk. Part of her wanted to run like hell—run for the car she knew was waiting for them in the port parking lot. Another part wanted to turn back, to dash toward Gill and demand answers. *Who has the boat? How do you know he's my friend? Did he talk to you? Did he use my name? Is his name David Lambley? Is his name David? Is his name—*

"Lark."

She nearly jumped at the sound of her name, at the sharpness of it as it left her brother's lips. Her hand flew to her lips to hold back a confession or a yelp or a mouthful of sick.

"What?" She eventually forced herself to look at Leo, but it was too late to mask her nerves.

"What's that guy talking about?" Leo insisted, to which Lark shook her head again. *I don't know.*

If it was David, how would she explain it? What would Leo think of her? What if it got back to her parents, her mother? It would be a nightmare she'd never live down. Except, if it was David...if there was even the slightest possibility that it really was him, it meant that Lark had gotten through to him, that Atticus had touched a nerve. What if—

"Hey." Leo was running out of patience. He looked surprisingly startled by the idea of a mystery friend floating around out there on the

bay.

"I have no idea," Lark told him through her fingers, trying like hell to play off her nerves. "I told you, that guy is weird. He probably thinks I'm someone else. Just forget it. Are we going to get coffee or what?" she asked, attempting to push them back in the right direction—the direction that was a sister and brother hanging out during a family vacation, ditching their parents and overspending on sub-par coffee in the name of escape.

The last thing she wanted was to ruin what very well may have been their last chance to hang out together. After this, Leo would run off to Thailand, and then what difference would it make if David had been in Raven's Head or not? Besides, even if David was there, even if he *had* followed her, maybe it was because he had realized what Lark had always known: he loved her just as much as she loved him. Perhaps he was playing at subterfuge because he was nervous she'd reject *him*. Maybe he was just awkward and didn't know how to approach her. Or, it could have been that this was all on purpose—a mystery for her to unravel until the time and place of his choosing, when all would become clear. *I'm here because I can't live without you. I'm here because this is meant to be.* Of course, the Twinkies. They were a gentle nudge. *Hey, it's me.* A peace offering. *My favorite for my favorite girl.*

Lark couldn't help it. She lifted her hand as if to rub at her mouth again, her nerves continuing to buzz like a livewire, her stomach twisting into a double-knot. Could it be? Had David really planned all of this as some sort of elaborate apology? With her fingers flitting against her lips, she tried to hide her smile from Leo. Because she'd figured it out, hadn't she? It *was* him. He'd come for her. He loved her, and he was here to prove it.

EZRA

GEMMA WAS STRETCHED out beneath him, her legs wrapped around his waist. He could see her short hair, first flaming red, then morphing into white-blonde, shifting to a deep chestnut, then going dark as midnight—every color alluring against the milk froth pallor of her skin. He gripped her bare hips as he thrust against her, her back arching, her head knocking against the cheap Motel 6 headboard. Reaching out, he scratched his nails down the length of her stomach, then grasped her right breast and pinched. She yelped, but it was the way she liked it. He pinched harder, jerking her hips forward, her figure little more than a sensual blur. She cried out, which only turned him on. He remembered the first time they'd played this game, the first time they'd torn off each other's clothes and gone at it at the local Holiday Inn. He'd been hesitant, but she'd encouraged him to scratch and pinch and bite. She'd pulled off his glasses and thrown them across the room. *Imagine me any way you want to.* She had been wild, untethered, bucking beneath him as he tried to keep up. A 180 from his regular life. From the routine. From what, at times, felt like a loveless marriage even though he hoped it wasn't. God, he hoped it wasn't…

She was writhing now, and Ezra sucked in air through his teeth. Leaning forward, he buried his right hand in her hair and made a fist. But rather than moaning in pleasure, she mewed.

"Ezra, stop…"

That's what she always said. *Stop.* What she meant was, *go for it. Do your worst.*

With her hair tangled between his fingers, he yanked her head back and she cried out again.

"Stop!"

He was shoved backward with a foot flat against his chest. Losing his balance, he threw an arm back to catch himself against the mattress, but he found no mattress beneath his groping palm. He hit the floor hard, his teeth clattering like silverware in a shaken drawer. A zing of pain shot down his back; a bitter reminder that no matter how young he felt, middle age had crept up on him, and old age would come on just as quick. Faster than he could anticipate, like one of those octogenarian marathon runners with bone-skinny limbs.

"Shit!" The curse escaped him before he could hold it back, the sudden ache of his lower back assuring him that youth had both been just yesterday and so long ago.

"What's wrong with you?"

It wasn't the demand that rattled him, but the voice. Not Gemma, but Poppy.

He scrambled for the bedside table, fumbling with his glasses and dropping them to the floor before finally shoving them onto his face. It was then that she came clear. Poppy's eyes glimmered with a mixture of rage and fear, pissed that he'd been so rough, scared that she didn't recognize the person she'd known for so long.

She rushed from atop the mattress, leaving him kneeling on a stranger's floor. Ezra watched his naked wife gather her clothes off the carpet like a nervous teenager preparing to flee.

"Poppy…" He wasn't sure what he was going to say, how he was going to spin this. All he knew was that silence would make it worse. But she cut him off.

"What's wrong with you?" she repeated, the question seeming more for her than him this time. A second later, her attention flashed up at him, confronting him directly. "Who was I just now?" she asked. "Because I certainly wasn't your wife."

She disappeared into the bathroom, and with the slam of the door, Ezra crumpled against the side of the bed with a murmured "shit."

It had been over eight months since he and Gemma had last shared an intimate encounter. After that, it had been nothing but yelling and cold stares. *I can't do this anymore,* he had told her. *Listen, Gemma, this ends now.*

Gemma hadn't taken it well. Pulling her right arm back, she had let fly hard enough to leave him seeing stars. That was the thing about

Gemma; everything she did was physical, extreme. Suddenly, rather than Ezra being the one doing the scratching and biting, he was on the receiving end of an altogether different experience.

Anyone else would have said, *Sayonara, you crazy bitch* and bailed, but Ezra and Gemma had been sharing their secret for nearly two years by then. Strange as it was, it was only after he told her they needed to stop seeing one another that he realized just how much he cared about her. Not love, no. But he cared enough to try to talk it out, enduring the fighting so they could part on somewhat amicable terms. He did it because it felt like the honorable way out; ironic, seeing as to how such an honorable man had been cheating on his wife. But mostly he did it because it felt safe. The affair had been a one-off. Ezra had never been one to take risks, which only made getting into a relationship with Gemma that much more absurd.

He had seen her at a few school functions, though Gemma wasn't a parent-teacher conference type of mom. But those shared sideways glances, no matter how rare, had been enough to plant the seed. Then, one day, he found her standing in his classroom long after school had let out. He'd been grading papers when she'd slid her hand across his desk, clearing it of everything before taking a seat, her high-heeled shoes atop his knees. There had been nothing beneath her coat.

Poppy and Gemma weren't what anyone would have called close friends, but they weren't anywhere near strangers either. Their kids went to school together, after all, and he was certain Poppy had Gemma's phone number programmed into her cell. That meant Gemma more than likely had Poppy's digits, too.

After Ezra dropped the bomb and told Gemma it was over, her next move was easy to predict. If he simply shrugged off her fury and told her to deal with it, she'd turn around and tell Poppy everything. If that happened, calling off their relationship to salvage the one he'd hobbled between himself and Poppy would have been pointless. If Gemma called the school, Ezra would lose his job. If she contacted Poppy, he would lose his family. But he wasn't helpless. He had his brother, Luca, which was just as good as having an ace up his sleeve.

Months before Ezra had pulled the plug on the affair, he'd pulled some strings instead. *I've got a friend who needs some legal help,* he'd explained to his brother. *Her kid is in trouble again. Something about parole.* Luca had refused at first, but Ezra wouldn't take no for an answer. Ezra wasn't a great liar, however, and it didn't take much for Luca to figure out Ezra's "friend" was actually his mistress. Luca had threatened to tell Poppy, to blow the lid off the whole damn thing. But he'd been bluffing, and in the end strings had been pulled and Poppy hadn't been told. Unfortunately, those strings had severed Luca and Ezra's relationship. The last thing Luca had told his kid brother was just how much of a piece of shit he thought Ezra was. But Gemma didn't know about Ezra and Luca's falling out, and Luca's favor kept her in check.

Mercifully, communication with Gemma had become virtually nonexistent over the past few weeks. The woman who used to text him a good twenty times per day had gone silent, and Ezra had convinced himself that Gemma was gone for good. Out of his life. Nothing but a ghost of his past mistakes.

Yet, there he was, picturing her while having sex with his wife. He couldn't remember the last time he and Poppy had made love. After today, he couldn't imagine the next time it would happen again. And while Ezra was usually quick to think on his feet, he wasn't sure how to claw his way out of this one. This time, he'd really fucked up.

"Hey, Poppy...?" He called out loud enough for her to hear him through the bathroom door. "I'm sorry. I was just messing around. I thought it might spice things up."

The bathroom door flew open and Poppy stepped out. She was back in her pajamas, stripping him of the privilege of seeing her unclothed. The shower hissed from within the weird Jack-and-Jill master bath—another thing in that house that didn't make sense, like the door in the corner of their room that opened to nothing but a wall behind it. Poppy marched past the bed and to her suitcase, which was propped open on the floor. Crouching, she shoved clothing aside, searching for fresh underwear, for a bra, a shirt, some pants.

"I just…I thought maybe changing things up would help," he murmured. "You know, reignite what we've lost."

POPPY

"BY HURTING ME?" Poppy shot him an incredulous look, disgusted by the way he was trying to lie his way out of this. She stood, her clothing held fast in her fists, and turned to face him fully. "I'm going to give you one shot, Ezra," she said. "One shot, so think very carefully about the next few words that come out of your mouth."

Ezra blinked at her, and for a moment she could see Leo reflected in the contours of her husband's face—youthful despite his middle age, tense and a little afraid. She could tell he was holding his breath, waiting for whatever was coming next.

"Are you having an affair?" She practically spit the question onto the Berber carpet between them, the words leaving a foul taste in her mouth. But with that acrid taste and the lurching of her heart came a sweeping sense of freedom, because she'd finally let the words spill past her lips. She'd spent the last few years convinced of his infidelity despite not having proof, searching his shirt collars for traces of lipstick or hints of someone else's perfume. But she'd never just come out and asked him, too afraid to hear his answer, too terrified to know the truth.

She watched him sit there, naked and stunned by her directness. His face looked almost foreign to her, his expression shocked, as though she'd slapped him hard across the face.

"It's a yes or no answer, Ezra," she told him, challenging his hesitation. "So, which is it? Or should I hop in the shower and give you more time to think it over?"

"No, I'm not," he assured her. "I would never."

Had he left it at a simple 'no', she would have been compelled to consider that, perhaps, her suspicions had been wrong. Innocent until proven guilty, she had yet to prove a thing. But it was that last bit—*I would never.* The lie was tangled between those three words. Poppy knew

Ezra had been tempted before. She knew he had made a pass at a teacher's aide once upon a time, when the kids were still small. She had proof of that because the woman had come to her. *I'm so sorry,* she had said. *I just had to tell you. You deserve to know. You two have kids.* But back then, Poppy had still been young and stupid. A mother of two elementary-aged children, she'd been terrified by the idea of losing him, so she hadn't breathed a word.

Poppy's past acceptance didn't change the fact that he'd almost cheated before. She knew he was capable of cheating again. 'I would never' suggested that his potential betrayal was all in her head, that she was crazy. And of all the things Poppy was sure of, it was that this wasn't just paranoia. She could see the lie swirling across his face, settling into his features like fog coming to rest across the water beyond the windows of their room.

She turned away from him and wordlessly stepped back into the bathroom, locking the door behind her. Throwing her clothes onto the bathroom counter, she exhaled a shaky breath, then shot a glance to the bathroom's other door. Who put a Jack-and-Jill as a master bathroom, she couldn't fathom, but there it was; another batshit design choice on the part of the house's architect. The second door led out into the hall. It looked closed, but upon closer inspection, it was unlatched. She pulled it shut and twisted the lock into place, then returned to the counter where she looked up at her reflection in a steamed-over mirror. But rather than glaring at herself, pissed that she'd waited so long to confront him, she gasped, blinking at what was developing before her eyes like an old Polaroid print. The steam from the shower was breathing life into an invisible word scribbled onto the mirror—a word that made Poppy wonder if, perhaps, all the stress really *was* making her go mad. Because a word being written on a mirror by a previous guest wouldn't have been a big deal, but this word was so pertinent to what had just transpired in the bedroom that it brought on a wave of vertigo so strong, she had to grab the edge of the counter for support.

Four letters just as profound as *love*.

Poppy's breath hitched in her throat as she stared ahead, unable to look away from that phantom declaration.

LIAR

Assuring her that it was exactly what Ezra was.

What he'd always been and would always be.

MANIFEST

LEO

THE COFFEE SHOP was packed. Leo typically hated crowds, but today it felt good to be surrounded by people. More secure. Better than what it had felt to be alone in the hall outside his bedroom the night before.

His gaze wandered the crowd, then paused upon the woman at the front of the line. She was decked out in expensive athleticwear, no doubt placing nothing short of the chaos theory as her coffee order. Next to her, a guy talking way too loud into his Bluetooth headset while surfing the web on his iPhone 9000. Leo watched a kid sitting at one of the tables, his mother's head buried in Facebook while her toddler stared at a propped-up tablet, flashing lights and technicolored cartoons dancing across his glazed-over eyes. Sensing he was being watched, the kid pulled his attention away from whatever mind-bending show he was watching and gave Leo a haunting stare. Leo looked away, his pulse amping up a tick.

In his dreams, there were moments when the coma would lift and Julien would open his eyes. But his gaze was always hollow, haunted like the kid's stare. There was never any recognition, never a joyous proclamation of *'hallelujah!'* or a hiss of breath that wheezed out *'Leeeeo'* into the cold silence of the hospital room. It was only ever a single blink of Julien's eyes from asleep to awake, and then an empty stare to the fluorescent tubes overhead, as though hoping they were the white light so many near-death survivors spoke of when they returned to Earth from the Great Beyond.

Except, Jules opening his eyes was nothing short of fantasy. Of the six months Julien had spent in a hospital bed, the veil never lifted. There was never any suggestion that, maybe, just maybe, the coma would dissipate enough to let the person trapped inside try to claw his way back to the surface. He was trapped, held underwater.

And while the hospital nightmares were bad, the lake dream was the worst. The glare of white hospital tile was replaced by a seemingly endless expanse of snow-covered tundra. Leo would look down at his feet and realize he was standing on inches-thick ice. He would linger there, his breath puffing out before him, his eyes scanning the vista while panic crept up his throat. And then, he'd hear the thumping.

Thump, thump, thump. The only sound out there in the cold, the snow deadening all else.

Thump, thump, thump. Like the thudding of his pulse.

Except, unless his heart had fallen to his feet, the vibrations weren't coming from him, but from the frozen lake beneath his boots.

Thump, thump, thump.

Eventually, Leo would look down and that's when he'd see him: Julien trapped beneath ice so thick his features were blurred like an ink blot stain.

Thump, thump, thump.

His fists pounding against the ice shelf, his mouth opening to scream, massive air bubbles rippling past his lips.

Thump, thump, thump.

Leo falling to his knees, his hands shoving snow aside to get a better view, his fingers frozen while clawing at the unbreakable boundary between them.

Thump, thump, thump.

Julien silently screaming, writhing in dark water. Leo screaming with him, the two of them like mirror images of each other—one in the real world, one trapped in an alternate universe.

"Leo."

He shuddered, then blinked at his sister's face. He expected to see the look he'd seen her wear a hundred thousand times by now, the one that so closely mimicked their mother's worry it was nothing short of eerie. But rather than looking into narrowed eyes, he found himself eye-to-eye with alarm, Lark's hand reaching up to catch him by the sleeve.

LARK

STANDING IN LINE with her brother close by, Lark hadn't thought anything of them when she first saw the couple occupying a well-loved sofa in one of the shop's crowded corners. She'd simply been people-watching when her attention fell onto the woman with her tangled black mess of hair, cozy on the couch, one long leg crossed over the other, the foot of a calf-high riding boot bobbing up and down beneath the hem of an odd-angled skirt. She struck Lark as both long-suffering and impatient. But then she realized who it was. And there, beside her, was the guy in the mirrored aviator shades—the one who had stared Lark down at the grocery store. He was giving an encore performance, boring a hole into Lark's chest as Dark Helena leaned into his ear to whisper some intimate secret. The way his face bloomed into a smirk turned Lark's stomach. Less than friendly. If anything, it was predatory—a hyena waiting for the pack of gazelles to thin.

She'd been hopeful only a half hour ago, but that hope was now souring on the back of her tongue. Despite his sunglasses, Lark was now much closer to her observer than she had been at Ouellette's; close enough to know those shades didn't hide a familiar face. She'd only seen a single photo of David, and she knew it could have been a random picture he'd found online, but she caught herself thinking it anyway: *that isn't David. That isn't him.*

Maybe David had hired two people to set his romantic plan of winning Lark back into motion. It was possible, right? This whole thing was crazy, so why not two people instead of one?

But that guy is snarling, she thought. *He's goddamn snarling, Lark.*

"Leo..." She whispered her brother's name despite the noise of the place—the grinding of beans, the hiss of steam, the dull roar of chit-chat and placed orders and baristas calling out names over the din. She squeezed his arm, trying to be as nonchalant as she could, never taking her eyes off the couple for longer than a second or two. "We need to go," she told him.

"What?" Leo pulled a face. *What are you talking about?*

"If it starts pouring while we're on that boat…" she began. "If the storm rolls in like Gill said…"

"Then we'll get wet," Leo said. "Or we'll wait it out."

Lark looked forward, then squeezed her eyes shut, imagining the boat sinking. Being struck by lightning. The ocean turning savage and swallowing them whole. She pictured Dark Helena sliding off the couch and sauntering across the coffee shop to stop a foot away from her and Leo. To do what, she had no idea, but she could feel it about to happen.

Lark's eyes shot open, her gaze darting back to Helena and her wingman. They were exactly where they had been, but it made no difference. Despite knowing she was safe next to Leo, safe in a crowded place, far safer than out on some crappy boat bobbing atop choppy water, she couldn't shake the urgency to get the hell out of there.

Go, her mind screamed. *This isn't right. You need to go.*

So, she grabbed Leo's hand and tried to pull him out of line like a determined child trying to lead an unreceptive parent. But, unlike how she had been willingly piloted away from Gill and his suggestion of hitching a ride on a speed boat belonging to Lark's mysterious "friend", Leo hardly budged.

"Don't be weird," Leo told her. "It'll be fine. We came all the way out here…"

"Leo." She nearly pleaded, her gaze jumping back to the couple. She was being far more nonchalant about it than she had been at the grocery store, but Lark could tell Dark Helena was watching. But Leo wasn't paying attention, too busy contemplating what he was going to order, concentrating on the hand-chalked coffee board that hung over the shop's small front counter. Not wanting to make a scene, Lark's mind bounded between options. She could grab Leo by the shoulder and tell him about David, or she could pivot on the soles of her boots, march over to Dark Helena and her sidekick, and demand to know what the fuck was going on. That, however, would put her at risk of public humiliation, and there was no way she was putting herself in that position. Or, she could choose the least terrifying way out and text David. *Are you behind this? This is starting to freak me out. If you want to talk, then—*

Yanking her phone out of her back pocket, she unlocked the screen for the first time since she and Leo had left Gill back at the dock, and that's when she saw it: one unread text message. Suddenly remembering that her phone had buzzed in her pocket, she'd been so distracted by Gill, so thrown by his mention of her friend with the speedboat, that the notification had slipped her mind. But now, as she stood next to her brother, her hand shook as she tapped the notification and navigated to her messaging app. She could still feel that guy snarling, could still sense both sets of eyes upon her, watching, waiting for a reaction.

Almost said 'hi' yesterday, the text read, *but got distracted by all those photos on the walls. Maybe tonight I'll ring again.*

Lark felt her heart loosen in her chest, sensed it dropping through the hollow of her ribcage to her feet. Just like on the dock only minutes before, the earth shifted, skewing to the right like a carnival ride. She increased her grip on Leo's arm if only to keep herself from drunkenly wavering amid the afternoon coffee crowd. Then, as if to purposefully spike her panic to an all-time high, her phone buzzed in the palm of her hand.

You're looking a little nervous, Lark. Maybe text Atticus for help?

She swallowed hard, pushing down the wave of nausea that was now back with a vengeance, threatening to take her to her knees in front of the entire store. Because if it wasn't David, how did he know about Atticus? It was impossible. Impossible...

"Leo..." She whispered, those two syllables feeling dry and soundless as they left her throat. *"Leo."* She tried again, her bottom lip suddenly trembling as she pulled on his sleeve. "I'm going to throw up. We need to go."

Looking up in hopes of meeting his gaze, she found that Leo was no longer staring at the menu board overhead. But he wasn't looking at *her*, either. His eyes were fixed on a point beyond her left shoulder. He was staring at the couch in the corner, exactly where Dark Helena and her wingman sat.

Leo's expression flickered between emotions like a lightbulb in a haunted house. Curious. Confounded. And then, something akin to surprise. His eyes widened. Realization fell across his features. Sickening dismay shrouded his face.

"Yeah," he said after a moment. "Okay." And without another word, he caught Lark by the hand and pulled her out of the shop.

LEO

HE WATCHED HIS SISTER grasp at the plank of wood that served as a seat while their boat hit white-capped waves. They were small, but the water was growing rougher with every passing minute, Leo's anxiety doubling with each hard-hitting crack of the bow.

They eventually hit a wave that left *By and By* shuddering at its seams. Leo had a good grip on the handle of the outboard motor, which kept him at least somewhat steady in his seat, but the impact sent Lark crashing into the side of the boat. For a heart-stopping moment he was sure she was about to go over.

"Lark!" Her name came tumbling past his lips as Lark exhaled a startled cry and slipped from her seat, quickly finding herself sitting flat on her ass in the hull. Scrambling to get up, her jeans and trench coat were soaked from the centimeter of water they'd taken on since leaving port.

"Are you okay?" he yelled, but she didn't respond. She was too busy leaning forward, her hands scrambling through the water at her feet.

"My phone," she gasped. "Oh shit, my phone!"

Leo's response was reflexive. He cut the motor and moved to help his sister, the panicked edge to her tone not helping his already rattled nerves. He spotted the cell and grabbed it, but it was too late. Lark snatched the waterlogged device from Leo's hands as though he'd purposefully dunked it into the bay.

Frantically pressing the power button, her screen remained dark. Her expression cycled through disbelief and horror until it finally settled on an emotion her brain deemed appropriate. Dropping her phone to her feet, she pushed her wet hands against her face and began to weep.

"Lark?" It would have struck him as an overreaction, but Leo knew there was more to his sister's dismay than losing access to her Facebook feed. He'd seen the apprehension reflected in her eyes back at the coffee shop, knew she was hiding something since Gill's mention of a mysterious friend.

"Oh my god," Lark cried. "What the fuck is happening? How am I going to text him now? How am I…just…" A sob tore out of her chest. "I have to figure this out," she whispered. "I have to figure this out!"

Leo watched his sister in silence, though the shudder of her shoulders made him lean in as he sat on his own bench seat. Closing the distance between himself and his younger sibling, he placed his hand on her shoulder, his own heart thudding hard against his chest.

"Figure what out?" he eventually asked, but he already suspected what was to come, because the Twinkies hadn't been a coincidence. No matter how much he had tried to explain it away, how hard he had wrestled with faulty logic, that box of snack cakes remained steadfast— not in the trash where he'd dumped them, but front and center on the kitchen island, as if purposefully placed there. Cruel. Deliberate. An amplification of his own angst.

Then there were the bedroom curtains. The thump against the wall. That goddamn shadow in the living room. That fucking scent.

"Remember when I was at the store with Dad and I texted you?" Lark asked, wiping at her eyes. "I said there was a woman."

"Marla Singer," Leo recalled.

"Marla Singer," she repeated, then swallowed as if gulping down the need to puke. "There was a guy, too. He was at the front of the store, waiting for her to finish something." Lark sniffled, trying to compose herself. "You know, like maybe waiting for her to throw some shit in someone else's cart without them noticing?"

Leo lifted his free hand, rubbing his palm across his mouth. She was talking about the couple he'd spotted over her shoulder at the coffee shop, about the dark-haired woman who met his gaze without so much as a sideways flinch and the guy whose mouth had coiled upward into a leering grin as they left.

"They're following me," she whispered, then shook her head and covered her face again. "I thought that maybe I knew who they were, thought that maybe it was…" She hesitated, her words lost in a newfound sob. "God, how could I have been so stupid?"

"Stupid about what?" Leo asked, his throat having gone dry despite the rain. Because what the hell did she mean they were following *her*? How did any of it make sense, what with the Twinkies? Lark had known Julien, sure, but they'd exchanged maybe a few sentences between them in the years Leo and Julien had been friends. Nothing as intimate as, *hey, know what my favorite food is? You'll never guess.*

"I can't…" she cried into her hands. "You'll think I'm an idiot."

"I won't," he told her, though there wasn't much conviction behind his assurance. Maybe there would have been if circumstances had been different, but the way the boat was rocking on those choppy waves was suddenly making him sick. His eyes burned against the queasiness that was clambering up his throat. And that wasn't even the worst of it.

The lapping of the waves against the boat threw him back into that hospital hallway—the one he was desperate to stop revisiting, the one he seemingly couldn't escape no matter how hard he tried—his ears ringing with the in-and-out hiss of Julien's vent. With the *thump, thump, thump* of Julien beating his fists against a sheet of ice. It was the same nausea that had overwhelmed him the moment Julien's mother rose from her chair, moved across the hospital room, and stopped in front of the machine that was keeping Julien alive. Leo had turned his gaze away, unable to watch her do what he knew was coming. It was when his attention had settled upon the vinyl-upholstered couch on the opposite side of the room—the piece of furniture he'd spent many evenings trying to sleep on, where he had sat for countless hours while waiting for his best friend to wake up. But there was someone else sitting in that spot the moment Julien's life was finally extinguished, someone who had been staring at Leo so intently it had felt as though he was holding Leo accountable for his little brother's death.

"Just tell me," Leo said. "Who did you think that guy was?"

"A guy I know," Lark whispered past her fingers. "A guy I fell for, that I met online. But it isn't him." She shook her head, her face momentarily going blank. When she looked back up at Leo, she appeared both terrified and confused. "But I'm getting texts," she told him. "Which means he's behind it. He has to be, right? They have my number. How else would they be able to—"

"What texts?" Leo asked, cutting her off. "Show me." He held out his hand, waiting for Lark to give him her phone only to remember that her cell was no longer part of the equation. It was drowning in salt water, skimming the bottom of the boat between her booted feet.

Sopping wet and shivering, Lark stared at the dead mobile phone with a helpless expression.

"He must have given them my number," she said softly. "But why would he—" When she looked up at Leo again, her eyes were wide and glistening with tears. "Allison warned me," she said, her bottom lip quivering again. "She said not to trust him, that he could be anybody. He wouldn't call me, wouldn't meet up. And then he just…" She shut her eyes, trying to keep her emotions in check. "…vanished," she whispered. "Like I never mattered. Like he couldn't have cared less."

"Vanished when?" Leo asked, surprised by the quake of his own voice, taken aback by the nauseating pitch of his stomach. It was the same roil of panicky hysteria he had felt when he'd watched Julien's mother move across the hospital room. He had wanted to scream, fighting with himself to both let it out and keep it in. Part of him wanted to lunge at Mrs. Bellamy, to grab her by her arms and snarl *don't you fucking dare.* Another part wanted to race her to the ventilator and flip the switch himself, to get it over with so that the ache could reach full bloom. The sooner it did, the sooner he could go numb.

Sitting there, staring at his sister's tear-swollen face, he felt those same things now. He wanted to pull Lark into his arms and comfort her, to tell her it was all going to be okay and that nothing was her fault. But the logical part of him knew none of that was true. Something was wrong, something was dangerous. There was no way Lark had set anything in motion of her own volition, but Leo knew his sister well enough to understand that she'd been played. *But I'm getting texts,* which meant they had her phone number. And how had they found her in Raven's Head? Certainly, they hadn't followed her all the way from South Carolina to Maine like something out of a low-budget stalker flick. Someone had provided the information, and that someone wasn't the mystery man she had fallen for. That someone was Lark, the girl who had a soft spot for telling strangers way too much.

Leo didn't know who Allison was, but she had been right. Lark's digital beau hadn't been who he said he was. The two people lurking out in the open, Lark's *friend with a speedboat,* they weren't here to do some creepy guy's bidding. There had only ever been one person, and Lark was right on the money with her conclusion: she had never mattered. This was bigger than her.

"When?" Leo asked again. "*When* did he disappear?"

Lark hesitated, but it made no difference. Leo already knew the answer, was already piecing the nightmare together one detail at a time.

"After Julien…" Lark said softly. "Like, the day after."

Leo pressed his hands to his rain-spattered face, dragging his palms down from his eyebrows to his chin. Letting his hands drop to his lap, he shook his head and exhaled an exasperated laugh. That was it, then. Confirmation, as if the Twinkies hadn't been enough.

"What?" Lark asked, spooked by his response.

"I know who it is," Leo said.

Lark blinked at him but stayed quiet, waiting with bated breath.

"Your friend with the speed boat? That's Felix Bellamy," he said.

"…and who is Felix Bellamy?" Lark asked.

"Julien's fuck-up of an older brother," Leo told her. "And Marla Singer? That's his mom."

POPPY

SHE CRIED IN THE SHOWER, ticking up the faucet toward the red letter 'H' a little more every minute. Eventually, the water bit rather than soothed. When she stepped out, the fog was nearly too thick to breathe. Her lungs cried out for a blast of cool air, but she refused to open the bathroom door even a crack. Ezra was out there, guaranteed.

So, rather than dealing with the situation at hand, Poppy stood naked and avoidant in front of the bathroom mirror, unable to see more than a blur of her own reflection through the mist as she drip-dried onto the soft bathmat underfoot. She breathed in steam and watched her likeness slowly reveal itself, a ghost surfacing from a thick and swirling fog. The water had left her skin red enough to suggest a second-degree burn, but she paid no attention to the angry tingle just beneath the surface of her skin. Her attention was rapt on that word, the one that someone had carefully printed onto the glass.

She couldn't imagine the universe lining up to cause such a coincidence. It seemed impossibly mind-bending in its parallelism, yet there it was. Staring at those four letters, she tried to imagine who had stayed at the bungalow before them. Had it been a husband and wife on the verge of collapse? A family in turmoil? A mother trying to white-knuckle some semblance of a close relationship with children who had turned distant long ago? Jesus, was this an alternate universe? Were the last people that stayed on the island *them?*

She blinked away a few tears, swiping at them with a still-wet hand, then reached out to the mirror with a trembling hand, carefully tracing the letters that had started to fade.

LIAR

She felt stupid for feeling so wounded. Ezra had been lying for a long time, so it made no sense to be overwhelmed by it now. Yet, it felt fresh; a deep cut created by a thousand small ones, torn open all over again.

Squeezing her eyes shut, she pressed the palm of her hand against the mirror and considered confronting him. She could tell him she wasn't sure whether she still loved him, could confess that she often thought of divorce. She could, but she wouldn't, because it would ruin her last chance with the kids. It would destroy any hope of reconciliation with him. That, and she recognized the key phrase: *she wasn't sure.* Not being certain meant that maybe she still loved him, but it was up to him to remind her just how that felt.

Jerking her hand to the right, she wiped the word away with a wet streak of condensation.

And it was then, as if signaling that it was unhappy with Ezra getting yet another easy out, that the universe spoke. Poppy jumped at a rumble so loud she literally felt it in the soles of her feet. She didn't understand what she was hearing at first. Had Ezra dropped something onto the floor? By the time a second growl vibrated the windows in their frames, Poppy suddenly realized what it was, and what it meant for her kids.

"Oh my god," she whispered, grabbing at a white bathrobe hanging from the back of one of the bathroom doors.

Growing up in South Carolina, she'd experienced plenty of heavy-hitting storms. Her family had taken tropical depressions and hurricanes head-on. Poppy still remembered the year her Uncle Bill—not quite right in the head—decided to take his boat on the water while half the state was boarding up their windows or fleeing west. Poppy didn't see her uncle for a good long while after that. For years an already water-shy Poppy imagined her uncle out there, his boat beaten by the waves, the clouds reaching down toward the water like God's two angry hands, dunking the boat beneath the sea. A decade later, she learned that Uncle Bill had been saved by the Coast Guard and was immediately driven by his wife to a rehab facility somewhere in the Virginia hills. But the news came too late and the damage had been done.

Poppy's Uncle Bill was the source of her aquaphobia, starting with the spill she'd taken off the back of his Bayliner as a kid. The stunt he had pulled with a category four hurricane only extended her fear to extreme weather. High winds, torrential downpours, hail; all of it sent her anxiety through the roof. That spike of adrenaline was the only reason Poppy jerked open the bathroom door and stumbled back into the bedroom, her hair sopping wet, that bathrobe half-open in her rush toward the windows.

Ezra was still in the room, dressed but no doubt waiting for her to surface, probably working on an apology. But rather than launching into whatever story he'd come up with, he looked about as freaked out as Poppy felt.

"Was that—" She began to ask a question she already knew the answer to when she was cut off by another snarl. Her eyes went wide and, despite herself, she looked to Ezra for comfort.

"Thunder," Ezra said, turning his spooked expression toward the windows overlooking the bay. They'd made it through their share of bad weather together, the worst of which had taken down a couple of massive oaks across the street from their house. They had not, however, been this isolated during one of these things before. Now, they were practically in the water…in the water…*in the water…*

"Jesus Christ, Ezra, they're out there…" she whispered, moving toward the glass.

For God's sake, she had *known* a storm was in the works. But she'd said nothing when Lark had come to her, insisting that the trip to Raven's head wasn't just for coffee, that she needed to go back to the grocery store. *I forgot pads, Mom. Jeez, do I have to spell it out?* Poppy had known it was a lie, knew that the whole point was to get away from being trapped in that house with their parents. Yet, it was the knowledge of being lied to, of being avoided, that had given rise to resentment. Angry at her daughter's inability to be honest, Poppy had waved a hand at Lark and let them go.

What kind of a mother am I?

Poppy's heart paused. For a handful of beats, the fear she felt for her children was overridden by the very real sensation of not being able to swallow. She gasped for breath, yet somehow wasn't able to pull in air.

Oh my god, what kind of a—

"Poppy?" Ezra turned to her, his eyes widening as he took in her twisting features.

Poppy's hands fluttered to her chest, batting at her collarbone as though trying to fill up her lungs. "The kids," she wheezed, her mind immediately racing to worst case scenarios, to that shitty little boat bobbing among the waves, overturned. Leo would make it because Leo was strong. But Lark was like Poppy; easily terrified, quick to panic. Because of Poppy's own fear, both of her children had been taught to swim before they had ever set foot in a kindergarten classroom. She knew Leo would use all those years of experience to his advantage, but Lark would freeze. Deep in her core, Poppy knew that in time of disaster, Lark would be the first to go.

By the time Poppy was able to draw in air, Ezra had crossed the room and now had his hands on her shoulders. He was peering into her face, as if giving her a stern look would somehow help her draw in a fortifying breath.

"The kids," Poppy repeated, stepping away from him. "We need to get to them. Now."

God, why hadn't she cancelled, or at least pushed back their reservation dates? Because the island had been solidly booked. The owner, Diedre, had said so in one of her AirBnB emails. Poppy knew the next opening might come too late, might be after Leo was gone, lost to her for good. So, selfishly, Poppy had shrugged off the warnings of a major storm, had excused bad weather as a reason to stay cooped up inside, indulging in hot cocoa and watching movies. Quintessential family time. What could be more perfect?

But this storm was beyond rain. It felt cosmic, like the word she'd discovered written onto the bathroom mirror. The universe was speaking. Aligning. Preparing.

Something was happening, and it made her want to scream.

EZRA

"THE KIDS. We need to get to them. Now."

Ezra's hand dropped to his side as his wife pulled away from his touch, moving toward the bedroom door.

"Poppy, how?" Ezra paused, switching tactics. "They're okay," he assured her. "They're in Raven's Head. If anything, they'll just wait it out there." Of course, he had no idea if that was the case. Leo may have decided to play the hero. Maybe they had piled into that sad excuse of a boat and decided to try to beat the storm back to the island. If they had gotten caught in it, it would be bad.

Not that any of that mattered. There was only one boat, which meant there was no way of getting to them, regardless of Poppy's fast-growing hysteria. Poppy flew out of the room, leaving him alone. Before going after her, he pulled his phone out of the pocket of his sweats and checked his signal strength. One lousy bar. It wasn't great, but it would be enough to get through to Gill. But first, he needed to make sure Poppy wasn't going to dive into the bay.

Catching up to her in the living room, he could already see her crumbling beneath the weight of her own anxiety. Ever since Leo had announced his plans to go to Thailand, she'd been spiraling toward a full-blown panic disorder. It was why he had choked back his impulse to freak out when she'd booked this place. Because if this was what Poppy needed to regroup, to take a breath and feel at least some semblance of control, if this was what she felt she needed to keep herself from falling apart, so be it. He'd eventually figure out how to pay the bill. Losing the kids, though—that hadn't been on anyone's itinerary.

Ezra knew Poppy didn't think much of him anymore. Hell, after this morning he doubted she thought anything of him at all, but he couldn't just stand there. With another crack of thunder, Poppy bellowed a cry and twisted away from the living room's bank of windows. She looked ready to bolt out of the house and down the pier, which was what prompted him to catch her by the shoulders and look her square in the eyes.

"Poppy," he said, steady as he could manage. "There's nothing you can do out there. They took the commuter, remember? I'll call them," he said, determined to prove that he could be better than he'd been. "If they're on the boat, I'll call the Coast Guard. It'll be okay. Just hold on a minute. Let me call."

What should have given Poppy comfort only elicited a stifled sob from her throat. She twisted away from him, pulling herself free of his grip, but he could see her face in the reflection of the glass. One hand was pressed over her mouth, her eyes glinting with tears. A moment later, lightning muted her image with a flash of white. A peal of thunder growled immediately after.

The storm was upon them. And while Ezra wished he could say he hadn't seen it coming, those dark and distant clouds had been looming upon his own horizon for months. And now they were here.

LEO

LARK DIDN'T HOLD BACK. She screamed when thunder clapped overhead, then clamped her hand over her mouth, same as she used to when she was a kid.

"We're almost there," Leo yelled at her above the wind and motor's whine. He wanted to follow it up with a reassuring promise. *Just a few more minutes* or *It's going to be okay,* but he hated those kinds of empty proclamations.

Mrs. Bellamy had badgered Julien's doctors for such pie-in-the-sky guarantees, seemingly convinced that if the words simply left their mouths, the lie would be rendered true. *He'll wake up any day now, ma'am. He'll open his eyes and he'll be fine. Good as new, same as he ever was.*

Sitting in Julien's hospital room for so long, there had been moments when Leo had wanted to scream at her, *don't you get it? It's not going to happen! This is it for him. For all of us. Julien isn't coming back.*

Perhaps that was akin to what he should have told Lark now. Out on the water in such weather, in such a dinky little boat, it may have very well been the end of them. If they hit some bad chop they'd be in the water before either one of them could react. Too far between the mainland and the island to make it back to either Raven's Head or the house, the Parrish children would die together, drowned the way Julien had drowned in Leo's most fearsome dreams.

Thump, thump, thump.

The water beat against the side of the boat as they continued to motor forward.

Thump, thump, thump.

Julien was reaching out to Leo from beneath the surface of the gulf, refusing to let him move on, to heal and forget.

Come on, he whispered. *Let's see what the hell is at the bottom of this bay. Otherwise, what's the point?*

But Julien was forced back beneath the waves when Leo's phone buzzed in his pocket, message after message coming through. And while he couldn't be sure, he knew who it must have been.

He and Jules had been sitting on the living room floor playing video games when Leo had set eyes on Felix for the very first time. Felix had marched through the house, looking both angry and intense. He had smirked at them both in passing, then pelted his kid brother square in the chest with a Twinkie snack cake.

"Don't choke," he had said.

Julien plucked the Twinkie from his lap and shrugged, but Felix was long gone by then, having disappeared down a hallway and out of sight, stomping all the way.

"He knows they're my favorite," Julien had murmured beneath his breath. "It's the only nice thing he ever does."

"Nice?" Leo hadn't been so sure. He'd only been all of ten years old then, but even then he knew an asshole when he saw one. Yeah, it was nice to get a special treat from a sibling, but it would have been even nicer had it not been thrown like a curveball directly at Julien's face.

"In his own way," Julien had said, then diverted his gaze. Despite Leo's youth, he knew sadness when he saw it. It was a deep sort of yearning. Leo could nearly smell the heartache brought on by things Julien had never spoken of, because boys aren't supposed to talk about stuff that hurts. That was "sissy stuff."

That had been it—nothing more than a quick passing glance and a Twinkie tossed at Julien's chest. Leo's introduction to Felix had been abrupt, but it had been enough to cement him in Leo's mind as his best buddy's prick of a big brother. The douche bag. The dick.

That wasn't to say that Julien never brought Felix up. Every so often there would be an aside about how Felix had called asking their mother for money, or how Felix has shown up at the house at night yelling about this thing or that. Once, Julien had to call 911 while hiding out upstairs, listening to Felix and their mother scream at one another until the cops arrived. Then there were the occasional utterances of Felix getting locked up for various infractions. One had been check fraud. Another had been a stolen car. Things started getting serious when those lesser crimes ballooned into stuff like breaking and entering and physical assault. Hell, it had only been a year before Julien's accident that drama had raged within the Bellamy household once again. There was at least one piece of good news in all of it: Felix was an absentee sibling. Julien saw him maybe every two or three years, which meant Leo saw him even less.

Until Julien's time at the hospital, when Leo had seen Felix every day for what felt like forever.

Three days after Julien landed in the ICU, Felix strode into his hospital room wearing a leather jacket and a pair of aviator sunglasses, dressed for a bar or a club, not a room where he'd find his little brother on life support. His nearly apathetic coolness made no difference to Mrs. Bellamy. She rushed to her eldest son and threw her arms around him as though she'd been awaiting his arrival with bated breath. And maybe she had been.

Her relief in seeing him did little to move Felix, however. He hardly reacted as he stood over Julien's bed. He simply stared across the room at Leo through the mirrored lenses of his shades. When he did finally move, it was to take a seat on the vinyl-upholstered couch at the far end of the room.

"Well," he had spoken after a minute of saying nothing. "This fucking sucks, doesn't it?" And then, as if it was of no consequence, Felix had pulled out his phone and begun to text someone.

Leo had sat in that room for a solid sixty-eight hours by then, but he had to excuse himself, forced to break vigil. Julien wouldn't have blamed him. Hell, Jules would have probably told him to go.

Yeah, Leo thought to himself now, squinting against the rain as it needled his face. *This does fucking suck.* Because what the hell was Felix doing in Raven's Head? Leo understood part of it: Felix had catfished Lark. But the *why* escaped him. It made no goddamn sense.

"Leo!" Lark cried out as they hit another series of choppy waves.

"We're almost there," Leo called out to her again, deciding to give in to just one placation. "We're going to be okay." It felt like the right thing to say. Had Julien opened his eyes in that hospital room, Leo would have told him the same thing. Meanwhile, Julien's doctors would have been standing behind Leo's shoulder, shaking their heads, disappointed by the lie. And for all Leo knew, Felix could have been behind his shoulder now, leering. *Oh, it's not going to be okay,* he'd hiss through his teeth. *It's not going to be anywhere fucking close.*

Lark twisted to look back at him, her hair so thoroughly whipped by the wind that it was little more than a matted tangle across her forehead.

"Promise me!" she yelled back, her face both afraid and full of hope.

It was then that it hit him square in the chest that he hadn't been able to do a damn thing to help his best friend. Even in his dreams, Julien died and died again. But right here, right now, he could save both himself and his sister. They'd make it back to that island if it was the last thing they did. Fuck Felix Bellamy. Fuck whatever reason had brought him there.

With that determination, Leo nodded at his sister.

"I promise," he told her—a promise he was going to keep. "Just hold on," he said. *Hold on. Hold on.*

POPPY

POPPY YELPED WHEN SHE spotted them on the horizon. Shoving past Ezra, she all but tripped down the hall as she bolted for the kitchen's side door, then burst out onto the deck and into the torrential downpour, disregarding the roll of thunder, blind to the lightning that streaked the sky. Her bare feet flew down the stairs and carried her the dozen yards it took to get to the pier. It was there that she saw her children more clearly through the deluge, huddled in a little boat, doing their best to pull up to the dock. Her heart both soared and broke at the sight of them—safe but still helpless. In that moment, Leo wasn't a high school graduate and Lark certainly wasn't coming up on her sixteenth birthday. Right then, her kids were eight and five, struggling, needing their mom.

She rushed down the length of the dock, her feet slapping wet planks. By the time she reached the boat, Lark had climbed onto steady ground, though she balanced on weary legs. Leo fought with the tie-out, but the wind was whipping at the hull. Somehow, the rain was growing heavier than it already was, threatening to drown them all. Poppy caught her daughter by the hand and yelled toward her son.

"It's good enough! Get out of the water!"

Naturally, Leo ignored her for a handful of seconds, but he ended up listening to at least one matriarch in the end. Mother Nature growled beneath Her breath, a rumble so low Poppy felt the air go electric with Her rage.

"Go!" She practically screamed the word at Lark, releasing her daughter's hand.

Lark didn't protest. She fell into a sprint, her long legs taking her down the dock faster than Poppy had expected.

Poppy turned back to Leo, who was now struggling to get onto the dock, the boat erratic beneath him. She dropped to her hands and knees, held out an arm.

"Leo," she said, her voice trembling despite her determination to keep her composure.

He met her gaze, and for a second she was sure he would refuse her help. *I can do it myself.* She could hear his mantra clear as a bell, the words he'd recited at her in anger and frustration for the last thirteen years. *I'm not a kid anymore.* It was a knife to the heart every time she heard it, every time she had to accept that it was becoming truer with every day that passed. *I know,* she wanted to yell at him. *Don't you know I know?!*

"Baby." Her arm remained jutting outward, her fingers outstretched. "Let me help," she told him. "Please."

She watched an expression she hadn't seen cross his face since he'd been small; a wobbly sort of apprehension, almost as though he were losing faith in himself, looking to her to help him find it again. Finally, their hands clasped together and Poppy pulled him forward, acting as a ballast as the world rocked beneath his feet.

The moment Leo was out of the boat, the sky split in two. The lightning was so close, they could smell ozone.

Suddenly, they were running together toward the house.

But they both stopped short when they spotted Lark standing at the foot of the deck's steps. Rather than having ducked beneath the awning, she stood drenched and miserable, her back to them, as if afraid to step inside.

"Lark?" Poppy yelled through the roaring rain, the veritable sheet of water muffling her voice. When Lark didn't respond, Poppy let her hand drop onto her daughter's shoulder. The response that came after was not what she expected.

Lark all but jumped out of her skin, veering around with wide and fearful eyes. What struck Poppy as most terrifying was her own lack of understanding, not knowing *why* Lark looked the way she did. Perhaps it had been the boat ride over. Maybe it was the shuddering roll of thunder or the camera-like flashes of lightning that veined the sky overhead. Maybe she was struggling with the aftershock, with the idea that she could have drowned out there. That both she and Leo could have died.

"Lark!" Poppy yelled her daughter's name, trying to snap her out of it. "Get inside!"

But Lark didn't move.

Leo took a few forward steps, leaned into her, and said something Poppy couldn't hear. It got Lark moving. She still looked dismayed but climbed the stairs, leaving a trail of water behind her as it sheeted off her long coat.

It was only when Poppy followed her children inside that she spotted Ezra deep inside the house. He hadn't run after Poppy when she had spotted the kids, and he hadn't gone outside when Lark had stopped just shy of the stairs. For a moment, Poppy was convinced that her husband had chosen that precise moment to give up on his family, on his life with them much the way Poppy often thought about giving up on him. But a second later she realized, Ezra hadn't followed because he was staring out at something on the water. It was a boat, half-hidden by the haze of the rain; a fast Bayliner, just like her uncle used to own. Someone was out in the gulf, which was strange given the weather; which was odd seeing as to how theirs was the only house around for miles.

LEO

AFTER FELIX'S APPEARANCE at the hospital, he and Leo didn't remain strangers for long.

While Leo had given up his post next to Julien's bed, it only took him a day to find himself back in that room. He had half-convinced himself that Felix would be gone by the time he got back but, surprisingly, Felix was still there, still sitting in the corner of that ugly vinyl hospital couch; present despite his attention being fixed on his phone, despite being absent for the majority of Julien's life, despite not giving a shit until then.

Spotting Felix upon that hospital couch, Leo hesitated at Julien's door, unsure whether to enter or vanish again. There was a chance Felix was camping out for a few days, using the free Wi-Fi. Mrs. Bellamy was nowhere to be found, and sharing the same space with Felix felt volatile, unsafe. But before Leo could back away from the door, Felix broke the tension. Glancing up from the blue glow of his cell, he gave a casual wave for Leo to come in. Leo forced an awkward smile and crossed the threshold, then shuffled to his usual chair.

"Cool nose ring," Felix said, and for a moment Leo almost laughed. It was the type of ice breaker you'd read about in *GQ* or *Men's Health*. *Lead with a compliment. Butter them up.*

"Yeah," Leo said, unsure of how else to respond. "Thanks."

"They let you go to school with that thing, or did you get it after graduation?"

"They let me." Leo shrugged.

"No shit?" Felix smirked. "I don't remember them being that lenient when I was there." His gaze momentarily drifted back to his phone, then up to Leo again. "But that was a while ago, so…" Felix mimicked Leo's shrug. "Times change, I guess."

It was easy to forget the age difference between the Bellamy brothers. Felix was never there, so the generational gap wasn't felt, but thirteen years was a big difference. It was enough time for one person to grow up while the other remained a child; for one to become a criminal while the other rushed toward a bright and hopeful future.

"What about your folks?" Felix asked, quirking an eyebrow. "They hit the roof?"

Leo frowned down at his hands, which rested in his lap. He wasn't the type to chitchat, and he certainly wasn't up to the task with the hiss of Julien's ventilator acting as a soundtrack.

"Yeah," Felix said after a moment. "I bet." And then, "So, what happened?"

"Um, my mom…yeah, she freaked out–"

"No," Felix cut him off, then nodded toward his brother. "To Julien," he said, and as he waited for Leo's response, Leo couldn't shake the oddly expectant expression that had settled into the contours of Felix's face. It was as though there was a correct reply. Felix was simply waiting to hear it. But Leo didn't know the answer to that question, so he simply shook his head in the negative and looked away from Felix's narrowed gaze.

"I don't know," Leo murmured. "They say that he lost control," he continued, punctuating what the police had relayed with a helpless shrug. It didn't feel right to discuss the accident in front of Julien, regardless of whether he could hear what was being said or not. Felix didn't share the same sentiment, however. He shifted his weight against the squeaky vinyl and exhaled a breath.

"They who?"

Leo glanced up, shook his head, puzzled by the follow-up. "The cops," he said. *Who else?*

"And he just…lost control," Felix repeated with a smug sort of look, like, *really? You believe that shit? You think he just veered off the road like, "whoops!"? A road he'd driven a million times?*

It was only then, with Felix looking so all-knowingly skeptical, that a question of circumstances slithered into Leo's thoughts and squeezed.

Lost control. It's what the police had said—or, at least what they had told Leo, anyway. There was no suggestion that there had been another vehicle involved. If anything, the cops were suspecting Julien of being at fault. Maybe he'd been drinking, or maybe he'd snorted something before climbing behind the wheel. Hell, you never knew with kids these days. Sex. Drugs. Tide Pods. Asinine YouTube challenges. As Felix had so plainly put it, times change. But Julien and Leo had been hanging out that night, stone sober. Julien had left Leo's house less than half an hour before a final voicemail showed up on Leo's phone.

Hey. We need to talk. You aren't going to believe this shit.

It was easy to tell the voicemail was left during Julien's last drive. He could hear the ambient noise of the car. The mysterious rattle that seemed to come from the glove box. The latest Jack White album on the stereo.

So, "yeah," Leo said, "just lost control."

Maybe he'd swerved to miss a deer. Perhaps he hadn't been paying attention because he'd been screwing around on his phone. Nobody would know for certain because Julien had been alone when he had missed the sharp right turn he'd taken a hundred thousand times before. It would have been his final resting place had it not been for the late-night commuter driving the rural highway, heading home from her shift as a nurse at the very hospital Julien would end up dying in.

Felix didn't say much else. It seemed that planting the seed of doubt in Leo's head had been victory enough. That, judging by the massive army-style duffle bag at Felix's feet, there would be an ample amount of time for small talk. The bag made it clear: Felix wasn't planning on leaving anytime soon.

It took a few weeks, but having Felix around eventually got less weird, and honestly, having someone else around was a relief. Leo had offered Mrs. Bellamy his condolences on what felt like an endless loop, but she continued to ignore him. Leo excused her behavior, of course. She was wracked with grief and worry. That, and she'd never been what anyone would have called warm. Even after so many years of being Julien's best friend, Leo had never felt welcome in their home. Sometimes he wondered if Mrs. Bellamy was the reason Julien's dad had never been in the picture, why Felix had taken off instead of remaining at home.

But regardless of the cause of the Bellamy's familial hardships, it was clear that Julien's mother loved her youngest son with everything she had. She looked positively ravaged with fear, terrified of what all his injuries would mean for his future. She kept asking doctors and nurses questions they couldn't answer. Would he be able to walk? Could plastic surgery fix the damage caused to his face? Leo sat silent as he listened to her beg for guarantees they simply couldn't give.

Felix, on the other hand, kept an unsettling level of cool. While Mrs. Bellamy refused to so much as look at Leo, Felix often stared. When their eyes happened to meet, Felix would offer up a disconcerting sort of smile. When Felix suggested buying Leo lunch one afternoon, Leo had hesitated, but Felix refused to take no for an answer.

Sitting in a booth inside a Chili's Grill and Bar, Leo had felt tense and awkward. And then Felix did something unexpected. He opened up, talking about his and Julien's childhoods, about how their dad had taken off when he was a teen and Jules had been a kid.

"It fucked me up, man," Felix confessed. "Figured it was better for me to stay away, you know? I'm damaged goods, but Julien could still make something of himself if he wasn't influenced by a piece of shit like me."

It had felt unnatural to hear something so genuine coming from a guy Leo had always considered to be the villain. But his confession swung the needle of opinion, and suddenly, rather than seeing Felix as just some asshole that had done nothing but hurt Julien with his absence and apathy, Felix became a human being—a guy who had been trying to protect his kid brother rather than wound him with his selfishness and indifference.

"What about you?" Felix asked. "Your family is cool with you practically living at Saint Francis?"

"They understand," Leo said.

"Yeah?" Felix shifted his weight against the booth seat, then smirked at the plate of nachos he'd ordered on a whim. "Funny, that. But I guess it makes sense."

Leo squinted at his paper drink coaster, unsure of what that was supposed to mean. But before he could dwell on it, Felix spoke up again.

"You're a good friend," he said. "The only one who comes to sit with him."

That affirmation gave Leo comfort. Before he knew it, he was opening up as well, talking more than he'd ever talked in his life, relaying the good times and the bad—all the stuff Felix had missed out on because he'd been off doing God only knew what. He talked about all the concerts he and Julien had gone to in Atlanta, Charleston, Charlotte…hell, Nashville. Leo introduced Felix to Julien's head-in-the-clouds dream of saving the world one beach at a time. The environmental marches. The letters penned to senators and congressmen. Thailand was supposed to be the pinnacle of Julien's efforts, a years-long international move that would allow him to work with some of the top environmentalists in the world. Leo was just the directionless loser who was tagging along, his sketchbook tucked beneath his arm, and even that had been Julien's idea.

What are you going to do, live at home forever? Go to some college you don't even want to go to? Come with me, man. Let's see what the hell else is out there. Otherwise, what's the point?

"So, Jules was going to make a difference," Felix mused. "And what happens? Someone nearly wipes him off the face of the Earth."

Leo furrowed his brow at that. "What do you mean *someone?*" Had the cops found evidence of something? Was there someone else involved? Had Leo not been looped in?

"Sorry," Felix said, shaking his head. "Some*thing,*" he corrected himself. "The accident, that's all I mean. It's a goddamn shame. The world needs guys like him, you know? Someone who actually tries to make the world a better place. But you should go, man…"

"Go?" Leo asked.

"Yeah, to Thailand. Do what Julien would have wanted. Pack up your shit and leave."

It was an oddly placed suggestion, but regardless of its awkward timing, just as Felix had planted the seed of doubt that there may have been more to Julien's accident, he inadvertently helped Leo decide that if Thailand lost Julien Bellamy, Leo would go to Thailand to honor his best friend's legacy. Because otherwise, as Julien had said, what's the point?

The two fell into texting one another. They ate together at least once a week and became close enough for Leo to talk to Felix about Amelia, about how the whole situation with Julien had taken a toll on him, how he wasn't sure if he felt the same way about her as he had in the past, how all he could think about was getting on a plane and flying to Bangkok. Or Phuket. Or Chiang Mai.

Months ticked by. Julien's condition failed to improve. Felix began to pull away just as quickly as he'd warmed up. By the time Mrs. Bellamy stood over Julien's ventilator with her finger hovering over the proverbial trigger, Leo and Felix had hardly spoken in weeks—not that Leo hadn't tried. But none of their back-and-forth banter or heart-to-heart talks mattered when the ventilator went silent. When it was finally over, Felix ghosted Leo so abruptly, it was like a light clicking off. One minute, Felix was an ally. The next, Leo's last link to Julien was gone in the dark.

Or so Leo had thought.

Would it have been better for the couple at the coffee shop to not have been the Bellamys but, instead, just a pair of creepy psychos nobody knew? Better, no. Less disturbing, yes. Something about Felix being behind this whole thing—catfishing Lark, tailing them out to Raven's Head, following Lark to the grocery store—the mere idea of Julien being tangled up in this whole thing by proxy turned Leo's stomach. It felt wrong, like an affront to the dead. It was Felix being the guy Leo always thought he was; the screwed-up outlier of a brother Julien hadn't deserved.

Then there was Mrs. Bellamy. Felix was fucked up enough that stalking wasn't beyond him. But Julien's *mother?* What were they playing at? What the hell was this all about?

As if reading his mind, Leo's phone vibrated in his pocket.

It's a shame you have to be a part of this, the text read. *But a debt is owed.*

Leo squeezed his cell in the palm of his hand, then closed his eyes and took a breath. Rather than finding some semblance of calm, he simply saw his sister's terrified face as she stood in the rain. He'd leaned into her after coming up the dock with their mother, murmured for her to get inside before they both had to explain what was going on. It seemed, however, that Lark had a good reason for being frozen in place. When Leo finally knocked on her bedroom door a few minutes after she'd disappeared upstairs, he found her still soaked, sitting on the edge of her bed, her waterlogged phone held fast in her hands.

"What?" he asked. "What's going on?"

It was then that Lark looked up at him. Trembling, she shook her head.

"Do you have any bars?" she asked.

"Hardly," he said.

"I don't want to be here," she told him.

"I know you don't," Leo said. "Let's just wait until tomorrow morning, and then we'll talk Mom and Dad into—"

"You didn't have anything weird happen to you last night?" she asked, cutting him off. "Because you looked pretty fucking spooked when I first saw you this morning."

Leo's mouth went dry. The bang against his wall. The curtains. The bell.

"Don't you get it?" Lark asked. "They were here, Leo. Upstairs. Last night. They were inside the house. We can't stay here. We have to go."

LARK

DAVID'S TIMING HAD been perfect.

Lark had been posting her writing on an online publishing app—a serialized fiction community of readers, writers, and a handful of agents and publishers, when David had randomly followed her account and left comments on every chapter she'd published. Not only had that meant that he'd read everything she'd written, but that he'd been invested enough to spend hours constructing thoughtful critiques. Maybe it should have been a little creepy, but Lark had been too flattered to see it that way. It was after Julien's accident, when all attention had been focused on Leo and his endless hospital visits. When nothing had been left for her.

Leo's veritable disappearance had left Lark feeling weird and vulnerable. She knew she should have been doing something to help her brother cope, but she couldn't bring herself to reach out to him. Perhaps it had been the fear of coming off as the needy little sister, or maybe she was afraid of that level of emotional pain. Leo had always been a hero to her, standing up to their parents when she didn't have the guts, always speaking his mind. Even now, at his most broken, he was saying "fuck you" with this Thailand thing. So maybe that was it. Faced with the idea of seeing her brother crushed beneath the weight of inevitable loss, Lark had turned away. Rather than offering solace to Leo, she sought comfort from a stranger instead.

David was two years older than her. He lived in some shitkicker Georgia town which he had left unnamed. She had found him smart, charming, and funny. Eventually, their conversations shifted from fiction and critiques to more personal talk. His jokes became flirtations. He asked a lot of questions, some of which had struck her as a little weird. *Is your parents' room upstairs next to yours?* But he always backed up his strange inquiries with reasoning that made her blush. *So, if I was to sneak in to see you, if we were to lock your bedroom door…*

Lark imagined it dozens of times: David creeping through the kitchen's back door. Sneaking up the stairs while holding his breath. Sliding into her room on silent feet. Locking the door behind him and crawling onto her bed while she slept. Her eyes would flutter open to find David gazing down at her from above. *Hi,* he'd say. She'd wrap her arms around his neck, her legs around his waist, and together they'd breathe heavy in the dark.

After a few months of talking, Lark threw caution to the wind. She gave David her cell number and they quickly moved away from social media and the writing community to constant texting. She asked him to call her, willed her phone to ring so they could talk about their favorite movies, their favorite books, what places they wanted to visit, where they wanted to live. But David never called. Whenever she'd try to call *him,* he'd never answer. He would, however, almost always immediately text her back.

Sorry, can't talk now. I'm at work. Or *I'm with the guys.* Or *I'm driving.* Or *I had my phone on do not disturb.*

About a month into his dodges, Lark got gutsy and confronted him.

Why are you doing this? If you didn't want this to go beyond the comments section, why did you string me along?

That time, it took him a while to respond. When he did, he fessed up.

Cancer. David's mother was dying, and his sense of humor was starting to fade.

Lark was hit with an overwhelming sense of guilt. God, she was an asshole. She and David had made a genuine connection. Hell, she was pretty sure she was in love with him. And yet, she was still selfish enough to ride him about not calling, about obfuscating, as though the only thing in the world that could have possibly mattered to him was her.

Before Lark knew it, they were talking about nothing but his sick mom. Lark would ask about her every day. As her condition became progressively worse, Lark sought out ways of comforting David without being there. Meanwhile, Leo was suffering in her presence, and she did nothing for him, because it was easier to offer compassion to a shadow than to flesh and bone.

She gave David the password to the family Netflix account. To Amazon Prime Video. At least that way he'd have something to do while sitting at his mother's bedside. She did the same for the family Spotify account, spending days curating playlists specifically for him. Every song meant something. Every lyric said what Lark couldn't. *I want you. I need you. Please, feel the same…*

Five months after it all started, David's mother died. He became distant and unresponsive, as though the loss had robbed him of his feelings for her. Lark cried for weeks, each day intensifying rather than diminishing her grief.

Then, during a day that was already too hard to bear, she spilled her guts to Allison about the mysterious stranger for whom she had fallen but had never met—the one that was breaking her heart.

"And he never answers when you call?" Allison had asked over a video call, her expressions so skeptical it made Lark question why they were friends. "Lark, he sounds like a catfish."

The matter-of-fact manner in which Allison broke down Lark and David's relationship was both artful and cruel. It left Lark not knowing whether to be thankful for her best friend's bluntness or furious that Allison refused to humor her, if even a little. Somewhere out there, David was suffering. Meanwhile, Lark was trying to hold it together, to not start sobbing in front of her computer. But Allison was all business.

"You need to stop talking to him," she said. "Like, right now. For all you know, you're talking to some fifty-year-old creeper who jerks off to your pics."

"You're an asshole," Lark fired back, and Allison shrugged.

"Fine," she said. "Meet up with him. And if he murders you…?"

"Shut up," Lark whispered, looking away from the screen and down to her hands. "Just shut up."

Allison was wrong. Lark was never more sure of anything in her life.

David was genuine. A dream come true.

The timing was bad, that's all. It wasn't his fault.

This was just testing the strength of their relationship. They'd get through it, and when they did, they'd both know it was the real deal.

I miss you. I want to meet.

It took David a full day to respond to her text.

Sorry, not now.

Please don't shut me out, she begged. *I know you're grieving, but I want to help.*

Hours went by.

Thanks. Not a good time.

His short, emotionless answers broke her heart.

Why are you pushing me away? Have I done something wrong?

Nothing.

A friend told me you aren't who you say you are, that it's the only reason why you'd act this way.

Finally, David responded:

Your friend is right.

The text stuttered her heart to a standstill. Anger bubbled up within her diaphragm, making it hard to breathe. He was screwing with her, trying to push her aside. His roughness was hard to take after months of what had felt like bliss, but maybe this was it, their first fight. Maybe this made it official: they were a couple, battling it out. *Or maybe he's telling the truth about being a liar,* she thought. Except, no. She refused to go down that path, refused to entertain the idea for even a second.

I don't believe you, she told him. Because Jesus Christ, what was wrong with her? Of *course* he didn't want to meet. His mother was still warm in the ground and here was Lark, demanding his undivided attention.

At first, his silence aggravated her. For the first time in her life, she suffered a fit of rage while locked away in her room. She tore her sheets from her bed, flung her pillows across the room, ripped posters off the walls, and threw her phone as hard as she could against the floor. She scooped a pillow up off the rug, pressed it against her face, and screamed, then stayed up all night considering what to do. Maybe blocking him from all her social media accounts would show him she didn't give a damn, just like him. Except, what would that do other than force him to forget her? No, she needed to get under his skin. But first, she needed to figure out how the hell to appeal to a ghost.

Sitting in front of her laptop, she stared at her Facebook feed while chewing on a nail. In what felt like almost an involuntary action, she logged out of her profile, hit 'CREATE AN ACCOUNT', and made Atticus Moore. If anything would force David out of the woodwork, it would be another guy. Someone who publicly took a liking to Lark across all the sites she frequented. Someone who was funny and charming. A replica of who David had once been.

Her plan failed. David remained invisible.

And yet, somehow, she found herself sitting on the edge of a bed miles outside of Raven's Head, soaked through with rain, desperate to believe that the guy Leo had said was someone named Felix wasn't also whomever David may have been.

Hearing the door click open, Lark didn't look up. She simply stared at the dead phone in her hands, listening to Leo slip in and quietly close the door behind him.

"What?" he asked. "What's going on?"

It was then that Lark looked up at him. Trembling, she shook her head.

"I don't want to be here," she said.

"I know you don't," Leo said. "Let's just wait until tomorrow morning, and then we'll talk Mom and Dad into—"

"You didn't have anything weird happen to you last night?" she asked, cutting him off. "Because you looked pretty fucking spooked when I first saw you this morning." Like he'd seen the same shadows she had. As though he'd heard that goddamn bell ring out in the hall.

She watched her brother's expression shift from stoic determination to something she'd only seen reflected in his eyes once before. It was panic. The same panic that had seized his features the night Julien finally died.

"Don't you get it?" Lark asked. "They were here, Leo. Upstairs. Last night. They were inside the house. We can't stay here. We have to go."

Leo stood motionless for a long moment, as though her words had frozen him in place.

Finally, he spoke.

"I know," he said. "I saw them, too."

SIGNAL

POPPY

IT HAD BEEN A FEW HOURS since the kids had made their way
back to the house, but Poppy's anxiety was still through the roof.
Attempting to calm her nerves, she'd tucked herself into the corner of
the couch with a cup of tea and Stephen King's latest release, but
relaxation eluded her. She kept looking up from her book, kept
blinking at the rain that was pounding against the living room's vast
windows, worried about what the evening would bring. The oncoming
darkness felt like an omen, a thing that could only bring catastrophe,
but she convinced herself it was only her agitation talking. *Cool it,* she
told herself. *We're fine.* Except, things didn't feel fine, and when both
her kids stepped into the living room an hour after full dark, Poppy
immediately knew something was up, something beyond their
harrowing sea voyage back home.

Seeing their reflections in the window glass, she turned her
attention away from the rain and regarded her children. Her mouth
went dry at the sight of them. These were two people she knew better
than anyone in the world, but who now looked staggeringly different
from how she remembered them. Perhaps it was the way the lamp on
the side table cast shadows across their faces, but they both looked
older, almost harried.

Lark was sallow enough to be anemic. Having changed out of her
soaked clothes and into her pajamas, even as she stood next to her
brother with her arms coiled across her midsection, she couldn't hide
the fact that she was shaking. Next to her, Leo was trying to be stoic
but unable to conceal his own unease. He, too, had changed clothes,
his fresh jeans and stretched-out cardigan giving him the appearance of
being ready to blow off the island at any given moment. He shifted his
weight from one Converse sneakered foot to the other—a subtle dance

he performed when he was nervous—and for half a second, Poppy found herself realizing that his shoes must have still been soaked with bay water and rain.

"Guys," Poppy finally spoke, prompting Ezra to look up from the TV. He was watching a random Arnold Schwarzenegger flick he'd found in a stack of DVDs; completely out of character for Ezra, but when he'd tried to load Netflix, the internet connection had been down.

"Sorry, but we need to talk," Leo said, the sleeves of his sweater so long they all but swallowed his hands.

Poppy's gaze drifted between her son and daughter, noting Lark's immediate and perhaps involuntary response to the sound of her brother's voice. Her bottom lip began to tremble. A moment later her hands flew up to cover her face. Poppy looked to Ezra, perhaps for guidance, maybe for support. *What's happening?*

"Lark?" Ezra's face twisted up in that overly-concerned way of his—an expression that, in one scenario could be reassuring, and in another could be infuriating. Ezra had an easy way with the kids, one that Poppy had often been jealous of because she had been forced to be the authoritarian. But Ezra? He'd always been the one they'd run to if they needed a parent in their corner, if they needed a *yes* to counter Mom's strict and final *no*. "What's up, kiddo?" Ezra clicked off the TV, then shifted against the overstuffed armchair he occupied to the left of the couch.

"I've done something stupid." Lark spoke shakily into her hands. "And now I'm in trouble."

Poppy stared.

"In really big trouble," Lark whispered.

Leo shook his head as if to say, *no, that's not how we agreed to present this. We were supposed to play it cool.*

But Lark was beyond keeping her composure. With her hands still concealing her face, she began to weep, to talk, spilling her guts onto the living room rug.

"You said I was addicted, and I am. You said the time I spent online was taking over my life, and it did." She paused, stammered. "It *has*," she corrected herself. "I know you don't get it, Mom." Her attention shifted upward, her gaze pausing on Poppy's face. "You don't have to get it. It's…" Lark shook her head again. "It's fine. I wish you could understand, but…"

"But." Poppy spoke up. She wanted to scream at them both. *What the hell is going on?!* But she kept her tone subdued. Lark was trying to come clean. The worst thing Poppy could do was get her defenses up and attack. "It's more than just writing, isn't it?" she asked, trying to be as gentle as she could be.

Lark looked away. A moment later, she began to weep again.

"Something is happening, and I don't know how to stop it."

Leo stared at his hands, seemingly afraid to look up as he wrung his fingers.

"What do you mean—" Ezra began, but Poppy cut him off.

"What kind of something?" she asked, pushing her book aside, moving to sit at attention. Her inquiry drew Leo's gaze. His eyes paused on her, then traveled back to his sister. *What are you doing?* he seemed to want to ask. *This isn't how this was supposed to play out, Lark. This isn't what we discussed.*

"I'm being stalked."

Lark's words just about stole Poppy's breath. At her left, she heard Ezra draw in a sharp intake of air. Leo reached up and pushed his fingers through his hair—same as his father did—then pivoted on the soles of his shoes as if ready to walk out of the room. But he didn't. A moment later he was facing forward again.

"Lark," he said, stern, ready to correct her, but Lark wasn't having it.

"No, Leo. Don't, okay? I did this. This is my fault—"

"It isn't—"

"I thought he was someone else, alright?" Lark cried.

"Because he lied to you," Leo reminded her.

"But then he disappeared," Lark told him. "He vanished and I got him to come back, okay? It's my fault, because after he lied, *I* lied. I'm no better than him. If I had just let him go we wouldn't be dealing with this right now. This is all me. I did this."

"Guys." Ezra held out his hands, as though such a simple gesture would somehow pause the conversation and make things come clear.

Poppy, however, was beyond such subtle signals. "Okay, stop," she said, her tone firm. "Start at the beginning. What's going on?"

"I met a guy," Lark whimpered. "We'd been talking online for a while. For months. And then things got…I don't know."

"Think," Poppy demanded.

"They got weird, okay?" Lark said.

"Got weird how?" Poppy asked, her words as taut as a piano wire. She didn't want to come right out and say it, but she was sure Lark knew what she was thinking. *I told you to be careful, told you it could be dangerous.* Hell, she'd told both her kids for years, relaying harrowing tales about teens being deceived, lured out to strange homes by too-good-to-be-true Craigslist ads only to be tortured, maimed, killed. Dramatic, sure, but nobody could claim that her worries were unwarranted. Facebook was full of articles about hapless kids being taken advantage of…or worse. She'd warned them both, but Leo wasn't her concern. Lark, though? Leave it to an almost sixteen-year-old to think that *she* would never be so stupid; as though nobody could possibly con *her* into driving out to some middle-of-nowhere house on the promise of sold out concert tickets or a cheap iPhone SE.

"Lark." Leo caught his sister by the arm, giving her a pointed look. Poppy narrowed her eyes at them both. It was odd seeing them displaying such a dynamic. Leo was trying to keep the situation under control, attempting to keep Lark in check while balancing his own restraint. That's when Poppy knew there was something more to what Lark was confessing, something that perhaps Lark didn't even grasp herself.

Lark wiped at her eyes with the back of her hand, then frowned at Leo, unhappy with how he was trying to corral her. Momentarily, Poppy was proud of her daughter. *Get him,* she thought. *Stand up for yourself.*

But when it came to a battle of siblings, Leo would always win. Despite his predisposition for art and introversion, he was a lot like his Uncle Luca. Strong. Convincing. He knew how to command a situation. Lark, it turned out, was a lot like Poppy: weak-willed and easy to lie to. Even easier to control.

"Why are you doing this?" Leo asked his sister. "I told you, Felix—"

Before he could finish his sentence, he looked down, distracted. Poppy could hear his phone vibrating in his pocket, because of course it was. Lark had hoisted herself up on the cross, but Leo wasn't free of digital addiction, either, and here was the proof. In the middle of this insane conversation, the buzzing of his phone could derail him, quick as a wink. Nothing was more important than an incoming text.

Trying to keep her cool, Poppy corrected her posture against the couch cushions. She took a breath, then shot Ezra a look to see whether he was going to jump in. But Ezra was now wearing an odd, indecipherable expression. She couldn't tell whether he was spooked or appalled or overwhelmed, but he was the least of her worries. Looking back to her kids, she posed a simple question, ready for some answers.

"Who the hell is Felix?"

LEO

WHEN LEO'S PHONE BUZZED against his thigh, he lost his train of thought. Hesitating, his gaze settled upon his mother, watching her expression shift between worry and impatience. Her attention jumped from one kid to the other, too busy trying to figure out what was happening to be pissed at either of them just yet.

Finally, she spoke, shaking Leo out of his torpor.

"Who the hell is Felix?"

And honestly, that was a great question. Did anyone actually know Felix Bellamy? Jesus, if Julien was still alive, would he know his own brother?

Felix was the guy who was in Raven's Head for God only knew what reason, the guy Lark and Leo were convinced had been inside the house the night before. Felix was the psycho who was texting Leo right now, and Leo was ignoring because of some no-cell-phone deal his mother had made. But it was easy to blame Felix for everything. He was, after all, the one with a criminal record the length of Leo's arm. What wasn't so simple was explaining why Julien's mother was in Raven's Head with him. *That* was what was nagging Leo the most, the fact that Mrs. Bellamy was in on whatever insanity was being played out.

"Screw it," he said, drew his out his phone, and peered at the text that had just come through.

We can hear you, Leo. Every word.

"Leo?" Mom was waiting for an answer.

Another buzz. Another message.

What will you tell her? Mother wants to know.

Mother.

So, they could see him right then, standing next to Lark, speaking to his mom.

Mother.

Or maybe Leo's hunch was right and Mrs. Bellamy was in on it. Hell, maybe she was behind the whole thing.

Maybe the text wasn't referring to Leo's mother, but to the only other mother tangled up in this thing.

"What the *fuck…?*"

There was a gasp of disapproval. "Leo!" Mom snapped, as though foul language would somehow render an already insane situation positively unacceptable.

"Hey, kiddo," Dad said. "Cool it."

But Leo didn't have time to worry about such trivial bullshit. He shook his head at his cell, not understanding how he could be reading what he was. *How* could they hear him? Was this place bugged? He shot a look at Lark. "Do you have your phone?"

"What?" She sniffed, seemingly baffled by his question. "No. It's back in the room. It's dead, remember?"

Leo looked back down at his cell, then to his mother. *Mother.* "Mom?"

Still flustered, Mom huffed out a breath at him, not understanding.

"Do you have your phone on you?" he asked, his skin crawling with the idea of Felix peering at them through the curtainless windows, through the boughs of spruce trees that partially surrounded the house. "Where is it?"

"In the bedroom," she told him. "Where *everyone's* should be. What does that—"

Her words trailed off as Leo turned his attention to the exposed ceiling beams. He had no idea what he was looking for or even if it was possible—someone could have hot mic'ed a rental property, right? The door had been unlocked when they had arrived. Leo had thought it weird then, but it was positively jarring now.

Except, it didn't add up. If it was just the house that was bugged, how had Felix known to find Leo and Lark at the coffee shop in Raven's Head? They had talked about it outside on the front porch, not inside. Unless…

It's me. The thought shook him, seizing his heart, forcing it to skip a beat. *It's* my *phone.*

He'd heard of apps that could surveil all sorts of things, from web searches to phone conversations and GPS coordinates—apps that ran on cell phones that never left the owners' hands. Julien had talked about that sort of stuff all the time, citing it as merely one of many reasons to go off grid and do something better with his life. *I mean, Christ,* Jules had scoffed, *look at Facebook. They know what I'm going to type before I even think it.*

Leo knew if a creeper wanted to spy on someone, all it took was a little effort. Besides, was he exempt from the vulnerabilities his sister wore so plainly? Hadn't there been moments when he'd left his phone unattended in Julien's hospital room while ducking out to speak to a nurse, or at the Chili's when he'd gone up to the bar to get both himself and Felix refills when the waitress had taken too long?

Leo's heart bounced into his throat as he jammed his finger against the power button on the side of his phone, holding it down. He shut it off and dropped it onto the coffee table as though it was white hot, then backed away from the table while wiping his palms against his jeans. "Shit," he whispered. "Oh, *goddamn…*"

When he looked up from his abandoned device, Lark was staring at him with wide eyes, imploring him to come out with it.

He shook his head at her. No, he wouldn't say a word, because what if they could still hear them? And then his breath hitched in his throat, because right then, a cell phone rang.

At first, Leo was sure it was his. It was a generic preloaded Android tone that every person over the age of forty seemed to have. Leo had never bothered to change it because he'd never cared about those types of things. As a matter of fact, he was pretty sure that he and his father shared—

A second ring.

Leo's eyes slowly followed the muffled sound to his right, to his dad, who was looking oddly frightened as he sat stock-still in an armchair next to the couch, the TV remote still held fast in his right hand.

"Ezra?" His mother's eyes flitted from one face to another, seeking out answers to a question she didn't know to ask. Rather than losing her temper, her tense expression softened around the edges, giving way to perplexed anxiety. "You guys are starting to scare me," she confessed, her tone quieter than usual. "Would someone please explain what's happening?"

Beyond looking about ready to crawl out of his skin, Dad didn't respond, probably because he had no idea what was going on either. It was why Leo had to speak up, had to snap their father out of his daze.

"Dad," he said. "Answer it." The command felt reflexive, born out of some primordial sense of self-preservation. But the strangeness of the situation wasn't lost on him. Felix had gotten Leo's phone number directly from Leo at the hospital. He'd gotten Lark's contact information from Lark, albeit under an alias. But their *dad?*

The phone rang again.

Lark exhaled a mew-like sound from deep within her throat.

"No," she said. "Daddy, don't."

"You have to answer it," Leo told him.

"No, he doesn't!" Lark fired back. "He doesn't have to do anything. Just stop, okay?"

"I can't," Leo told her, because they had to figure out what the hell was going on. The fact that their father's cell phone was ringing was proof that there was more to this than either of them knew. The mystery was no longer *who.* Leo was certain of the culprit's identity. The mystery was *why.* And the only way to get that answer was to go to the source. If answering the call brought them one step closer to piecing together this godforsaken puzzle, they had to answer the fucking call.

"I know who it is," Lark said, turning her attention to their parents. "I fell in love with him, okay? Then he decided he didn't care anymore and I couldn't handle it, so I made someone up. A crush to make him jealous. I antagonized him." She turned her gaze to their mother. "I'm an idiot, alright? You don't have to say it because I already know. You warned me and I didn't listen and now—"

The phone continued to ring.

"Lark, fucking *can it.*" Leo fired the command at her, finally having heard enough. He was sick of her going on about how this had to do with some stupid love affair. No matter who Felix had spoken to or how he had gotten his information or why the hell both he and Mrs. Bellamy were in Raven's Head, Julien was the key to this. Not Lark. Not her broken heart. Not even Leo. Julien.

Lark stared at Leo with a blank expression, stunned into silence by his callous reaction. A moment later, she was crying again.

"They're calling back," their dad murmured, the first call having gone to voicemail. He was holding the phone out and away from him the way someone might hold a dead thing or a rotten piece of fruit. His expression was a weird mix of dread and knowing. Leo wanted to yell at him to answer it, but it would have been pointless. The longer Leo watched his father, the more it seemed like his dad was ready to chuck his phone across the room in disgust.

"He said his name was David," Lark wept. "He said he lived in Georgia. How was I supposed to know he was a liar?" She looked up at them all, imploring. "How was I supposed to know?" she asked, her tear-swollen gaze settling upon their mother. "Would *you* have known?"

Mom's expression went momentarily dark. A second later, she finally broke her silence.

"How does he know that we're here, Lark?" she asked. "Did you tell him?"

"No." Lark shook her head, abruptly breaking eye contact with them all. "I mean, I was going to but—"

"Wait, what?" Leo held up a hand. *Shut up, Everyone, just wait.* "You were going to tell him how?" He gave Lark his full attention. She'd never breathed a word of this before. "A text? A call?"

Lark continue to shake her head in the negative, trying to swallow her sobs.

"Then how?" he asked, insistent. *"Think."*

"An email!" she finally yelled. "Jesus, who cares? I was going to send it, but I never did. What difference does it make?"

"But you wrote it," Leo surmised. "Did you delete it?"

"No, I just…I don't remember. I think I just closed out of it," she said. "Why?"

Leo closed his eyes and took a steadying breath, picturing it: Felix accessing Lark's account, reading her emails, perusing all the messages their mother had forwarded to them over the past few weeks. Details about Raven's Head, about the very house they were standing in now. Suddenly, the unlocked front door made sense. The message their mother had forwarded from the AirBnB host had the passcode right there in black and white.

"Leo, why?!" Lark insisted.

"Because if you just close out of it, the message goes into your drafts," Leo told her. "It doesn't just disappear."

Lark blanched.

"He has your password, doesn't he?" Leo asked. He hated asking, but he'd heard of this sort of thing before: girls giving guys their passwords to show their boyfriends how devoted and trusting and faithful they were. *See? You can know everything about me. I love you that much. I've got nothing to hide.*

"To my email?" Lark asked, sniffling against the back of her hand. "No, just to my—" She stopped as if suddenly realizing what she'd done. Yeah, she'd given him her password, just to another site. Except that didn't matter when your password was the same for everything. He'd complained to her about it when she'd asked him for help with her computer. He'd even installed a password generator on her laptop and phone. She had promised to use it, but clearly, that hadn't happened. Surprise, surprise.

Leo covered his face with his hands.

"…oh no…" Lark breathed the words into the room, her voice small, suddenly sounding like a child who'd just broken a priceless family heirloom.

Do you have any idea what could happen if someone got access to your account? Leo had asked her. *They could erase you, Lark. Like you never existed.*

What had her response been? She'd rolled her eyes at him as if to say, *oh, the Internet is so dangerous! Please, you sound just like Mom.*

"…wait, 'oh no' what?" Their mother asked, forever a step behind the conversation. "Lark? What did you do?"

"Shit," Dad whispered, then turned away from the group. A moment later, his phone rang again, pushing Leo to the brink. Letting his hands fall from his face and to his sides, he marched over to his father, snatched the phone out of his hand, and accepted the call.

"I know it's you," Leo said. "I just don't know why."

There was a pause on the line, and then the sound of a cocksure smirk.

"Tell Lark 'no hard feelings'," the voice said. "She was a means to an end, that's all."

And then, just like that, the line went dead.

Leo held his father's phone out to stare at the screen, blinking as the single bar disappeared. A moment later, the WiFi signal—weak as it was—vanished as well.

EZRA

FELIX.

Ezra hadn't heard that name in months, but he knew it. Christ, he *knew* it. Yet, somehow, he managed to convince himself that it couldn't be *that* Felix. No, absolutely not. It had to be someone else. Because this all started with Lark, right? Isn't that what his daughter had just confessed? She had met some random guy, had led him on. Stupid, sure, but she was just a kid living in a digital age. He remembered his own days on AOL, cruising chat rooms. It had been easy to get lost within the masquerade—secret personas, endless conversations, wishful thinking, too much trust.

No, this wasn't that Felix. *Just a coincidence,* he told himself. *Gemma isn't that crazy. She wouldn't send her kid after me because I called off some lousy affair.* Except, Gemma was about as crazy as they came. Ezra had known about that long before they had ever started their flirtations. In fact, it had been part of the allure. The opposite of Poppy. A thrill he couldn't resist.

He got his first taste of Gemma's eccentricity at a cheap motel, her biting and scratching, mewing and hissing like some feral cat. After their second or third "date" and lying naked beneath cheap and questionably clean sheets, she had puffed on a cigarette and told him she'd been a witch in a past life. She'd also been at Jonestown, ladling Kool-Aid into paper cups. She relayed these former incarnations, then rolled onto her stomach, propped her chin up on her palm like a schoolgirl, and offered him a Cheshire grin. *All my pasts are threaded through with violence, so you better watch out.* And then there was the question he had yet to shake: *have you ever wanted to hurt one of your students? Just lay into them for mouthing off, beat them down until they're lying on the floor begging for you to stop, weeping like the baby they were only fifteen years ago?* Ezra had been taken aback by the inquiry. He hadn't gotten a chance to respond before Gemma had mumbled a muffled promise around the filter of a burning cigarette. *Mouthing off or not, if anyone ever hurt one of my kids, I'd fucking kill 'em…*

Ezra recalled all of this within the span of a single heartbeat—one that hit as hard as a punch to the chest. When he finally refocused his attention and rejoined the room, he was greeted by his phone being chucked hard against the couch cushion by his son.

Leo turned away from everyone, his fingers tangled in his dark brown hair. His body language reflected how Ezra had felt the night he left Gemma's place for the last time. Freaked out. Borderline manic. Unsure of what to do. Pulled over along the side of a dark road, pacing back and forth through the twin beams of his headlights.

Oh shit. Oh fuck. Oh my God. Oh Christ.

"How could they have Dad's number?" Lark asked, her tone so soft Ezra could just about hear her desire to become invisible, to simply disappear the way he had wanted to that night in early spring.

"Because you gave it to them," Leo murmured. "If they have access to your account, they have access to everything. Emails. Contacts. Phone numbers."

Was that all it took; a single unlatched window to bring the entire digital house down? Ezra had stopped asking Poppy about those annoying Google notices warning him about new logins to her account. There had been a lot of them lately, but he hadn't brought it up because every one had been legitimate in the past. And now, he and Poppy were hardly speaking. That, and he had more important things to think about, like how to get things back on track with his family. Like how to ghost Gemma for good. Like how he was going to pay for three days on a private island. Like Felix.

Ezra didn't realize he was shivering until he noticed Leo staring at him in that way of his. The kid was trying to decipher something, or maybe he'd already figured it out. But no, that was impossible. This was one secret Ezra would take to his grave.

Before Leo read too much into things, his attention drifted back to his sister. Lark's sobbing had newfound vigor.

"I'm so sorry," she said between heaving, broken breaths. "I'm—

so—sorry. I—didn't—know…"

Of course she didn't. No one did.

That was the silver lining around this black cloud.

Despite the twisting of his heart, his secret was safe.

Safe because the dead couldn't speak.

POPPY

"LEO."

Poppy waited for her son to look up from his frantic search through the kitchen drawers. But Leo refused to pause his hunt for whatever it was he was looking for, refused to acknowledge her at all. For all she knew, he hadn't heard her in his panic, and it *was* panic. She recognized the expression on his face the way one recognizes an unwelcome visitor. It was the same look she wore so many times while staring into her own eyes, trying to calm herself before anxiety was given the chance to wrap around her throat, stealing her every breath.

"Would you please stop for a minute?" she asked, that familiar disquiet coiling around her ankles, starting its upward slither. "Please," she begged him, reaching out to catch hold of his arm.

Again, he failed to look her way. It was then that the mother in her fell away and Poppy—the girl she had once been—burst through the surface. The tough grunge kid with pink-dyed hair and tattered jeans. The girl who had pilgrimaged to Seattle after Kurt Cobain had been killed. The chick who had secretly celebrated when Leo had bought a Pearl Jam T-shirt at some random shop at the mall.

"Hey," she said, snapping her fingers at him. "Look at me." And while her tone was as sharp as a blade, she felt nothing if not afraid. But she concealed it well, and Leo froze, her ire momentarily stopping him in his tracks. He blinked while she kept hold of his arm, her grip tightening rather than letting go.

"Tell me what's happening," she demanded. "Who is Felix?"

He stared at her for a long moment, his face blank and scared. This situation was rendering him silent. She could see it in his eyes—he wanted to speak, but something was keeping him gagged.

"Just tell me," she said softly, her grip on his arm relaxing.

"Julien's brother," Leo said, though it was so softly spoken she nearly missed it.

Poppy vaguely remembered the stories. Something about Julien's brother never being around, but when he was, he was mean and abrasive; something about him and Julien's mother fighting. She recalled Leo coming to her once. *If Julien needs to live somewhere else for a while, can he come here?* A better mother would have seen that as a red flag, because what the hell was going on in Julien's life that he'd have to find another home?

Julien never did end up needing a new place to live. Leo's inquiry into his friend's well-being faded from memory like most small things do. At least until now, when the recollection came crawling out of the shadows—a dismissed, unheeded thought limping into the light, sharp teeth glinting like knives.

Poppy furrowed her brow, suddenly more confused than ever. "He and Lark were..." Were what? A couple? Didn't Lark say the guy's name was David?

"She didn't know it was him," Leo said. "It started with me, with the hospital. He was there. We talked a lot. Then Julien was gone, and so was Felix."

"Until just now," she said.

"Yeah," Leo murmured, rifling through another drawer. "Until just now." It was then that he held up what he'd been searching for. A flashlight.

"What's that for?" Poppy asked. But Leo didn't have to answer her. Her heart was already flip-flopping inside her chest because she knew exactly what her son intended, she just didn't want to believe it to be true.

"It takes nearly twenty minutes to get to Raven's Head," Leo began. "Twenty minutes to get back. Only two people can fit on that boat at a time." He kept his voice down as if not wanting to be overheard. "One person would have to come back three times to get all four of us out of here. And that's in the dark and without a spotlight. In the pouring rain. It's impossible."

Then there was the fact that, even if it *were* possible, Poppy would have been hard pressed to set foot onto that dinghy, regardless of whatever dangers lurked in the shadows of their rental home. Yet, she dismissed that truth and refuted Leo's logic anyway. She had to stop him. There was no way she could let him go out there.

"This is an island," she reminded him. "It's an *island*, Leo."

Leo widened his eyes at her, then motioned with his free hand to tell her to keep her voice down.

"Why?" Poppy asked. "Are they listening?"

Leo didn't respond to that, only clicked the flashlight on.

"Leo?" Lark stepped into the kitchen, still recovering from her fit of tears. Her face was puffy, her eyes red and rimmed in smeared black kohl. Every other breath she took hitched in her throat. With her arms coiled tightly across her chest, she lingered between the kitchen and living room, seemingly unsure of whether she wanted to know what was going on or be left in the dark.

"You aren't going out there," Poppy said flatly, but she knew full well that Leo was going to do whatever he pleased. He was a Taurus. Stubborn. Determined. Part of her was proud of him for his fierce independence. Despite his recent hardships, he was full of fight. But part of her wanted to squelch that self-reliance if only to keep him close. Close meant safe, and what the hell was out there anyway? Or, more accurately, who?

"Really?" Leo challenged, albeit beneath his breath. "Does that mean you're getting on the boat?"

"What? Leo, you aren't—" Lark stared at the flashlight, rejecting the possibility.

"Why would you do that?" Poppy asked. "What's the point? They aren't *here*, right?"

She watched her children exchange a look.

"No," she said, refusing to believe it. *This is a goddamn island*, she told herself. There was one dock. One way to the house. There were windows everywhere. Locks on the doors. They were secluded out in there in the middle of the bay, nobody but the Parrishes for miles because that's what they were paying for. That was the whole fucking point.

Except, the way her kids were looking at each other made her skin crawl.

"It's impossible," she told them with a shake of the head. "I'm not getting on the boat because there's nobody here."

"And why not?" Leo asked. "They can park a boat around the backside of the island somewhere where we can't see it. There are enough trees out there to make a campsite without anyone knowing, right? It's a big island…"

Lark covered her mouth with a hand, as if trying to suppress another cry.

"You're just assuming he'd go that far," Poppy assured him— wishful thinking put into words. "Did he *tell* you he's here? And even if he had, why would you believe him? You said he's a liar. He lied to Lark. So why—"

"Because they were inside the house," Leo said, cutting her off, no longer concerned with the volume of his voice. "Lark saw them. So did I."

Poppy's muscles stiffened. She lost her breath.

They. Them. It was more than just Felix, then?

They were inside the house.

"That's impossible," Poppy repeated, but her resolve was gone. "The house was locked," she said softly, determined to keep talking, still searching for the right series of words to convince her son not to go out into the rain.

"They have access to Lark's account," Leo reminded her. "Mom, you forwarded us every email you got about this place for weeks. The address. Photos of every room. Aerials of the island. Don't you remember? One of those emails included the lock code to the front door."

Reaching out to steady herself against the kitchen island, she shook her head, desperate to believe this was just some far-fetched joke. Nobody had snuck in and crept around while everyone slept. But if they had, what an ideal home to lurk in. The bizarre layout. The endless doors, like that weird Jack-and-Jill bathroom just off the master suite.

That's when it hit her. Suddenly, Poppy felt that she might vomit, because she'd seen them too, hadn't she? That word, *liar,* scrawled across the mirror. It had been perfect because whoever had written it had been listening. They had known. Knew. Knew *everything.*

"What the hell is this?" she whispered, still unable to fully wrap her mind around the possibility.

Giving her daughter her full attention, Poppy was momentarily overwhelmed by a rush of indignation. She'd warned Lark about things like this. She had asked nicely. She'd yelled, then pleaded and cursed and ignored. She'd even tried to bribe, but no matter what she had attempted, she had been left feeling helpless, watching her little girl's light fade beneath the blue glow of a tiny screen. And now, even with Lark's phone waterlogged and broken, it was still there, haunting them. Whatever Lark had done on that device, whatever it was she had set in motion…it was with them, inside the house, lurking in the shadows, smiling within the enveloping darkness, waiting like a wolf.

LARK

"WHAT THE HELL IS THIS?" Lark's mother whispered. A moment later, her gaze met Lark's. "I said it would swallow you, didn't I? Except, it isn't just you now, Lark."

Lark tried to maintain eye contact, but she was looking away before she could stop herself. Her stomach twisted around her mother's thinly veiled accusation, because she had overheard Leo from the other room. She'd listened to him explain that he and Felix had been associated long before Felix had come for her, disguised as David. And yet, that didn't make a damn bit of difference. It was clear upon whose shoulders their mother placed the blame.

A part of her couldn't help but believe that this was her fault. Sure, maybe it had all started as a joke. Perhaps Felix and Leo had a falling out and Felix thought, *hey, I'll screw with his kid sister. Why not?* People were bizarre; they did crazy shit. But rather than leaving it alone, Lark had pushed "David" too far, demanding his undivided attention. Maybe that's what had triggered Felix into taking the joke a dozen steps further than even he had anticipated. That, or perhaps it had been Lark's fake boyfriend—an attempt to provoke a response. *You want a reaction?* Felix had probably thought… *I'll show you a reaction. Here we go...*

Except, if that was the explanation, why was Felix's mother with him?

"If you aren't getting on the boat, that means I'm going," Leo said to their mother, prompting Lark to look up again. Her gaze settled onto her brother, that flashlight still in his hand.

She didn't get it. He was going out into the dark, and if he found who he was looking for…then what? Would a fistfight solve this? Was it possible to talk it out? Was this even about what Lark thought it was about? She was suddenly reminded of the insidious smile that had crept across Felix's mouth when she'd spotted him at the coffee shop, and that grin had said it all. He was dangerous. He loved being in Raven's

Head, creeping around corners only to make himself obvious. *Peek-a-boo,* his expression had read. It was the smile of someone who was unhinged.

"You aren't," their mother said, reaching for the flashlight. "It's insane." She was right. If Felix was out there, there was no way Leo was coming back, at least not alone. Rather than losing him to Thailand, Lark would lose him to some psycho whom *she* had goaded, whom she had *loved.* Unless she went with him.

The rumble of thunder shook her from the inside out. She jumped, suddenly feeling as though she was about to vomit. "Jesus," she whispered, pressing a hand to her forehead. "Oh, Jesus…"

If she was right that all roads led back to her, perhaps Felix would take her instead of Leo. He'd take her instead. He'd take her…

"Leo, wait," she said, allowing her hand to fall to her side. "God, wait…"

When she looked up, she met his eyes with a weak sort of smile.

"I'm coming with you," she said. "If he's out there, he can face us both."

"You've lost your mind," Leo said, turning away from her. But rather than backing down, his refusal only set her in motion. She crossed the length of the kitchen at a pace that surprised her—quick, determined steps led her toward him, a newfound sense of determination burning hot within her chest.

"And how do you propose to stop me?" Lark asked. "I'll just follow you out there."

"You'll get lost," Leo protested. "You won't keep up."

"Because you're going to run?" she asked. "Are you suddenly some sort of marathon sprinter? And will you be running from him or from me?"

Leo exhaled a laugh. "You think you can provoke me into letting you come along? Why? So we can both get killed?"

Hearing the worst-case scenario spoken aloud forced panic to scramble up her windpipe, because Leo saying it so bluntly meant it could really happen. This whole crazy situation was real. The unimaginable was upon them.

"Yeah." Lark forced the word out, spitting it onto the floorboards between them. "Yeah, *exactly*. So we can both get killed. I don't want to die, Leo, but I also don't want you to die alone."

"Oh my God," their mother gasped, momentarily pressing her hands over her ears. *I'm not hearing this.* "Both of you, stop it! No one is going out there!" She closed the distance between them, reached forward, and yanked the flashlight out of Leo's hand. "No one is going anywhere. We're staying here, inside, understand? Inside, where it's safe!"

"Safe?" Leo snorted. "Do you ever listen, Mom? We *saw them inside*. I came downstairs last night and I saw someone in the living room, standing in the—" Leo stopped, as if realizing something. A moment later he was pivoting on the soles of his sneakers, marching back into the aforementioned living room. Lark watched him from the kitchen's threshold, her fingers folded hard against her mouth as he stalked toward a specific spot in the room; the spot, she assumed, he'd seen whomever it was that had been standing there in the dark. Maybe Felix. Perhaps Dark Helena. She tried to imagine the shadow they must have cast. Had they moved or simply stood motionless, hoping Leo wouldn't notice? Or had they purposefully waited for him, playing what was starting to feel more and more like a game?

Leo was standing in the corner now, his brow furrowed, facing the wall.

"What are you doing?" Mom asked, then turned her attention to Lark. "What's he doing?"

Lark shook her head. *I don't know.*

"I saw them," Leo said. "Out of nowhere, and then into nowhere..." He lifted a hand, pressed his palm against the wall.

"But they didn't do anything, Leo," Lark reminded him. "If they wanted to hurt us, why didn't they do it last night? I mean, right? They would have done it by now." Her answer came quickly, much like the flashes of lightning that veined white-hot across the dark sky beyond the glass. Felix had led her on for months under the ruse of being someone he wasn't. He *wanted* to scare them, and maybe that's all there was to this. A scare.

A soft click sounded from where Leo stood.

"That's right," their mother agreed. "They didn't do anything because this is *nonsense*. We're going to wait for morning. We'll stay together, all of us here in the living room. If the storm has passed, your father will take the boat to Raven's Head and get the Coast Guard to come get us. Okay?"

Neither Lark nor Leo responded.

"Answer me, goddamnit!" their mother barked. She turned, throwing the heavy flashlight across the kitchen as if to accentuate her demand. It hit the hardwood with a startling crack, then rolled into the shadows of the hall that led to the master suite. Lark jumped at the noise. She felt Leo tense up despite being across the room. Even their father exclaimed an alarmed "oh shit" from beside the bank of living room windows. Except, rather than turning to face them or asking what had been thrown, he simply repeated himself.

"Oh shit."

Lark furrowed her eyebrows at that.

"Oh *shit.*" The same words, but with a completely different tone, an entirely different meaning.

Lark's attention jumped back to Leo, looking for guidance, desperate to squelch the hysteria that was starting to eke its way up her throat. Leo, however, was no help. She watched something shift within the subtle contours of her brother's face; a tensing of his features, a twitch of the corner of his mouth. It was recognition that this was worse than he expected, an understanding that the situation had escalated, that there was no way out.

"Ezra?" Mom pivoted on the soles of her slipper socks. After a moment, she swept past Lark and moved toward the windows. Lark trailed behind her, if only to not be left alone.

It was there, in the dimly lit living room, that Dad stood at one of the house's many giant windows, his silhouette outlined in the dancing warmth of an orange glow coming off the bay. The sun had set hours before in a similar tangerine hue, but this was no sunset.

Lark slowly stepped around her parents to get a better view, her heart stopping at what she saw. Because the water was on fire.

No, not the water. The boat.

The commuter bobbed up and down, continuing to burn despite the wind and rain, still tied to the pier. Like a Scandinavian death pyre, their only way off the island was now little more than a wind-whipped flame.

And when she turned her head to look for Leo, she found him standing in the same spot in the living room where she'd seen him last. Except, only moments before, he'd been standing in a corner. But now, he was standing in front of an open door.

A door where one hadn't been before.

LEO

LEO SPRINTED DOWN the deck's steps and into the downpour, the flashlight his mother had chucked across the kitchen back in his grip. Yet, despite his speed, Lark grabbed at the sleeve of his shirt; a drowning girl desperate to keep her head above water. She was keeping up with him, grasping at his arm with no intention of letting go. He stopped a few yards shy of the house and turned to squint at her through the rain. *This isn't about you. How many times are you going to make me say it?* But before anything hurtful could slither past his lips, he was forced into silence by the determination on her face.

She glared at him through the darkness, her eyes narrowed not against the wind or rain but against Leo's ego. *I told you I'm coming with you,* her expression read. *I'm tired of being pushed around.*

"I don't care what you want," she told him, her voice half-stolen by the wind coming off the water. "I'm just as much a part of this as you are, Leo. He dragged me into this. I have just as much right to get even with that asshole as you do."

Leo was tempted to yell at her to go back, but she wasn't wrong. What had Leo done beyond sitting at Julien's bedside, hoping for a miracle? And Lark; if anything, she'd offered Felix—or David, or whatever the hell he wanted to call himself—at least some semblance of comfort during a rough-as-hell time. Neither one of them deserved this.

And why is Julien's mom involved? Why is she here?

Even if Leo had yelled toward Lark and she could hear him over the rain, he'd have been drowned out by their mother, who was screaming at them from the open kitchen door at the top of the stairs.

"Get back here!" she screeched from beneath the covered porch. It was as though she hadn't gaped at the house's secret living room passageway only seconds before; as though the idea of someone occupying the house right along with them—slinking through the spaces in the walls— was beyond her comprehension, beyond anything she could possibly fathom or accept.

Mother, Leo thought. *Mom, screaming into the dark. Into the wind.*

Maybe it was the cold rain rolling down the back of his neck, or perhaps it was the numbing chill carried on an occasional gust of air; whatever it was, the discomfort forced Leo to see the situation for what it was. This wasn't about Lark and her gullibility; not about her broken heart or even the fact that she'd egged Felix on. It wasn't about Leo, either; not about the six months he'd spent in a straight-backed chair, tormented by a creeping sense of loss. This wasn't even about Julien. How could it have been? Julien was dead.

No, this whole thing was about one person and one person only.

Gemma Bellamy. The woman with nothing left to lose.

Suddenly, worst case scenarios came flooding forth like a river undammed. Turning to look up at his mother's silhouette, he could hardly make out her face through the shadows, but he didn't have to see her expression to sense her fear. It was coming off her like soundwaves. Like radiation or heat. She practically vibrated with apprehension, determined to keep her kids safe while her children recklessly defied her. But Poppy Parrish had good reason to be afraid, because while Leo had no proof to back up his suspicion, his gut assured him that Gemma was capable of far more than any of them could imagine. And that feeling? It was the only reason he hesitated as he stood there in the pouring rain, replaying the scene he'd never unsee inside his head. Gemma approaching Julien's bed. Reaching for the ventilator. Ushering in a silence that would never stop.

POPPY

SHE YELLED AT THEM, but they didn't listen. She just about dropped to her knees and prayed they'd turn around, but Poppy had never believed in God. As the age-old argument went, if there was an Almighty, why was there suffering, starvation, blight? Why were there people wanting to harm her children? Was it because she'd rejected the church as a girl, dyed her hair pink as a teen, slept with whomever she felt like in college, or refused to drag her own kids out of bed every Sunday morning to sit in a pew? Imagine a vicious God holding a grudge against a woman and her family because they failed to drop five bucks into the offering basket every week. Hell, if that's all it took to get on His shit list, the Great and Heavenly Father could kiss her heavenly ass.

Poppy knew she had more faults than she could count, but she knew none of them were bad enough to leave her standing out on the porch of a strange and secluded house—a house that she hadn't known about until it had mysteriously popped up on her Facebook feed—while the two halves of her heart wandered into the darkness with a single flashlight between them.

Her anxiety had become comfortably familiar over the years. Sometimes it seemed to her that she only felt normal when she was on edge. But now, as she listened to the rain beat against the porch roof, staring ahead into a vast emptiness of darkness, that easy familiarity shifted to match the magnitude of the night that was taking her children away. Poppy felt no comfort in the panic that squeezed the blood from her heart. Any semblance of solace was gone. All that was left was all-consuming dread. *This will not end well.* The thought circled her head like a vulture. *This will not end well.* And if she lost either Leo or Lark, there would be nothing left to do but tie stones to her ankles and sink to the bottom of the bay.

She watched the beam of Leo's flashlight bounce up and down

until the trees blotted out its glow. The moment it disappeared was the moment she was sure she would scream until she burst. Scream until her anguish tore a hole in the universe, until it swallowed her whole.

But rather than screaming, she turned to step back inside in a daze. Her throat felt raw from shouting. She felt soaked despite not having stood out in the rain. Pausing in the open doorway of the rental property that had once struck her as nothing but picturesque, she stared through the foyer and into the living room she hoped to never see again. She tried to remember who had posted the AirBnB listing that had led her to this nightmare, but couldn't recall if it had been a friend or simply an ad. She'd accused Lark of letting her online life alter the trajectory of her reality, and yet Poppy had been the one who had sprung for this place as blindly as Lark had fallen for a faceless, voiceless boy. She'd been thrilled when the owners had gotten back to her within minutes of sending in the rental request. *We've been booked up,* Diedre Allan had written her, *but you're in a bit of luck.* It had felt like kismet, as though the Parrishes were meant to be here. Now, it felt nothing short of malevolent. Vengeful. Nefarious.

Secret doorways. Tunnels snaking through the walls. It all by design.

The Parrishes were indeed meant to be here, but not for the reasons Poppy had hoped.

Ezra was on the opposite side of the house, his attention still fixed on the dark water. Poppy stared at his back, suddenly overwhelmed with a sense of helplessness. Seeing him there, distracted and distant, assured her that this was the end. Even if she woke up tomorrow morning to learn this whole thing was a terrible dream, Poppy and Ezra's marriage wouldn't survive the night. Because here she was, desperate and terrified, and Ezra couldn't be bothered to look up from his phone, which she could see glowing in the palm of his hand in the window's reflection. And just like that, she found herself at the threshold of the one thing she had always feared: being alone.

She considered marching across the house, reeling back, and pounding her fist into Ezra's shoulder. At least then he would be forced to acknowledge the betrayal she felt. She thought about sinking her nails into the meat of his forearms, demanding to know why he hadn't run after their children, why hadn't he for once acted like the champion and defender that he was supposed to be. But what good would any of that do? It was too late to run after the kids. They were gone, lost in the rain and lightning and trees. But what about her? Why hadn't *she* run into the woods to drag her children home? She was just as capable of fighting for the kids' safety as he was, and yet she'd only stood on the porch, yelling.

Her stomach churned around her ever-growing anxiety. It was a feeling she'd always been able to manage, but tonight had proven that the relationship between Poppy and her fear had changed for the worse. That near-constant tremor she felt at the bottom of her heart was now amplified. The soft tuning-fork hum of horror was now elevated to an ear-shattering pitch, so loud she could hardly think straight. Poppy squeezed her eyes shut against the thought of it—the fact that, after a lifetime of battling the quake of her nerves, she found herself losing the fight at the worst possible time. Lark and Leo were out there, marching toward God only knew what, and Poppy had let them go because she'd been afraid.

The kids saw them inside.

With her insides tangled in knots and her heart contracted as tight as a fist, Poppy turned away from her husband and stared down the dark hallway that led toward the master suite. Inhaling a shaky breath, she looked over her shoulder, waiting for Ezra to finally notice her, praying that he'd say her name. But he was still fiddling with his phone, looking rather frustrated with whatever it was he was trying to achieve.

"Ezra," she said, his name leaving her lips in a quiver. When he looked up, she shook her head at him, knowing she'd never find the right words to convey her dismay. "The world is falling apart," she finally told him. "Are you going to do anything to stop it?"

He looked down, then looked away without a word. Poppy did the same, a sob suddenly grabbing hold of her throat.

We're supposed to be here, she thought, glancing up the staircase through a sheen of helpless tears. Climbing the risers in her mind's eye, she recollected the photos and maritime artifacts that lined the walls, the books that seemed to fill every empty space, perfect for distracting the eye from mysterious seams. She remembered exploring the second floor when they had first arrived, when Ezra and Lark had boated into town for groceries and Leo had hidden himself away in one of the house's many strange rooms, when things had still felt hopeful. And finally, she saw herself climbing the rickety ladder into the attic, recalled the space that had looked like a makeshift camp. The Coleman lantern. The sleeping bags.

We're supposed to be here.

A wave of heat washed over her like flames dancing across the bay. She felt her legs go wobbly with her sharp and shaky inhale of breath. The Post-It Note that had appeared inside one of the cabinets. She hadn't seen it the afternoon they'd arrived because it hadn't been there.

The word on the mirror. The result of eavesdropping. Pitch perfect. Cruel.

Maybe they're up there now, she thought. *Maybe they're just waiting for one of us to find them, to bring an end to this game.* That possibility should have sent her reeling, but Poppy steeled her nerves instead, because if they were inside, it meant they weren't out in the woods. The idea of Lark and Leo being safe pushed Poppy to wipe at her eyes and take a few brave forward steps, stopping only when the toes of her wool socks kissed the edge of the bottom stair. And it was there, standing at the base of the risers while gazing up, that Poppy shut her eyes and took a deep and steadying breath. If they *were* up there, this was a climb up to the gallows. If they *were* up there, what would come next?

EZRA

IT WAS AS THOUGH THE ISLAND had blipped off the map, absorbed by some Bermuda Triangle darkness where no calls or texts could go in or out. Still standing at the window, Ezra looked up from his phone and peered through the night to the end of the dock. Poppy's question had wrenched his heart, but what the hell was he supposed to do? Tell her everything? Swim to shore? The boat was still on fire out there, though the flames had receded from blazing pillars to smoldering embers, glowing like Jack-o-lantern eyes.

He didn't know why it was so hard to accept Gemma as capable of this level of derangement, yet here he was. He blinked down at his phone again, somehow convinced that if he only waited long enough, cell service would return. And if it did, then what? Would he call her, threaten her, insist that if she refused to back down his fancy lawyer brother would make sure Felix rotted in jail? Or, perhaps, she'd call *him*. Better yet, she'd call Poppy, revealing all.

Squeezing his phone in helpless frustration, he finally turned away from the window to face an empty room. If there was a chance Gemma was going to tell Poppy everything, what difference did it make if he came clean? But Poppy was gone. He thought back to her screaming at the kids out on the front porch, determined to keep them where they were. Of course, they hadn't listened. Ezra hadn't answered his wife's question because he hadn't known what to say, but he knew his silence had been a betrayal. And now he imagined Poppy, desperate and hurt, going after Lark and Leo, because if Ezra wasn't going to do anything, the least *she* could do was bring them back to the house.

"Shit," he murmured. Ezra was alone inside the house. He had to go out there, had to find his family and make sure they were okay. Stepping fast across the living room, he still couldn't put together how any of this could have possibly come to pass. Because he'd been alone. Pulling onto the soft shoulder of a rural road, he'd been *alone*.

If, however, that was true, how the hell had he ended up here?

"Jesus," he whispered, grabbing his coat off the wall hook in the kitchen. "No way she knows," he whispered. "No way."

But what if she did? There would be no coming back from it, not unless Ezra could turn the tables somehow.

"They're threatening us," he murmured to himself, pulling on his coat. "Felix is a convicted felon." Meanwhile, Ezra was an upstanding citizen, well-connected. If Gemma and Felix showed up on the front porch steps in the dead of night, if they strong-armed their way inside, if things escalated…

If push came to shove, Ezra was sure his brother would be on his side. Nobody in their right mind would hold it against him for protecting his family.

Gemma and Felix had burned the boat. Felix was stalking Lark and had been for months. The Bellamys would arrive and make a show of it, stall to make it dramatic just the way Gemma liked. Rather than just dropping the bomb, she'd dance around the subject, push for maximum tension. *I warned you, Ezra.* That would be Ezra's window of opportunity. *My past is threaded through with violence.* He'd strike before she could.

Ezra paused in the open kitchen doorway, his eyebrows furrowed behind plastic frames. Only a lunatic would strand a family out on an island for God only knew how long. What if there was an accident and they had to rush to Raven's Head to get to a hospital?

"She's put us all at risk," he told himself.

If that boat caught the dock on fire, if the fire spread to the island, if the Parrishes burned, it would have been murder.

That was it, then. The logic of it.

Whatever Ezra did in retaliation would be nothing short of self-defense.

POPPY

SHE TREMBLED AS SHE MADE her way along the upstairs hallway. Part of her wanted to rush back down the stairs and insist that Ezra come up with her. She pictured him standing in that empty living room, still clinging to his phone, too quiet for her liking. His relative silence throughout this entire fiasco struck her as unnerving. Here she was, losing her mind, and he just stood there, staring out at the bay. Except, she knew that wasn't fair. Surely, he was having his own reaction to the circumstances, right? *But you resent him for it,* she thought, *because he isn't responding the way you want him to.* If she was honest with herself, that was the root of their problems. Ezra had been making a genuine attempt at being better, especially after what had happened to Julien. It seemed to Poppy that, with what Leo had gone through, it had reminded Ezra of what was important, of what they were all about to lose. Still, the littlest things continued to rub her the wrong way. The way he shifted his weight or ran his fingers through his hair. The way he adjusted his glasses or chewed his food or sighed or breathed. Her brain was trying to convince her heart that it was no longer right, that they no longer fit, that she had to let him go. Yet, her idiot heart continued to hold on.

Reaching the end of the hall, she looked up at the door in the ceiling, hiding away the pull-down attic stairs. Her gaze fixed itself on the chain that hung down, the small brass ring that implored her to slip her finger through it and pull. It was just long enough to reach if she balanced on her tiptoes. *And what will you do if there really is someone up there?* she wondered. *Arm yourself, at least.* But even if she had a loaded gun, she would have been no match for anyone who knew how to use a weapon. Years ago, when a self-defense trend had swept the nation, a friend had suggested meeting at the local shooting range to unload a few rounds into a paper target. Poppy had declined, skipping the blazing guns and sticking to sun salutations instead. *Some good that will do you now,* she thought. *Namas-fucking-te.*

She continued to scan the place. At least she'd look a little more threatening and capable if she were holding something she could swing. It all came down to optics, right? If she *felt* dangerous, she could fool herself into believing it was true.

Taking a single backward step, she searched the hall, pausing upon a heavy-looking candlestick sitting atop a stack of books. She wrapped her fingers around its neck, testing its weight in her palm, though she doubted it would do her any good. It was short. If her assailant was close enough for Poppy to take a swing and connect, she was done for. Surely, there was a more appropriate weapon among all that nautical junk, but she wasn't in the mindset to take the time to look. Frankly, she was sure if she didn't get this over with within the next few seconds, she'd either back out and run downstairs like some damsel in distress or fall into the clutches of a full-blown panic attack.

With the candlestick in hand, she once again turned her attention to the downward-hanging ceiling chain. If she pulled that trap door open and brought the ladder down, there would be no going back. She could still turn around, go sit with Ezra in the living room—at least then she wouldn't be alone. But where would that get her? Where would it get any of them? *To exactly where you are now,* she told herself. *Awaiting inevitable disaster.*

"Okay," she said, taking a few quick breaths. "Christ, okay…"

And then, without giving herself time to stall any longer, she reached up, grabbed the chain with her right hand, and jerked down the trap door.

The fold-down ladder didn't like being pulled at such a breakneck pace. It buckled and unfolded with a bang, its feet coming to rest hard against the floor. Poppy pressed a hand to her chest, startled by how violent the ladder's descent had been. Had she been standing a few inches to the right, the thing would have either taken off her head or made a fine powder of the bones in her foot. But she escaped unscathed, and before she could think better of it, she began to climb, desperate to outpace her nerves.

Half expecting to see some maniac squatting like a gargoyle in the shadows of that attic, she pictured the Joker, or Pennywise—the new one with the independently roving eyes and long-toothed smile. *I'll never understand why so many people love Tim Curry's version,* she had told her kids while walking out of the theater. That had been one of the last times she had felt connected to them both; Lark and Leo goofing off, reciting their favorite lines from the new *IT* remake. In that moment, Poppy had been blissfully happy, just her and the two halves that made up her full heart. The same heart that was now pounding against the curve of her ribs.

Squeezing her eyes shut, she braced herself and took the final few stairs upward, the rungs painfully hard against her socked feet. Her eyes flew open as her head popped up from the attic floor, imagining someone smashing her teeth in with an old toaster, or teeing her head off with one of the golf clubs she had seen while snooping around.

With her breath stuck in her throat, she frantically took in her surroundings, straining to see in the dark. Her left hand continued to keep a vise grip on the top rung of the ladder while her right squeezed the candlestick tight enough to make her fingers ache.

"Hello?" The word escaped her in a weak whisper. Stupid to think that, had someone been up there, they'd actually respond; stupid because all her question managed to do was reveal just how afraid she was. *You idiot,* she thought. Who in their right mind said *hello?* She should have threatened them, yelled something akin to *I've got a gun* or *I took jujitsu and man, when I find you, you're fucked!* She should have been tough, because when it came to horror, it was the fear-stricken girl that split up from the group that always got murdered first.

Thankfully, there was no sign of anyone lurking up there—at least not that she could see. She held her breath and strained to listen, but she couldn't hear anything beyond the rain pounding on the roof. She considered climbing all the way up, searching the place for signs of it having been inhabited since she'd seen it last, but her thoughts did an abrupt U-turn and she was suddenly thinking about the kids again, about how they were out in the woods. If there was nobody in the attic, it meant they were out there in the darkness, stalking her children.

The mere thought of it allowed her fear to grab her by the throat and squeeze. *You've lived your whole life with me,* it said. *But tonight's the night I finally kill you. They'll bury you in a fetal position. Poppy Parrish, dead of fright. You wait and see.*

Except, no. She narrowed her eyes at her own invasive thoughts. *No.* Just because there was nobody up in the attic didn't mean Poppy was done. She'd go through the rooms one-by-one, uncover all those goddamn secret passageways. She'd tear the place apart and find them…

"Find them," she said, descending the attic ladder one rung at a time. "If they're inside, you have to find them."

Except, the moment her feet hit the hallway carpet, she came to realize two things.

The first: she should have gone up into the attic and grabbed a golf club.

The second: someone was standing behind her, and it wasn't Ezra. She could feel it in her bones.

EZRA

JERKING AT WHAT SOUNDED like something crashing against the upstairs floor, Ezra's gaze darted up from his phone and shot through the kitchen toward the stairs.

"What the hell was that?" He was surprised by how breathless he sounded, how jittery he felt as he did an about-face away from the open kitchen door.

His first instinct was to yell. *Who's up there? What's going on?* But his throat constricted around the idea of it before any sound could escape. If his family was outside in the rain, he should have been the only one inside the house. Which meant…

"Oh, *fuck*."

He just about choked on his pulse, because this was it. This was how it was going to happen.

He imagined the worst, most unhinged thing he could think up.

Gemma descending the stairs wearing some bizarre cultist robe. *I'm a witch, and not one of those Salem girls…*

Felix drawing a pentagram on the floor in the center of the living room.

Ezra being knocked out or maimed or injured enough to be forced to lie down at the symbol's center while Gemma hovered over him, a sacrificial dagger held over her head.

Was that what this had come to? Would Gemma really take it that far?

And why wouldn't she? he wondered. *You deserve it for what you did.*

There was murmuring from the second floor. A man's voice.

Ezra swallowed hard. He turned again, then rushed onto the covered portion of the deck, determined to leave the house. But he hesitated, sure that if Gemma was so inclined, goddamnit, she'd find him. Besides, what about Poppy and the kids? The island was big. What if they came back and he was gone? *Nonsense,* he thought. *The island is an island. I can find them...*

"Find them," he whispered, his nerves so alive that the slightest breeze across the back of his neck felt like a gale; so hypersensitive he could feel a single hair atop his head shift out of place.

"Find them," he repeated, sure that if he said it enough his lizard brain would kick in and he'd become the alpha male Poppy had always wanted him to be. The action hero. The one who swoops in and saves the day.

"Find them," he said again, still not moving, that mantra suddenly taking on a different meaning. Here he was, planning to run when, only minutes ago, he'd been psyching himself up to do what needed to be done in the name of self-defense. Did he really think that dashing out into the rain and warning Poppy and the kids not to come back would come off as heroic?

"*Stop* them," he murmured, the hand that wasn't gripping his phone slowly curling into a fist. Taking a deep breath, he stifled his panic enough to focus on his plan, same as he'd done the night he'd veered off the highway and onto the soft shoulder just shy of the trees. Maybe it was something in his blood—the same thing that Luca had. Fearlessness. Grit.

The frightened Ezra took a step back while the cool, premeditating Ezra moved away from the drenched porch steps and back inside, toward the source of the sound, toward conflict rather than away.

They were upstairs, that he knew. Someone had dropped something on the floor, revealing their position. Hell, maybe they didn't know Ezra was inside, assuming that he'd gone into the rain with his family. Wouldn't it be a surprise, then, to find Ezra armed and ready to defend his wife and kids?

His attention shifted to the kitchen counters. Someone had pulled a handful of drawers open and failed to push them closed. Probably Leo. Having every intention of climbing up the stairs, he stepped around the kitchen island, heading for the butcher block next to the stove. But when he made a move to grab the largest chef's knife of the bunch, he came up empty. It was missing, as were its decently sized brothers. It was then that Ezra remembered Poppy tossing them into the dishwasher after breakfast. The only blades in the block were a set of six steak knives, a couple of small paring blades, and a 12" serrated breadknife.

That dishwasher was quietly whooshing beneath the countertop. After the kids had returned from Raven's Head, Poppy had nursed her pensive state by compulsively cleaning the place.

"Goddamnit." The word escaped as a hiss from between his teeth. He considered yanking the dishwasher door open, but he wasn't sure if that would work. The stupid thing would beep or sound some sort of alarm, which would only serve as a honing beacon for Gemma and her crazy fucking kid. That, and they'd be white hot. No use grabbing one of those knives unless he was prepared to arm himself with an oven mitt as well.

"Son of a *bitch*," he hissed again, then drew the bread knife from the block. He tested one of the serrated points against the pad of his thumb as he turned toward the stairs. It wasn't dull, but it wasn't anywhere near as sharp as he wanted. It did, however, look pretty menacing with its impressive length and jagged teeth; not something anyone would enjoy having bite through their forearm or slice across their leg. As he silently stalked toward the stairs, he decided that it didn't matter. He'd take Gemma by surprise, grab whatever weapon she had, and use that. The knife was a backup plan. Just another way out of a desperate situation.

He began to climb, his mind spinning a hundred different scenarios at once. But his upward climb was halted as abruptly as his thoughts were derailed. Because overhead, there was a scream; a sound he'd heard at least a dozen times during hot South Carolina summers, when the Palmetto bugs skittered into the living room through the crack in the chimney flue.

Upstairs, the scream hadn't been Gemma.

It was unmistakably Poppy.

Which meant that she'd never gone out into the rain.

She's always been in the house.

And they had found her before he had found them.

RAVAGE

POPPY

"HI THERE."

It was all the stranger said.

Poppy gasped, the sensation a strange and strangling blend of terror and disbelief, because there was a man she didn't know standing before her, and he was wearing a darkly disorienting smile. It was the person—or one of the people—who had been lurking within the walls of their rental house, hiding behind the shiplap and plaster since the moment the Parrishes had arrived. A borderless shadow, able to exist anywhere and everywhere all at once. A phantom. A curse.

Fighting to pull in a breath, her eyes searched the man's face, sure that if she stared hard enough she'd be able to identify him. Waiting for recognition, she was shocked when it did in fact come, but not in the way she had expected. Instead of remembering him from some random run-in, his features began to shift ever so slightly until, rather than peering into the face of an intruder, she was looking into the eyes of a boy she'd known for years.

Julien Bellamy.

Poppy blinked, shaking off the ghost she knew couldn't have been. When her vision cleared, Julien was gone, replaced by sharp angles and hard eyes. *Felix.* The name blared like a siren inside her head. *It's him. The one Leo had worried about so long ago. The one that has broken Lark's heart.*

Poppy's gaping surprise shifted. She narrowed her eyes.

"Uh-oh," Felix murmured, cocking his head to the side—a move that always reminded her of a dimwitted dog. "Looks like Mama Bear is awake."

That term made Poppy tense. She'd always found it dull; something that belonged scripted on a wall next to words like 'hope' and 'gather'. But if Felix was using "Mama Bear" to mean that Poppy's fear had suddenly been consumed by her desire to maim her aggressor, he was spot on. The fingers of her right hand tightened around the neck of the candlestick. Her teeth clamped down hard, gnashing behind the hard line of her mouth. She stared at him for another moment, then took a step back to give herself enough room to swing.

The moment she lifted her right arm to wield her weapon, a hot and jarring sting bloomed fast beneath her shoulder blade. It was only when Poppy turned that she realized she and Felix hadn't been alone. Because there, behind her, stood Gemma Bellamy. And in her hand, Gemma held the knife she'd just used to stab Poppy in the back.

LARK

LARK WAS FREEZING, her pajamas soaked through, but no amount of trembling would break her. She dutifully trudged behind Leo, her gaze focused on the beam of their flashlight, her shoulders pulled high up to her ears. Part of her hoped their search would come up empty; just a pair of siblings flirting with pneumonia during a cold autumn night. But something about the whole thing, from the way Leo was carrying himself to the fact that he hadn't spoken a word to her since they'd left the house, assured her that they'd find something. Perhaps not Felix, but a discovery would be made. Leo was too determined to let them go back emptyhanded, and that's what worried her most.

What would come to pass if Leo and Felix came face-to-face? Would it be nothing more than an upfront conversation, completely civilized and disarmingly polite? Or would it be a full-fledged rolled-up-sleeves beatdown in the pouring rain?

Lark imagined Felix pummeling Leo to within an inch of his life, Felix pulling Leo's head back and mashing her brother's face into the mud, trying to drown him on dry land. She pictured the roles reversed, Felix flailing beneath Leo's tall, wiry frame, his arms gesticulating like the wings of a wounded bird. She pictured both of those scenarios equally because she didn't know which to picture. The further they trudged into the trees, the more she became aware of the fact that she had no idea who Felix was or what he was capable of. The more that realization sank in, the more it weighed down her feet until, finally, she was no longer keeping up with her brother. Rather, she watched him gain distance on her, the beam of his flashlight beginning to dim.

Lark's eyes fluttered against the dark, then she raised her voice to yell above the roaring rain. "Leo, wait."

Half-expecting him to have not heard her, she was surprised to see him stop and look over his shoulder. She could hardly make out his face, the moon's glow swallowed by the clouds overhead, so she imagined what he must have looked like instead; water sheeting off his face, his expression strained, looking just as cold and miserable as she felt.

"Forget David," she told him, then paused with a wince. "No…not David," she corrected herself. "Forget Felix." She was scared to think of what would come to pass if they found him. It was the last thing she wanted for reasons she didn't want to admit, even to herself. "Remember what Gill said? My friend with the speedboat? He's not my friend, Leo. But there's a speedboat. If we find it, we can leave." *Leave,* she thought, *without confrontation. Go without having this whole thing play out.* "Wherever it is, we'll find it. This island isn't that big, right? If they're here, we can find it."

She waited for Leo to respond, but he didn't.

"We can pull it around to the dock," she told him. "I'll run in and get Mom and Dad and we can finally get the hell out of here. If David—" She stopped, squeezed her eyes shut, exhaled a breath. "…*Felix* isn't near the boat when we find it, *he'll* be the one who's stuck."

And it would serve him right, wouldn't it? For all the heartache she'd suffered, for the fact that he'd gone to such lengths to scare her because of her stupid, misguided attempt at winning him back.

Leo continued to stand mute, but Lark knew him well enough. He hadn't given her an immediate 'no', which meant he was considering this new plan. She watched him stare into the distance, as though he could see more than a handful of yards through the deluge. Finally, he spoke. "We should skim the island perimeter."

It was the opposite of what they were doing now, which was simply marching toward the island's heart.

"What are you going to do to him if we find him?" The question left her lips before she could rationalize why she was asking it. That, and there was concern in her voice, almost as though her subconscious was giving her a winking nudge. *Sure, you can pretend you want to strand him out here. You can tell yourself David was nothing but a figment of your imagination. But you know it's bullshit, Lark.*

She was freaked out by the idea of Leo and Felix running into one another, but the idea of meeting him face-to-face herself wasn't as terrifying as it should have been. Despite everything, there was still magic in that possibility. Because what if, during that meeting, Felix realized what Lark had known all this time—that they had something special, that they had made a connection, that they were meant to be? What if, faced with the task of looking into her eyes, Felix came to understand that this whole Raven's Head thing was nothing short of a fiasco; that despite the lies he had told her, he did in fact love her? What if he could see that she still loved him?

"What *can* I do?" Leo asked, his question a stark reminder that what she was imagining didn't fit what Leo knew Felix to be.

"I don't know," she said, the full weight of realization suddenly hitting her hard.

She had no idea what they were in the middle of.

Clueless as to where all of this could go.

She didn't know who Felix was or why he was there.

Why his mother was there.

What they wanted or what they could do.

And then, as if picking up on her uncertainty, the universe answered by breathing out a scream.

Lark stiffened at the sound of it. Staring at her brother, she waited for him to turn and continue walking, to not respond to the wail because it had been nothing but an auditory hallucination. Just distant thunder. Only the rain. But rather than turning away, Leo's eyes widened. They stared at one another for a long moment, holding their breaths. Finally, Lark broke their silence.

"Was that Mom?" The idea of it turned her stomach. To think that something was happening back at the house, that she and Leo were out in the woods while their mother was screaming somewhere inside that place...

Lark pressed a wet hand over her mouth to hold back her own cry. Her mom, goddamn her. They'd been nothing if at each other's throats for the past year, but Lark loved her, regardless. And now, hearing that scream…

"Oh my God," Lark gasped into her palm. "Oh my God, Leo, what are we supposed to do?"

"Go back," he said, grabbing her by the wrist. "Now."

"And do what?" she asked, afraid, so scared that she was wringing her arm out of his grasp.

"I don't know," he told her. But before his uncertainty could terrify her even more, they were both running through the trees, their sneakers slipping out from under them as they squelched through the mud.

And as they ran toward the house, Lark decided that she would convince Felix he didn't have to go through with whatever it was he and his mother had planned. Maybe he'd take one look at her and fall in love all over again. Hell, maybe he'd lay his eyes on her and laugh. But she couldn't let those sorts of what-ifs get in the way of what she knew was her responsibility. She couldn't keep being afraid to live life, her *real* life, the one her mother so desperately wanted for her. Whatever happened back at the house, Lark would take it head-on. Because this was her fault. Her problem. Felix was hers to tame.

LEO

THE LAST TIME LEO had heard a woman wail was at Julien's funeral. There had been a chorus of sobbing, of sniffling and broken sighs, though the congregation had been mostly silent throughout the service. Leo had kept to his own soundlessness by bowing his head and averting his eyes, afraid that looking directly at his best friend's coffin would cause it to burst into flame. Appropriate, since Julien was going into the fire after the final sermon was said; erased from the face of the earth, reduced to five pounds of smoldering ash.

The idea of it had Leo squeezing his eyes shut, his hands clasped tight in his lap if only to keep himself from grabbing the pew in front of him and shaking it, shaking it, goddamn *shaking* it until it splintered and disintegrated in his hands. He wanted to scream through the entirety of Julien's funeral, wanted to stand up among blubbering relatives and praying hands and crack open his own chest, where a swirling mass of blackbirds would spiral away from where his heart should have been. But he was beat to it by a cry of anguished mourning cutting through the din.

Julien's mother collapsed next to her son's coffin, looking as though she was about to faint. She took a few ornate flower arrangements down with her as she crumpled to the ground. A vase toppled over, spilling water down the steps of the pulpit. Another rolled and shattered, transforming the sound of her broken heart into a cacophony of choking gasps and breaking glass. A handful of people rushed to her side, sliding their hands beneath her arms, pulling her to her feet like a broken doll. Many looked frantically about them, as if searching for a doctor who could mend a mother's devastation; looking for a first responder who knew how to soothe the hysteria that accompanied bottomless despair.

Lark covered her mouth while Leo stared at the service program his sister had crumpled into scrap paper in her hand. Julien's name was printed at the top in a graceful font. *In loving memory.* It was all that was left; pictures of the past flickering against the backs of Leo's eyelids, recollections that he knew would change with every playback until they only vaguely represented the reality that he had lived. Those memories would fade like old photographs, eventually nothing but faint traces of what had once been so vivid and alive.

He covered his eyes with his left hand, trying to block out Mrs. Bellamy's screams, trying to imagine himself anywhere but where he was just then. When he felt fingers squeeze his right, he found his mother's palm atop of his own.

It's okay, sweetheart, she whispered beneath Mrs. Bellamy's cries. *We're safe.* As if, somewhere within that chapel, an unspoken danger hid in plain sight. *We're safe.*

Those were the words that circled through his head as he and Lark ran back toward the house. *We're safe.* Even when Lark yelped as she caught a spruce branch across the curve of her cheek. *We're safe.* Even when his sneaker snagged on a root buried in the mud and he crashed to his knees, his right ankle exploding in pain.

"Oh my god, are you okay?" Lark slid into the mud next to him, and suddenly her hands were on him the way all those hands had scrambled across Mrs. Bellamy's trembling arms. "Are you hurt?" she asked, then immediately switched gears, focusing on what needed to be done. "Come on, get up," she told him. "We've got to go, Leo. Hurry, please."

But rather than pulling himself back to his feet, he stalled. What was the point of getting up unless it was to keep running? Maybe if they hadn't been trapped on an island he would have had more of an inclination to push himself to stand. Perhaps if there was a way to escape, he would have convinced himself to keep moving until he was as far away from this life as he could get. *Thailand,* he thought. *Just get through this and it's waiting. Get through this one last thing and you can forget it all.*

And there was a lot to forget, like the hospital, its smells, the rhythmic hiss of Julien's vent. That sound had so thoroughly burned itself into his brain he could still hear it now, maybe half a mile ahead of them. He knew it was a hallucination, knew his brain was stuck on this endless loop of replaying the same scenes, the same sounds. In, out. Inhale, exhale. The bay breathing like a beast in the storm.

"Leo." Lark pleaded, desperate as she tried to yank him up and out of the mud. "Please, get up!"

He did, but only because she sounded so scared. When it came to his own emotions, he was resigned to whatever was about to happen. The situation felt finite, as though it had been set into motion long ago. Something about the rain, the darkness, the island itself—it all felt like a disastrous sort of destiny. It was the very thing he had convinced himself of during Julien's final days: that no amount of waiting would have changed the outcome of his best friend's fate. Now, it was Leo's turn. He had yet to understand how, but he knew for certain that somehow, both his and Julien's destruction were intertwined.

Leo limped along as Lark pulled him forward, the beam of the flashlight in his free hand nearly obscured by muck. Ever other step felt like fire, and by the time the house appeared in the distance, he was sure his ankle was broken. He could still walk, but it was a blinding sort of pain. He tried to push through, but before he knew it his sister was nudging herself beneath his arm, propping him up despite her small frame.

"I don't know why he'd do this," she said after a long while, her words breathless with the effort she was putting in to keep Leo upright and moving. "I mean, would he go through the trouble if he really didn't care? Why would he bother? He wouldn't, right? If he's here, it must mean something, right?"

Leo didn't reply, not liking where Lark's head was at. She wasn't thinking straight, probably delirious with cold, exertion, and fear. Felix wasn't in Raven's Head because he was somehow choking on his oversized heart, and he certainly hadn't dragged his mother along with him to meet his girlfriend on the fly. They were there to get even.

But revenge was a sort of caring, too, wasn't it?

Because when grief putrefied, all that was left was the black sludge of vengeance.

POPPY

BEFORE SHE KNEW what was happening, she was on her knees in the upstairs hallway, gasping against a pain so foreign she wasn't sure if it was a numbing sort of cold or a blinding heat. A moment later, a tickle trailed down her back, creeping beneath the waistband of her wide-legged lounge pants, nudging its way past the top of her underwear. Reflexively, she reached back to stifle the sensation. Her palm came back wet. The sight of her blood glistening against the curves of her fingers sent a shockwave through her system, because this was really happening. It was no longer a possibility. This was now.

Her bottom lip trembled as she stared at her red-stained fingers, another scream doing a slow climb up her throat. As soon as she could catch her breath, it would tear itself free of her body and shake the walls. But before she could suck in air and shatter the windows with anguished disbelief, she was caught off-guard by the sight of Ezra standing at the top of the stairs.

He was wearing his parka but no shoes, as though he'd been debating going outside. Her gaze settled on his face, and at first she was sure she was imagining things—maybe losing too much blood. He wore an expression Poppy had never seen before, rendering him nearly unrecognizable for half a beat. It was a startling mask of unfettered rage. And in his hand, glinting in the dim hallway light, was the longest, meanest knife Poppy had ever seen. The blade had teeth like a ghoul. It could have been a saw, serrated and ready to slice in half whomever came near.

She watched her husband's gaze flit between the two people that loomed over her huddled and kneeling frame, and for a moment she was sure he was about to show his teeth and snarl. A moment later, his attention jumped to her face, and something miraculous occurred. His anger seemed to dissolve, and his expression bloomed with a heartbreaking sort of sorrow. For the first time in years—the two of them suspended in terrified disbelief—she was reminded of the man she'd fallen in love with so long ago. She'd been crazy about him. He could light her up with his laugh, with a touch, with a flash of his easy smile. All at once, Poppy was twenty years younger and Ezra was her everything.

As Poppy knelt there—bleeding and breathing in heaving, silent sobs—she remembered the way he'd scoop her up and spin her around. She recalled the way his face had looked when Leo had been born, or the way he'd gently lay a blanket over her when she'd fallen asleep on the couch, exhausted by an endless relay of bottles and diapers. All the hurt feelings and resentments that had collected in the dusty corners of their relationship were wiped clean by the idea of losing it all. Him. The kids. Her life. It was enough to bring it all full-circle and remind her of what was important, assuring her that anything could be fixed. If they made it out of this, *anything* could be fixed…

"Gemma." The name escaped Ezra's lips.

Despite Leo and Julien's friendship, Gemma Bellamy was a woman Poppy had always held at arm's length. Poppy and Gemma had regarded each other at school functions for the past several years, of course. Poppy even had Gemma's phone number programmed into her phone in case of an emergency. Julien had given it to her years ago, when he and Leo had gone on a Blueridge Mountain camping trip. But that didn't mean Poppy *knew* Gemma. Gemma had always struck Poppy as volatile, if not a little manic and off-kilter. Years had passed, yet the two women remained strangers to one another. That was what made the familiarity with which Ezra addressed Gemma so confusing.

Had Leo not reminded Poppy who Felix was less than an hour before, there was no doubt she would have drawn a blank when she'd set eyes on both him and his mother. *Especially* his mother. Gemma, the chameleon. Last Poppy had seen her, Gemma's hair had been a red lick of fire atop her head. Now, it was dyed black and looked as though it had been chopped short by a pair of dull kitchen shears. Gemma looked older, too; understandably ravaged by the loss she had endured. But Ezra? Poppy doubted she'd ever witnessed him interact with

Gemma himself. And yet, there he was, clearly on the up-and-up on who both she and Felix were.

Poppy's mind started to spin scenarios, but her thoughts were derailed by a bitter laugh.

"You look shocked to see me, Ezra," Gemma said, bemused.

"I am," Ezra staggered. "I…we…" He was searching for words and failing. Poppy could hardly blame him. The moment she saw Gemma and Felix surrounding her, she had lost all thought.

"Do you like the house?" Gemma asked, casting a glance to the wall at her right. "A bit cluttered, but from what my aunt tells me, the tourists love it." She shifted her weight from one riding boot to the other, then gave Poppy a thoughtful smile. "Easy to book, right? Even though they're typically full-up this time of year. I guess someone put a good word in for the Parrishes, talked about how nice of a family they are, how much they need a break after such an awful year."

Poppy's mouth went dry. She covered it with a hand to hold back a sob, not wanting to draw attention to herself. But Ezra took care of that for her. Shaking off his torpor, he finally found his voice.

"What do you want?"

"What do I want?" Gemma's expression hardened. "My youngest son is dead, Ezra. So, maybe we can start with that. Can you imagine it? That awful feeling…" She turned her gaze to Poppy, as if trying to connect with her, mother to mother. "Try to imagine it," she said, her voice dropping an octave, lulling to a hush. "Try, for just one second, and perhaps then you'll begin to understand what someone like me could want."

Poppy shook her head, knowing that human imagination could only stretch so far. No matter how much she tried, she'd never be able to match the despair Gemma must have felt. And she would never want to. Not in a million years.

"I'm so sorry about Julien," Poppy whispered, her words weak and breathless, shaky beneath the stinging of her back. "But why are you punishing us? What does what happened to Julien have to do with my family?"

Gemma's expression shifted, flickering from grief-stricken and angry to something almost indecipherable. Poppy squinted as she attempted to read the disconcerting far-away look.

"What does it have to do with your family?" Gemma repeated, then canted her head, her gaze drifting from Poppy's confusion to Ezra, who was still frozen at the top of the stairs. "Or, perhaps, what *doesn't* it have to do with you…"

Poppy shook her head, not understanding. "What does that—"

Before she could finish her question, she watched Gemma lift her right arm. The knife in Gemma's hand glinted in the dim hallway light, Poppy's blood miring its blade. For the briefest of moments, Poppy understood that this was the end, the last moment she'd ever experience. She'd never see her kids again. That thought was what finally pushed a scream from deep within her lungs. Watching Gemma make her move, Poppy lifted both her arms in a protective gesture and howled.

EZRA

POPPY'S SCREAM was like a chain cinching around his heart. The moment she cried out, he couldn't breathe, but also couldn't stop himself from falling forward into a run.

With his parka billowing out behind him and the serrated knife held tight in his right hand, he lunged toward both Gemma and Felix. Startled by Ezra's sudden movement, Gemma stumbled back and away from Poppy, who was still protecting her face with both arms held aloft. But before Ezra could reach either of them, he was thrown off-balance, body-checked by Felix into the nearest wall.

Ezra hit the wall hard with a grunt, his coat cushioning some of the impact. But it was enough to send his knife skittering to his feet, accompanied by a menagerie of photographs and nautical knick-knacks tumbling to the floor. Ezra scrambled to sweep the knife up, but Felix was too quick. He kicked it away with the tip of a work boot, sending it and a variety of décor down the hall. A moment later, he was grabbing Ezra by the arm, twisting hard until Ezra was forced to spin around, his arm pinned behind his back.

Ezra struggled, managing to wrench his arm free of his coat sleeve, finding freedom for the briefest of moments. But it was a short-lived victory. Felix seized him again, this time in an even more menacing grasp, assuring him that even the slightest of movements would result in a dislocated shoulder, or worse.

His gaze darted back to his bleeding, crying wife. He couldn't tell whether Gemma had stabbed Poppy again, or whether Poppy was weeping because she was petrified.

"What the hell do you want with her?" Ezra spit the words onto the hallway carpet. "Poppy has nothing to do with this," he said. "Neither do my kids."

It was enough to get Gemma to step away from his wife. Though, that left Gemma meandering down the hall toward Ezra instead, that knife catching the light as her hips swayed from left to right. She stopped directly in front of him, Felix still holding tight to Ezra's arm. Leaning in, she just about let her bottom lip graze his own. Ezra inhaled her scent, shaken by the realization that he suddenly recognized the faint traces of what he'd been smelling throughout the house since they had arrived. It was the perfume he had bought her for her birthday—an eclectic mix of cloves and star anise. *For the Witch,* he'd written on the attached card. *You've put a spell on me.*

That scent made Ezra's mouth go sour as she lingered there, a mere breath from his face.

"My kid didn't have anything to do with it either, Ezra," she finally said. "But that didn't keep you from running him down, did it?"

Ezra swallowed hard in response.

"Speaking of, where *are* your kids?" Gemma took a backward step, tipping her head skyward to listen past the rain. And then, as if on cue, there was the sound of yelling from outside.

"Mom?!"

The moment Ezra heard Lark's voice, his heart sank to his feet. But before he could be overwhelmed with the chaos that was about to unfold, he exhaled a gasp as Gemma sank the knife she held deep into his shoulder, just right of his heart.

LARK

"MOM?!"

Lark stumbled into the house, her mud-covered pajama bottoms sloughing water onto the floor. The moment her muck-coated boots hit the hardwood, they began to slide out from beneath her. She caught herself on the doorframe and shot a look over her shoulder to make sure Leo was still behind her.

"Mom!" It felt like she was screaming, but her ears told a different story. What should have been a bellow came out sounding weak and frightened, as though all that fear and running had stolen her sense of urgency. But nothing could have been further from the truth. The marathon had made things finally come clear. Lark was ready to make things right between herself and her mother. They'd spent way too long butting heads; far too many months glowering at one another and murmuring beneath their breath. No matter which way Lark spun it, the fact of the matter was, her mom had hit the nail on its head. Lark had gotten sucked into a life she'd been convinced had been real. Turns out, it had been nothing but a façade; a pretty candy-colored shell concealing a rancid core.

Rather than dashing further into the house, Lark's need to seek out her mother was tamped by the need to stay with her brother. That, and there was a noise upstairs. A grunt, like someone being punched in the gut.

Lark spun around, her gaze fixed on Leo's face. Leo was, however, still outside on the porch where the rain was the loudest. Lark widened her eyes and held up a hand to tell him to wait. *Did you hear that?* she mouthed, then pointed upward while holding her breath.

Leo mutely shook his head. No, he hadn't heard anything.

With both siblings staring at one another, a wail came from overhead.

"Lark, Leo, *run!*"

Their mother's warbled scream grabbed hold of Lark's insides and shook. Suddenly, Lark was trembling from shoulders to feet as though a switch had been thrown. It was an involuntary spasm, a flood of adrenaline that left her teeth chattering and her body shivering, like spontaneous hypothermia. Then there was the almost uncontrollable need to scream in response to her mother's cry. This was beyond terror. It was deeper, as though Lark's sense of horror had somehow materialized outside her body and crawled back in; like being possessed by her own sense of panic and dismay.

Upstairs, there was a commotion. Someone was coming down, and Lark was willing to bet it wasn't Mom or Dad.

Pivoting on muddy boots, she grabbed hold of Leo's bicep and charged back out onto the deck, down the stairs, and into the rain. Because even though part of her was screaming not to run, to stay and fight and help...not listening to her mother had gotten her into this situation in the first place. It felt wrong to challenge her request now. *A final request,* she thought, then immediately shook off the notion.

No. That was impossible.

It wouldn't go that far.

It couldn't.

It can't.

Lark started to make a beeline for the trees she and Leo had recently broken free of, but Leo could only move so fast. He was limping behind her, and she was pretty sure he was calling her name— *Lark, Lark!*—but she could hardly hear him, her own heartbeat deafeningly loud.

Eventually, she lost her grip on Leo's arm, slick with mud and rain. She continued to stumble toward the trees for a few seconds longer before coming to a stop. When she turned, she realized Leo wasn't the only one behind her. A man a good deal taller and heavier than her brother was taking a graceful leap over the deck's railing like an Olympic runner clearing the final hurdle before the finish line. Rainwater and mud splashed up around Felix's feet as he landed without so much as a stumble. It was then, just as Felix dashed up to

Leo and hooked an arm around his neck, that Lark exhaled her own desperate cry.

"No!" she screamed. And then she fell into a run. Not away and into the trees, but back toward her brother. Toward Felix. Toward the only solution she knew.

Stop him, she thought. *Let him take you and it'll be done.*

LEO

HE KNEW WHAT WAS COMING before it happened. He saw it in Lark's face, in the way her features twisted with a sense of startled fright. Felix had finally made his grand entrance. A second later, Leo was being jerked backward, practically crumpling to the ground as his good leg was swept out from beneath him, his broken ankle spearing him through with a flash of white-hot pain.

Lark's scream cut through the rain.

"No!"

Rather than trying to flee, Lark was running back toward the house, toward Leo and Felix and whatever nightmare awaited them inside.

"Lark, stop!" The words left him in what felt like an involuntary reflex.

But Lark didn't stop. She kept coming at them, leaping onto Felix's back the moment she reached them both. Leo stumbled away from them as Felix was left stunned and unprepared.

"Stop it!" Lark screamed, her fists pummeling Felix about the shoulders and head. "You fucking psycho! You traitor! I loved you, you piece of shit!"

Felix reached around, grabbing Lark by an arm. He gave it a vicious pull, and as she cried out, he shoved her to the ground. She landed in the mud, slipping as she scrambled back to her feet like a newborn colt. As soon as she was upright again, she threw herself at him a second time. But Felix was ready this time, and rather than taking more punches, he instead placed a hand on top of Lark's shoulder, extended his arm outward, and smirked when Lark could no longer reach him. Her arms swung wildly but only caught air. She screamed in frustration as she continued to struggle against a stiff-armed hold.

"I fucking *loved* you!" Lark yelled at him, clawing at the arm that was keeping her at bay. "What the hell do you want that you haven't already taken from me? Leave us alone, you son of a bitch!"

One second, Felix was laughing. The next, his expression went deadly serious, not liking Lark's choice of insult. Had it not been so dark out, Leo would have sworn Felix looked genuinely offended. And then it clicked.

Son of a bitch.

It got under Felix's skin.

This whole thing was bigger than Julien. Darker. This was about Gemma. It all circled back to Mom.

"…wait…" Leo spoke the word into the rain. He lifted his hands as if to say *hold on, give me a minute to figure this out.*

Rather than waiting, Felix seized Lark by the neck, his fingers easily wrapping clear around to the bumps of her vertebrae. Leo watched his sister's expression shift from furiously determined to startled, then terrified. Her features strained as Felix lifted her up off the ground, her boots dangling inches from the mud, kicking, seeking out the ground.

"Felix!" Leo yelled the name into the storm.

Felix's gaze snapped to Leo's face. Lark continued to struggle, her fingers clawing at Felix's arm.

"Let her go. Please!" Leo continued to hold his hands aloft in surrender. "Let's talk, alright? Whatever this is about, she has nothing to do with it."

Felix glowered, but a moment later he dropped Lark to the ground, then gave Leo his full attention. He didn't bother regarding Lark as he stepped away from her, didn't seem to notice her pawing at her neck as she choked, gasping for air.

"Okay," Felix said, closing the distance between Leo and himself. "You're up."

Felix snatched Leo by the arm and pulled him back toward the house.

"What? Why? What do you mean I'm—" Leo stumbled forward, struggling to keep his footing as he limped along. "Jesus, what did I do?" He shook his head, tried to pull away, to stall, but Felix wouldn't stop. He kept on, like an executioner dragging the damned to the noose.

"Goddamnit, would you wait a minute?" Leo shouted. "What the hell is this about? You know Julien was like a brother to me! Whatever I did…"

It was then that Felix stopped, his grip on Leo's arm increasing seven-fold. He turned and pulled Leo forward, both suddenly standing chest-to-chest.

"You didn't do a fucking thing, so shut the fuck up about it." Felix just about snarled the words. "I was asked to do this and I'm doing it, alright? It's a tough break, that's all. Someone's got to pay and *you're up.*"

"What—" Leo shook his head. "I don't understand."

But Felix was pulling him along again, dragging him through the mud toward a house that no longer looked idyllic, but doomed.

"Just tell me!" Leo pleaded, his feet clomping up the porch steps toward the open front door. "Please, just explain!"

Felix gave Leo a forceful shove forward, and suddenly dark became light. The rain disappeared. The cold was replaced with warmth. Leo crashed to his hands and knees against planks of hardwood, and before he saw his mother, he could hear her weeping. Wincing against the brightness of the kitchen, Leo looked up to see his mother half-covered in blood. His father stood stark still, startled and pale. And he saw Julien's mother, Gemma, standing behind him, holding the tip of a knife against his father's jugular vein.

"There's no way to explain, Leo," Gemma said after a moment, her eyes fixed on his slumped and broken frame. "I suggested your mother try to imagine how it feels, but imagining such a thing is impossible. You were there, and even *you* can't comprehend it. It's beyond the scope of human capability. It's why we decided to come here, why Felix and I made the trip."

"Why?" Leo whispered, somehow already knowing the answer, a sob slowly climbing up his throat.

"To make the impossible possible," Gemma explained. "To help you understand."

POPPY

TO MAKE THE IMPOSSIBLE possible.

Poppy could no longer feel the burning sting that had settled in just below her right shoulder blade. She could hardly think straight, Gemma's words causing reality to bend around her like a fisheye lens. Suddenly, she understood—not everything, but more than she had a moment before. She knew why Gemma and Felix had tracked her family down. To pay tribute, not with poetry or prayers, but with blood and sacrifice. The house had been specially selected for Gemma's sick game of hide-and-seek.

Wordlessly, Poppy shook her head in refusal, not wanting to believe that what had just entered her mind was possible. No, it was too far-fetched. Too cinematic. Too much like some thriller she would have curled up to watch on the couch while nursing a cup of tea. That, and the puzzle still wasn't complete. A piece was missing. It still didn't make sense.

Her gaze darted to Leo and Felix. Leo was on his hands and knees just beyond the open front door. Seeing him that way made her heart ache, made her want to scream. He looked like he'd crawled through miles of mud, returning from wherever it was he and Lark had gone, where he and Lark should have stayed. Felix loomed to the side of him, soaked with rain. He looked irritated, almost impatient as he paced a few steps in one direction before changing course. He didn't, however, look concerned that Leo would try to make a break for it, and didn't appear too worried about Ezra or Poppy, either. That lack of concern was what relit Poppy's fire. Only an arrogant bastard would assume that the Parrishes would just lie down and die. If, when Felix looked at Poppy, all he saw was a helpless victim, he had another thing coming. He wanted to see her go Mama Bear? Bring it on.

She clenched her teeth, then shot a look over to Ezra and Gemma. Ezra's knife was missing, abandoned somewhere in the upstairs hall.

She'd watched him drop it when Gemma had pressed the tip of her own blade to his throat. That had been just before Lark had yelled into the hush of the house and Felix had dashed down to greet her; just before Poppy had screamed for her daughter to run. Gemma had forced them both to the ground floor under the threat of cutting Ezra from ear to ear; the only reason Poppy hadn't tried to fight. And so here they all were, downstairs, when suddenly all she wanted was to be upstairs again. That was where the knife was with its dull but glinting teeth. It's where the attic was, home to golf clubs and old metal toasters. Hell, she'd be happy just to get that fucking candlestick back in her hands.

She wasn't sure what she was doing. Provocation felt like a last resort. But maybe if she could distract them, she could dash up the stairs and grab something to defend her family with.

"You want to help us understand," Poppy said. "But Gemma, nobody here gets your goddamn point."

Gemma lifted an eyebrow from behind Ezra's shoulder, and for a moment she almost looked impressed with Poppy's gumption. That look was short-lived, however, quickly replaced with the quiver of an upturned lip and a flash of teeth, with a look of aggravation, of disgust.

"Oh, your husband here understands," Gemma countered, spitting the words as though they tasted putrid and decayed. "And from the look of it, he's damn good at keeping a secret. Or maybe you're just that blind, just that *dumb*. You have no idea what kind of a man you're married to. If you did, I doubt you'd be here now."

Poppy blinked, surprised by the sting of those words, taken off-guard by all those old, ugly feelings—the ones she'd been wrestling with for so long; the ones that had finally convinced her that this was it, that she and Ezra had given it a good run but it was time to pack it in.

"Ezra and I have been having an affair."

Poppy had expected to hear that confession for years now, but she assumed it would come from Ezra himself. She'd imagined herself spitting in his face, reeling back and slapping him hard enough to make her arm numb for days. In every scenario, she was screaming and furious. Yet, at that very moment, hearing those words come from Gemma rather than him, all Poppy felt was disorienting despair.

There's no time for this, logic screamed inside her head. *Fall apart later. Get it together now.*

And yet, her heart clenched like a fist, threatening to petrify within her chest. Because how could he? How *dare* he? And with Gemma, of all people. With the mother of their son's best friend.

Holy shit, Ezra. I knew you'd stoop low, she wanted to say, *but this sets a new bar.*

"Holy shit."

She heard the words inside her head spoken aloud, yet her lips didn't move.

"Oh, holy *shit.*"

Poppy furrowed her brow, then dared turn her gaze from Gemma and Ezra to look at her son. And it was there, upon Leo's face, that she discovered a look of both realization and disbelief.

LEO

"HOLY SHIT."

No. This can't be real, Leo thought. *This is crazy.*

And then Julien's words reverberated within his ears.

You aren't going to believe this shit. You aren't going to believe…

It was the last message Julien had left on Leo's voicemail, possibly the last words he'd spoken to anyone before he'd veered off the highway, bounced down the steep incline of a soft shoulder, and wrapped the front end of his car around the trunk of a tree. Julien's message had sounded breathless and urgent; a warning to Leo that he was in route, heading Leo's way with mind-bending news. But he never made it. Something, or someone, had caused him do something stupid…like swerve, or lose his concentration, or drive too fast on that shitty little narrow road.

Something.

Or someone.

Someone, like…

"Oh, holy *shit*." The involuntary exclamation was forced out of him by the quaking in his chest. Because could it be possible?

It's a tough break, that's all. Someone's got to pay. You're up.

Leo dared to look up from the floor between his hands, his attention fixing itself on his father's face, desperate to see the truth. He waited, wordlessly pleading with his dad to say it wasn't so, to say *something* that would assure Leo the scenario he was putting together was completely off-base. So ridiculous it was laughable. So out-of-left-field it was a step shy of idiotic. Impossible. Completely fucking nuts. But all Leo got was an avoided gaze. His dad kept his eyes averted, either knowing that the truth would be written across his face or that Leo already knew, that the last piece of the puzzle had finally fallen into place.

"Oh my god." Leo looked away, suddenly sure he was going to

vomit.

His eyes jumped to his mother. Jesus, had she known all this time? Terrified that he'd see guilt in her eyes, he was almost spooked to find her staring at him. But all he saw was confusion—at least at first. Once their eyes met, it was as though the reality of it dawned on her as well. The disbelief he was feeling slithered across her face as she struggled to accept the truth. And that truth? It meant they had been living a lie. Sharing a house with a monster. A killer. A fraud.

Seeing his mother share in the same shock he was feeling allowed him a moment to remember his father sitting next to him during Julien's funeral. His father, looking sad and scared, his jaw set and his eyes forward as worlds crumbled and lives fell apart.

"The truth always comes to the surface," Gemma said, drawing Leo's attention back in again. She was speaking to Leo's father, her voice wavering with emotion, though Leo couldn't tell if it was grief or rage. "You thought nobody had seen, thought you could just walk away from it as if it had never happened. Maybe it's because you'd helped us, because if I dared accuse you, you'd pull some strings and Felix would be put away, right? Would that be beyond you, Ezra? Would you take both of my boys away?"

Wait, was Gemma talking about Leo's Uncle Luca? Was *that* why the family hadn't seen him in nearly a year? Dad had demanded his brother help him bail out his mistress's kid? Leo shot a look up at Felix, searching his aggressor's face for answers, but Felix gave nothing away. He did, however, look as though he was reconsidering something, as though he was suddenly feeling in over his head and had no idea how to find his way out. For a flash of a moment, Leo could relate. How many times had he felt that very way with his own mother? This trip was a perfect example. He'd given in to make her happy, to stop her from harping him. *Looks like Felix has it worse, though,* he thought.

And if what Gemma was saying was true, if she believed that Leo's father could put Felix away, it meant that none of this stopped with Julien. This wasn't just about what had happened on that highway. This had to do with the future, too, which meant there was no going back. The Bellamys had no choice but to leave no survivors behind.

"You were right, you know," Gemma continued, on the verge of tears now. "You did get away with it. You turned your back on it as though it had never happened. Nobody knew. Not your wife. Not Leo. And if I went to the police, if I told them what I knew? Who would believe someone like me over the brother of a fancy attorney?" Her voice broke and for a split-second Leo felt his allegiance waver. Gemma wasn't a bad person, she was just broken. Damaged. Grieving. Betrayed, just like him.

Suddenly, all Leo wanted was to jump up from where he was kneeling and lunge not at Gemma or Felix, but at his own father. Maybe if he helped them murder his dad, they could all get on with their lives. A sort of poetic justice.

Except, that wasn't what the Bellamys had in mind.

"You can't ever fully understand the pain you've caused," Gemma said, "but you can at least experience a fraction of it."

She nodded at Felix, and before Leo knew what was happening, Felix had him back in a headlock. Leo's mother screamed. His dad yelled something that Leo couldn't quite make out, like "stop" or "don't" or "wait."

"An eye for an eye," Gemma said.

And then Leo gasped, the tip of a blade easing its way between his ribs.

LARK

LARK'S HEART SKIPPED a beat as she watched Felix drag Leo inside the house. She lingered in the rain, not because she was having second thoughts of going inside—no, her mind was made up about that. She hesitated because she knew running in there on nothing but impulse and adrenaline would get her—and maybe her entire family— killed.

There was still a chance she could talk Felix down. Though, after how he'd lifted her off the ground, she was guessing love wouldn't factor into that equation. She'd be damned if she let all this play out without speaking to him face-to-face, but she certainly couldn't do it without protection. It was then that, staring at the glowing windows of the house through the pouring rain, she decided on her destination. She had to get upstairs.

She skulked around trees and shrubs, keeping to the darkest of the evening's shadows in case someone peeked out a window to see where she was. The closer she got to that open door, the more she could hear.

"You can't ever fully understand the pain you've caused, but you can at least experience a fraction of it. An eye for an eye."

Lark's eyes went wide as her mother bellowed a blood-curdling scream. For a moment, she forgot she was trying to keep herself hidden and clumsily clamored up the side of the deck's railing, slipping and falling onto the planks with a thud. But nobody noticed because her mother was wailing in a way that made her skin crawl. It was the sound of an animal being garroted. Of being burned alive. It was the sound of being flayed, internal organs exposed. It was the cacophony of dying, there was no doubt.

It took all of Lark's self-control to keep herself from barreling through the door and trying to stop what must have been happening in her absence. When her father started yelling: *No! Stop it! Don't touch him!* Lark lost her determination to stay the course. "Him" meant Leo.

Something awful was happening to her brother, and she had to intervene.

Taking a steadying breath, she ran inside.

She didn't pause to see what was happening around her, knowing better than anyone that she was powerless to contain the situation, at least for now. Instead, she used the chaos to her advantage and bolted for the stairs.

Half-expecting someone to grab her by the ankle as she took the risers two-by-two, nobody did despite the horror movie cliché. Because here comes the hapless Girl Wonder, running up the stairs rather than beelining into the safety of the trees. Felix and Dark Helena were probably blinking at each other in a daze, wondering what the hell the point of going upstairs could be. Lark was trapping herself up there. A moment ago, she had been free.

But what else could she have done? Hidden until everything was over—*until everyone was dead?* Waited for help to arrive—*and gone back to what? To whom?* Now, she was stuck in a situation she wanted no part of, but one solitary fact continued to burn bright in her mind: whatever the hell was going on downstairs was her fault, and it was her job to right her idiotic love-sick wrongs.

Reaching the second floor, she paused in momentary hesitation, her gaze settling on a knife—long and serrated, like the kind she used to cut breakfast bagels down the middle before school. She left it where it was, her muddy boots propelling her toward her intended destination. Because there, in the middle of the hallway wall and mounted near the ceiling, was Lark's coup de grace. The boat paddle. As long as nobody had a gun, she knew she could inflict some serious damage with that thing.

Downstairs, her mother was sobbing. Leo and her father were silent.

"Lark." Her name coiled up the stairwell.

It was an odd sensation to hear her name leave Felix's lips. Odd and surprising, because he wasn't taunting her like some psycho killer madman. *Come out, come out, wherever you are.* Something about the way it was spoken sounded reluctant, as though he was calling up to her because he'd been told to do it, not because he actually wanted her to come down. Again, the possibility flashed bright as daylight against the backs of her eyelids: maybe he really did care. Perhaps this was all a big mistake and he wasn't a willing participant in any of this. Maybe he was a victim, just like her. Like Leo. Like her whole family.

Right, and he'd been a victim when he nearly choked you to death out there in the rain, right?

She blinked at the boat paddle, then stretched her arms up to reach it, but it was too goddamn high. Spinning around, she looked for a table or foot stool—something she could use to give herself a boost. Her attention settled on a stack of books along one of the window ledges. A second later she was yanking those hardcovers down from their perch, piling one on top of the other before taking a precarious upward step. The stack wobbled, but she righted herself a moment before her hands fell onto the boat paddle's handle. It was suspended on two inverted display hooks, which meant she had to push the paddle up before it would come down.

She shoved her palms against the paddle's handle, giving it as much of a boost toward the ceiling as she could. For a moment, the paddle didn't budge, and Lark's heart stuttered to a stop. What if it was nailed to the wall? What if it was impossible to get down by hand? Didn't people who had tons of crap displayed in their houses do things like that? Distracted by the possibility of her plan falling through, she shot a look down the hall, her gaze pausing on the knife that remained on the floor. Would that even work? *Like a saw,* she thought, then winced at the idea of dragging those serrated teeth across someone's flesh. No, she wanted no part in something so bloody. She just needed the damn paddle. Knocking someone out was one thing. Sawing them in half like something out of *The Texas Chainsaw Massacre* was altogether another.

"Lark, I have to go up there if you don't come down on your own," Felix warned.

She looked back to the wall in front of her, then gritted her teeth and forced the heels of both palms hard against the bottom edge of the paddle. Half-expecting it not to move, she was left startled when it flew upward with surprising force. The stack of books shifted beneath her feet. She scrambled for purchase, groping at the wall for anything that could save her. But instead of salvation, she found herself on her back, breathless and disoriented, a small framed photograph held fast in her right hand. The boat paddle came crashing down on top of her a moment later, hitting her hard across the chin. She immediately tasted blood, and as she sat up, she could sense it pooling behind the bottom ridge of her teeth. She gagged, then turned her head and spit blood across a stranger's carpet, across a photo of three men standing next to a boat. She nearly reached for the photograph to wipe down the glass, but before she could do something so absurd in a situation so extreme, she found herself staring at Felix, who was now standing at the top of the stairs.

Their eyes met, and for a moment she hoped again, hoped for one last time, willed him to see her for who she had been to him for all those months. Surely, she had to have meant *something.* They'd spend hours texting, talking about their hopes, their aspirations. Even if everything he had told her was a lie, her compassion must have resonated with him. *Don't you remember me?* she wanted to ask, hoping her expression conveyed her thoughts. *You* know *me, Felix. And I know you. Just stop to remember. Just remember. Just…*

Rather than sharing a moment of understanding, Felix took a handful of forward steps—not toward her, but to sweep up the knife that had been left lying on the floor. Seeing that knife in his hand assured her of two things. The first: she could wait until the end of time, but Felix wasn't going to reciprocate her feelings. The second: Plan B was now off the table. Felix had the knife. Which meant Plan A had to work. Her eyes darted to the paddle lying across her lap.

Suddenly remembering the task at hand, Lark scrambled to her feet, taking the boat paddle with her. And before she gave Felix a chance to respond, she charged him, reeled back, and swung with a garbled, bloody-mouthed scream.

LEO

THE SCREAMS WERE STARTING to meld into one another, seeming to come from every direction, as if in stereo. The only reason Leo knew Lark's cry had come from her was because it had come from upstairs, not a few yards away. And while their mother sounded terrified, overhead, it was the definitive tone of heartbreak. Upstairs, Lark was taking part in the same fight, but for her, it was an altogether different kind of battle.

Felix had left Leo slumped on the floor, half-propped up next to the kitchen island with the door behind him wide open to the rain. It seemed that Felix knew as well as Leo: if Leo decided to run, he'd hit the deck stairs, stumble, and crash to the mud where he'd wait for either Felix or Gemma to put him out of his misery. And yet, despite his current state—his ankle screaming its own sort of wail, his palms decorated with blood—Lark's cry managed to twist his stomach into a knot. He didn't want to imagine what Felix was doing to his sister up there, didn't want to think of the awful things he might be compelled to inflict.

Leo's mother looked as though she was trying to yell in response to Lark's cry, but sound refused to come from her throat. Leo turned his gaze away, unable to keep his eyes on her horrified expression. She looked like someone watching a ship go down. Like someone watching a zeppelin light up. Or a plane nosedive. Or a helicopter explode.

Leo's dad, on the other hand, let out an oddly strangled-sounding groan from deep within his throat, but he managed to keep himself subdued, that knife still held fast against his throat. Any struggle would have prompted Gemma to lose her cool.

It appeared that the Bellamys had the upper hand. Two of the Parrishes were wounded. One was being held at knifepoint. And only imagination could tell what was happening to Lark upstairs.

At least, until something went clunking down the risers from overhead.

Leo blinked at the breadknife that landed just shy of his mother's feet. If there was such a thing as a miracle, this was it. Jesus himself was saying, *you all clearly need some goddamn help.*

"Don't you touch that," Gemma barked in warning. "So much as reach for it and I'll slit his throat." She yanked Leo's father back with an arm across his chest, as if in a dare.

Leo squeezed his eyes shut, knowing that no matter what happened next, blood would be spilled. After all, Gemma and Felix couldn't leave survivors, and Leo knew Gemma well enough to anticipate this scenario only going one way. He had, after all, occupied the same tiny room with her for half a year's time. She had had good days, as though something reassured her that everything would turn out alright. But Leo had also watched her struggle as she spent hours with her face in her hands, silently weeping as she waited for yet another result from a useless round of tests. He had witnessed her live her life like an open wound, and the person she held captive now was the source of her pain. Leo knew the only way his dad was walking out of this alive was if Gemma lost her nerve, and he doubted she would. She had been courageous enough to press her finger against the power button of Julien's ventilator. There was no reason for her to fear anything else.

And yet, in a blink of an instant, the last thing Leo wanted was to bear witness to his father's assassination. Somehow, even after discovering what he had done, how he had derailed *Leo's* life, Leo couldn't handle the idea of watching the person he had forever called his dad die. But he couldn't ignore the opportunity, either. Whatever Lark had done upstairs, it had afforded them a shot at survival, however slim.

With his gaze fixed on his mom, he purposefully gave the knife near her feet a hard stare. *Pick it up,* the look said. *Because even if he dies, we can still live.*

"I'm not joking!" Gemma shouted, as though sensing both Poppy and Leo's defiance. "I'll kill him right—"

She was cut off by a second scream from upstairs. Either Lark was being killed or she'd gone savage. It was a guttural yell. A war cry. Before Gemma could regain her bearings, the thudding of something else falling down the stairs had everyone turning their heads, eyes wide, mouths gaping. This time, it certainly wasn't a knife. Whatever was coming down was as heavy as a sack of bricks.

When Felix hit the floor, Leo's mother swept up the breadknife and skittered away, putting a safe distance between herself and the man that was clutching his face at the base of the stairs. Blood oozed from between Felix's fingers and down his neck. When he pulled his hands away, it was Gemma's turn to shriek.

A wide gash slashed Felix's face from his ear down to the corner of his mouth. The bone of his cheek glistened beneath a coating of red, as did a few of his teeth. Lark had opened him up like a gory flower waking to an early spring, and it was a wonder he hadn't been knocked out by the impact of whatever Lark had managed upstairs. But no, Felix was wide awake. His eyes were wild, almost feral as he tried to process what had just happened, trying to figure out what the hell was going on.

Meanwhile, Gemma kept screaming. It was then that Leo's father made his move. He grabbed Gemma's wrist and yanked the knife away from his own throat, then twisted her arm hard enough to turn her agonized wail for Felix into a yelp of pain. Gemma's knife clattered to the floor, and before Leo's father leaned down to scoop it up, he pushed her against the nearest wall. Leo's mouth went dry as he watched his dad bury his fingers in her short dark hair. He saw it all happening before his eyes within a flash of an instant: Gemma's face slamming into the shiplap over and over until God only knew what would result. But before Leo's premonition could come to pass, his dad was seized by a snarling Felix.

Felix positioned himself the same as when he'd taken Leo hostage outside. With Leo's dad's head in the crook of his elbow, Felix's free hand came up as if to snap his neck. Leo shut his eyes and looked away, not able to bring himself to witness what he was sure came next.

It was only then, when he'd shut out the world, that he heard his sister speak.

"Felix," she said. "Or should I call you David? I'm so excited to finally meet you."

A second later, like the shudder of thunder outside, there came another hard crack.

VANISH

LARK

LARK HAD MEANT TO hit him in the head, but she was caught off guard when Felix turned her way. The gash across his face was like something out of a slasher flick. She gawked at what she'd done to him, not having meant to wound him so badly. She'd caught his cheek with the edge of the boat paddle, that she knew. But she hadn't seen what she'd done because he'd stumbled backward and fallen down the stairs—hadn't seen it until just then.

Disoriented by the bloody mess that had stained the full front of his shirt, she lost her focus and her aim landed low. The paddle caught Felix on the shoulder, the hit landing flat surface to flesh. Rather than gifting him a broken arm, the impact was as effective as a flat-handed slap. Thankfully, Felix let her dad go anyway. But rather than writhing in pain and pawing at his arm, Felix came at Lark with unbridled fury burning behind his eyes.

Lark couldn't bring herself to look away from the horrific state of his face. Jesus, he would never look the same again. Even if he found an incredible surgeon, there was no coming back from something like that. And then there was that idea she couldn't shake, the possibility that all of this—Raven's Head, the island, the house—had never been Felix's idea in the first place. It's why his mother was here. She was behind it all. Lark only wished she knew why.

"Oh my God." She heard the words leave her lips. Having found empowerment upstairs, she'd felt incredible when she'd come downstairs, about to give Felix his knock-out blow. For a few fleeting moments, Lark had discovered what it felt like to be in charge, to be more than what others thought of her. And yet, as soon as she saw Felix coming for her, she crawled back into her shell.

"I'm so sorry," she whispered, her hands held out in front of her, a victim awaiting an inevitable blow. She stumbled backward as he charged her, teeth bared, blood-covered hands falling onto her shoulders.

"I'm sorry," she repeated, as though the apology would somehow placate the disfigured man before her. "I didn't mean—"

"Do it." The command came from behind him, those two words hard and direct; a master demanding obedience. "Show them," said Dark Helena, and before Lark could furrow her eyebrows in confusion, all sound became muffled as Felix's hands fell over her ears.

POPPY

LARK'S COLLAPSE was a heavy sort of falling, as though someone had stood a cadaver on end before letting it go. She hit the floor hard enough to rattle the dishes in the kitchen cupboards. For a moment, it was all Poppy could think about—the fact that the cups and plates had jumped despite the cabinets being yards away.

She had heard people talk about death in such a way before—about how when you first see it, when it first hits you, you focus on the most trivial of details. A father checking the exact mileage on a kid's mangled motorcycle. A sister staring at the cartoon pattern of her deceased brother's boxer briefs. A mother straightening a strangled daughter's hair before the coroner arrives. For Poppy, it was the dishes. She was unable to stop thinking about their clatter until her gaze froze upon what little of Lark's face was exposed from behind a cascade of black box-dyed hair. And there, staring back at her, was an eye. Wide open. Bright but unseeing. Present yet distant. Forever gone.

Something within Poppy shifted. The itch of hysteria seized her heart and squeezed. She drew in breath, ready to scream, sure that when she finally did it would be loud enough to tear her in two. She was a dying star. A supernova. It was the end of everything. Her heart, a black hole.

When the scream came, it was disembodied. The scream wasn't hers.

Behind Ezra, Gemma cried out; broken, hopeless, lost. "Now you know," she bleated, beating a fist against her sternum as if attempting to shed the sorrow from her own heart. "Now you know!"

Poppy just about screamed right along with her, but her stronger side rejected the invitation. Rather than being buried by her own anguish, her fingers tightened around the hilt of the knife in her hand, hard enough to make her knuckles go white. Gemma screamed in misplaced mourning while Ezra stood stiff and unmoving, looking genuinely horrified. Leo was still on the floor, a hand pressed over a bleeding wound that might take him from Poppy, too.

Amid the chaos, Poppy inhaled a breath and slowly rose to her feet. She pushed past the pain, that knife held fast against her hip.

LEO

LEO ONLY NOTICED HIS MOTHER swaying like a wind-whipped sapling when she took a few steps toward Felix. With her head tilted downward and her chin nearly resting against her chest, strands of blood-clotted hair framed her face, and Leo had to do a double take. Was this person he was seeing really his mother? She looked positively menacing, fueled by vengeance strong enough to raise the dead from their graves. The knife she held no longer struck him as the last option of an empty butcher block. That knife, glinting in her hand, was now nothing short of a saw.

Felix didn't hear her stepping up behind him, not with his own mother howling in renewed mourning from across the room. He probably couldn't have sensed her because that part of his intuition had been dulled by Lark's handiwork. Hell, the longer Leo watched the scene unfold, the more Felix appeared to be swaying too, as if on the verge of passing out, having lost too much blood. And when Gemma finally paused her screaming long enough to realize what was about to happen, Felix was too slow to react. Perhaps if she'd yelled *behind you* rather than…

"Felix, watch out!"

…maybe then he would have turned.

But rather than veering around, Felix looked nothing short of puzzled before, a second later, Leo's mother responded to the riddle Felix couldn't quite figure out.

The way the knife pulled across Felix's throat forced Leo's gaze away. Rather than a clean cut, the serrated blade tore at his flesh with as much grace as a dog shaking its prey. But the scene was a car crash, and Leo couldn't keep his eyes averted for long. When he glanced back up, Felix was pawing at a ragged wound that was geysering blood, his eyes fixed on Leo's face. For the briefest of moments, Leo saw disbelief reflected in Felix's face—flat-out doubt that what was happening was real. Ironic, seeing as Leo had felt that very same way, refusing to accept that Gemma and Felix would come after him and his family when all Leo had done was love Julien more than he'd loved any other friend he'd ever known.

It can't be, Leo had thought so many times.

This isn't happening, Felix's expression screamed.

They wouldn't, Leo had thought.

It's not supposed to end this way, Felix's eyes insisted.

But Leo and Felix weren't the only ones reeling with disbelief. On the other side of the room, Gemma began screaming at a different pitch. Her sorrow was replaced with horror, and before she could stop herself, she was wrenching free of Dad's grasp and rushing across the room to her eldest son's side. But by the time she reached him, Felix had slumped to the floor, his hands groping at the yawning wound beneath his chin. He sputtered and gaped, gasping for air that couldn't route itself down a severed windpipe; choking as he aspirated blood. Gemma's hands flew forward, her palms uselessly pressing themselves on top of Felix's own. It was a fruitless effort to stop the waterfall of crimson that was now sheeting down the front of Felix's shirt. And as it continued to flow, Gemma stopped screaming and began to yelp like a wounded dog.

"Felix! Felix! Felix!"

Over and over like a siren. Like the ear-splitting blip of a heart monitor that had forever bored itself into the wrinkles of Leo's brain.

"Don't go! Don't go! Don't go!"

Leo's heart twisted within the cage of his chest. No doubt, there would be another funeral to attend. Another casket to weep beside. Another group of groping hands to avoid as they reached out, trying to help. *It's okay, sweetheart. We're safe. We're safe. We're safe.*

And now, somewhere in the shadows of the afterlife, Julien would finally get to spend time with his big brother. Now, instead of Felix running off into the night, instead of disappearing off the face of the earth, only returning to cause trouble, he and Julien would be united, waiting for their mother so they could finally be the happy family they deserved to be.

With his eyes shut tight, Leo's bottom lip began to tremble at the sound of Felix's gurgling gasps, at Gemma's pleading cries for him not to leave her, to not force her into living a broken life alone. No matter how the cards fell now, Leo couldn't help but remind himself that this was Julien's family. The last of whom connected him to the living. The final strand keeping him anchored to the world Leo knew.

Leo couldn't help but revisit the last few moments he'd spent in Julien's hospital room, couldn't help but remember how Gemma had held her head high despite the tears that streamed down her face. He recalled how he and Felix had connected, how they had shared meals and hours of silence next to Julien's bed. It hadn't mattered that Felix had been preoccupied with his phone, always reading something, always texting someone. In hindsight, Leo couldn't help but conclude that he'd been reading Lark's writing, talking to her as David while Leo sat less than a yard or two away. Hell, the way Felix had vanished after Julien's death was proof that he'd been using Leo the same as he'd been using Lark; nothing but a source of information, a way to help his mother plot her revenge.

And yet, Leo couldn't manage to focus on those things. The anger and betrayal he should have felt was lost on him. He was shoved back in time and place, standing just shy of the curve in the road Julien had failed to clear, his attention fixed on yellow police tape and the mangled car he'd ridden in hundreds of times. He found himself staring at his hands, his life passing in slow motion as his family moved around him at ten times their speed—his parents, his sister, all of them zipping about while all Leo did was stand in place, statuesque, replaying Julien's final voicemail inside his head on a loop.

You aren't going to believe this shit. You aren't going to believe...

The wet gurgling coming from Felix's throat made Leo think of Julien's lake, of the thick sheet of ice standing between him and his best friend. The sound of Felix trying to stay alive didn't last long. When those wet lapping noises finally came to an end, Leo looked up, but it wasn't Felix's sudden silence that pulled him away from Julien's pounding fists. It was Gemma's pleading "No!" that forced his eyes open; not *no, don't go,* but *no, don't touch me.*

Leo's father had Gemma by the hair again. She scrambled for purchase as he yanked her away from Felix's lifeless body, her bloodied hands reaching up to claw at his wrists.

It can't be.

Leo felt the floor tilt beneath him as he watched a strange amalgamation of rage and anticipation flash across his father's face. His stomach lurched as he spotted the knife Gemma had held to his dad's throat now held fast in his father's hand.

This isn't happening.

Leo's father yanked Gemma up to her feet, and for a second, Leo was sure he was going to launch into some kind of speech; something about how Gemma had gone to such trouble to pay tribute to Julien, but now her tribute would be little more than a blood sacrifice to Lark. Like something out of Shakespeare. A life for a life for a life for a life.

Just as Leo had held fast to hope during Julien's darkest hours, he couldn't help but hope now. Whether the accident had been caused by Julien's erratic driving or Leo's dad genuinely trying to run him off the road…that would forever be left to question. What Leo did know, however, was that his father hadn't physically touched Julien to get the result he'd achieved. He hadn't pulled Julien out of his car and flashed a knife across his periphery. He hadn't held Julien captive by the hair while Julien pleaded for his life, like he was doing to Gemma now. Because that wasn't Leo's father. No matter his mistakes, Leo's dad wasn't a killer. What was unfolding before him was nothing but an illusion. A hallucination. A fever dream.

"Do it," Gemma cried out, weeping yet still managing to sound fierce. "What have you left me with? What do I have left, Ezra? Tell me!"

The glint of a blade, which Leo's father had been holding against her back, now came around her front.

He wouldn't, Leo thought, suddenly seeing his dad laughing next to the grill with his Uncle Luca. Remembering him dancing to crappy '90s music he claimed was "the best" just because it was what he'd listened to all through high school. Recalling how his father had taught him how to drive stick shift, how to change the oil in the car, how to swap out a tire. Remembering Christmas mornings and how Dad would immediately put on whatever clothes he'd gotten, which always left him looking like a clown in pajamas; multiple pairs of socks, joke T-shirts, and the obligatory necktie. Sunday morning chocolate chip banana pancakes. Bruce Willis action movie marathons. Singing Radiohead's "Creep" at the top of his lungs in the car.

He wouldn't, Leo thought again. Not his dad. No way.

He wouldn't. Even though he did, sinking the knife hilt-deep into Gemma's stomach.

Leo stared open-mouthed as they seemed to dance together, swaying back and forth while Leo's father embraced Julien's mom in an almost loving way from behind. They remained that way for a few beats before, readjusted his grip, rather than pulling the knife out and away, Dad jerked the knife upward, tearing a hole in Gemma's belly from navel to sternum.

Leo could hardly see Gemma or Felix or even Lark by the time the third body hit the floor, his vision swimming behind a sheen of tears and dismay. His mind was elsewhere again, months in the past, remembering how his father had reached out and placed a hand on Leo's shoulder the day after Julien's accident; recalling how he'd uttered some generic assertion that everything would be fine, that it would all work itself out.

It's okay, sweetheart, Mom had said.

We're safe, she had promised. *We're safe. We're safe.*

And yet, here they were.

Here they were.

Here they were.

EZRA

EZRA STOOD STARING at Gemma's corpse, as if waiting for her to sit up and leer at him. The longer he stared the more convinced he was that he could see her breathing, but he knew that was impossible. The wet sheen of her innards that had spilled out onto the floor assured him that she was dead. Gutted. Like the witch she'd claimed to have once been.

That was when it all flashed before him. Arriving at the Bellamy house. Asking Gemma to stop texting, to stop calling, to stop it all because it was over. Gemma screaming, beating her fists against his chest. Ezra catching her by the wrists, trying to calm her. *Stop, Gemma. Please…* That was when the kitchen door leading out to the garage had opened, when Julien had stepped inside. The kid had stopped dead in his tracks as he took in the scene, and there had been a horrible moment—a half-second pause when Julien hadn't comprehended who or what he was seeing. But it was swiftly followed by recognition. *Holy shit,* Julien's expression had read. *Mr. Parrish?* The moment Julien had turned and rushed back out the door was the moment Ezra had released Gemma and turned to run after her son. Had Gemma not grabbed him, he'd have been able to stop Julien before he'd jumped in his car and taken off down the road. But Gemma had latched on to his wrist and refused to let go. If she hadn't been so insistent, perhaps none of this would have ever come to pass.

But now she was dead, just like her two sons.

She was dead, and it wasn't Ezra's fault.

It wasn't his fault. It wasn't his goddamn—

The stink of iron and sweat brought him back around. With the white noise of the rain loud in his ears, his attention paused on Lark, still as a photograph. His baby girl lay flat on her stomach, her arms and legs splayed out like a fallen star. With her head turned at a severe angle, her face was half-concealed by the splay of her dark wet hair.

Her eyes were wide open, somehow still alert. Still beautiful enough to make his heart swell and then sink, because she didn't move. Didn't blink. That stillness was enough to bring him back to earth.

The knife fell from his fingers, clanking hard against the floor.

When he looked up, he saw sheet-white phantoms of his wife and son. They were alive, thank God. Had he not intervened, there was no telling how this would have ended.

Leo was huddled on the floor, one hand over whatever injury Felix had inflicted upon him. Poppy stood only feet from where Felix had fallen, her socks soaking up his blood. For a snap of an instant, his own stab wound flared like a firework, threatening to double him over in agony. He couldn't believe that what his family had just gone through had really occurred. Yet, the proof was right there in front of him.

Felix crumpled in a heap.

Gemma's body, an empty husk.

Lark. Poor, beautiful Lark.

Ezra took a few stumbling backward steps until he felt his shoulder blades kiss the wall, then slid down to the floor to sit. It was only then that he dared to meet Poppy's gaze. He wanted to speak, but he held his silence instead, trusting that she could see what he was sure was reflected in his eyes: he had been left with no choice. Gemma had to die. For what she'd planned, what she'd set into motion. For what had been done to their daughter, their little girl.

This wasn't his fault.

Wasn't his fault.

This wasn't Ezra's fault.

It wasn't him.

POPPY

POPPY WAITED FOR EZRA to speak, but all he did was stare. It was a move he pulled when things got tough, the ace he flashed when he wanted redemption but didn't want to struggle through an explanation. It was an urgent, expectant look that said, *you're my wife, you're supposed to know what I'm thinking.* For most of their marriage, she had believed that bullshit to be true.

It was her job to know her husband well enough to read his mind, to not need him to speak to be understood. She was supposed to know how to decipher a single look, and for years, she had felt that her inability to master such a parlor trick was a domestic shortcoming. She wasn't the best cook, often forgot to move the laundry from the washer to the dryer, hated dusting, and could have been a better, more attentive mother. But despite all of that, Ezra had loved her enough to overlook her failings. So, in instances like these, it was only right for Poppy to pretend that she'd been gifted the power of telepathy. It felt like the least she could do.

But that had been then, before the breakdown of their relationship, before that nagging sense of not being the only woman in Ezra's life. This was now, after learning the truth. There would be no more pretending. At least not here, not now, not from her.

Standing motionless, she stared back at him with an intensity she hoped *he* would understand. *I know everything,* her gaze said. *I know it all and it can't be undone.* But as far as knowing what to do next, she didn't know. Their phones had no service. The boat had burned. Leo was wounded. Lark was gone.

Part of her wanted to sit down just as Ezra had—back against the wall—and weep until she died. But it was Leo's quiet gasping that pulled her away from that breakdown and forced her back into the present. Leo was still on the floor, still bleeding, still *breathing.* He needed her help.

Those gasps were eerily reminiscent of what he'd sounded like the night of Julien's accident, the night he'd found out through the grapevine that his best friend was in critical condition in the ICU. It was the sound of a heart breaking, tearing in half bit by bit; the sound she'd heard coming from Leo the night he'd come home from the hospital, when he'd tried to punch his fist through the front door.

Those had been the moments when Poppy had hated whoever had hurt Julien most, when she had told herself that if she had only known their identity, she would have done awful things to avenge the pain Julien's accident had caused her own son. They were the times when she had considered what she would have done to keep it all from happening, to protect Leo from living through such pain. Watching Leo's personality disappear a little at a time, there hadn't been a day that had passed when Poppy hadn't lamented her own helplessness. Because mothers were supposed to protect their children, and whoever had cut Julien down had stolen away her ability to keep Leo's heart whole.

Poppy shut her eyes, allowing the tears to cut through smears of blood she was sure decorated her cheeks. She felt her bottom lip tremble only to catch it between her teeth. After giving herself a moment to recover, she looked back to Ezra, offering him her own urgent and expectant look.

She moved toward him then, her socks leaving tracks of blood in her wake, abandoning on the kitchen island the knife that had torn open Felix's throat. When she reached him, she lowered herself to the floor and rocked onto her knees, less than a foot away from where her husband sat. That's where she remained for a long while, waiting for Ezra to speak first.

"We need to find a way to reach the police," he finally said, his voice trembling, his hands shaking in his lap. "Tell them what happened. Explain that this was all self-defense."

Poppy looked down to the floor between them, then glanced back to Ezra a moment later. "And Julien?" she asked softly. "Was that self-defense, too?"

Ezra's expression shifted as quick as a lightning flash. Trauma was abruptly replaced with an indignant look. She imagined his thoughts: was she serious? Did she hear herself? Had she sleepwalked through this whole ordeal? Gemma and Felix had tried to kill their family, had planned to exterminate them all. And yet, here was Poppy, asking him if a confession would accompany their self-defense plea.

"What are you talking about?" he finally asked. "You can't possibly believe her, Poppy." His gaze jumped to Gemma, then back to her again. "Are you kidding? You think this is my fault?"

Poppy pressed her lips together in a tentative line, but she couldn't help but wince when Ezra's voice broke with emotion.

"I didn't touch him, Poppy. You've got to believe me. This story Gemma was spinning, she just made the whole thing up. They needed an excuse to be here, didn't they? What better reason than to blame me for what happened…"

"It wasn't your fault," Poppy said, agreeing.

"That's right," Ezra insisted. "He was in his car, I was in mine. It's not my fault he was doing eighty down a highway where the posted limit is forty-five."

"But when he ran off the road?" Poppy asked softly.

"I didn't run him off the road." Ezra's tone shifted; less pleading, far more annoyed. "I just told you—"

"You were in your car," Poppy said, "and he was in his. But you said he was doing eighty."

Ezra's jaw squared with tension.

"You wouldn't know how fast he was going had you not being doing eighty as well. You were tailing him."

He narrowed his eyes but looked away, his entire body coiling up as if ready to spring.

"Ezra," she said softly. "Look up. Look at our son."

She turned her head to glance back at Leo, who had curled up against the kitchen island, his knees against his chest, his arms wrapped around his legs. Leo was peering through rain-dampened hair at both his parents, his face a mask of unmistakable distress, inevitably imagining the goings-on of that fateful evening. The high-speed chase. The swerve. The sound of metal meeting bark. And then there was the question of what Ezra had done after he realized what had happened, after he'd seen Julien's taillights burning red in the dark. Had he pulled over? Gotten out of the car? Had he run down the embankment to see if he could help, and when he realized what all of it would mean, had he driven away?

"Accidents happen," Poppy said, turning her attention back to Ezra. "You didn't want any of this."

"That's right," Ezra whispered, and finally, Poppy could see his remorse. But as quick as she saw it, she reminded herself that it was nothing next to taking the life of a high school kid, nothing compared to their son's sorrow.

"So, you lied," Poppy said. "Pretended that it hadn't been you who had caused Julien's accident; that you weren't the one who had done this—" She motioned back toward Leo. "—to our son. You did it to protect yourself."

"No." Ezra shook his head. "Us. I did it to protect *us*."

"And the affair," Poppy continued. "Was that for us, too?"

Ezra shook his head. "It's not like that," he insisted. "I was calling it off, but she was insistent. I kept telling her to leave me alone, to stop calling. I told her for *months*, Poppy, but she kept at it. She was fucking crazy. I mean, look!" He waved an arm around them, inviting her to take in the carnage he was so convinced she'd missed. "She came after us. What was I supposed to do? Let her?"

"And she came after us, why? Because she couldn't stand the idea of losing you?" Poppy sighed the question into the space between them, her fingers grazing the hilt of the knife Ezra had used to end Gemma's life. "Ezra," she said after a moment, holding his stare with her own. "She came after us because you killed her son. And because of your deceit, now Lark is—" She paused, unable to finish that sentence. She squeezed her eyes shut and looked away, sweeping the knife up off the floor. "For years, you've been tearing me apart a little at a time." Poppy ran the tip of the knife against the floor, as if attempting to carve her initials into the wood beneath it. "I often wondered what I'd done wrong, what I could have done to make you happier." She exhaled a soft laugh at that. "But now I understand that there was nothing I could have done, because I'd done nothing wrong. You punched your fist through our son's chest and tore out his heart to protect a lie. And now you'd lie again, say that it was self-defense, all while standing over your own daughter's grave."

"Mom…"

It came from behind her, from Leo, but it was little more than a dreamy and distant whisper inside her head.

"Mom, wait…"

She exhaled, her eyes rolling upward to spot the glint of the blade in her periphery. A swift forward motion sank it deep into Ezra's leg, perfectly choreographed with Leo's prayer of *please*.

At first, Ezra blinked down with a stunned sort of gasp. Poppy had shoved that knife down to its hilt, careful with her aim. She could read his agony, but she also made out the confusion that flashed across his face. Because if she'd meant to kill him, why hadn't she stabbed him in the chest? In the neck? Why hadn't she repeated what she'd done with Felix and slashed his throat?

Poppy scooted away from him, her hands sliding through Gemma's blood as she pushed herself away. It was then, as she put distance between herself and Ezra, that she saw panic sweep across his face.

Distracted by the knife sheathed deep within his flesh, his hands instinctively flew to its handle. In a growing frenzy, he did what came naturally, and just as one would swipe an insect off their arm, Ezra yanked the knife out of its resting place and let it skitter across the floorboards. There was no thought to whether he should keep it close at hand, whether he would need to protect himself from another attack; not a hint of retaliation marring the alarm that had settled into the corners of his eyes. But it wouldn't have mattered if revenge had crossed his mind.

Poppy settled in next to Leo and tucked his head against her shoulder. "Don't look," she whispered into his hair. "It's going to be okay," she told him. "Just don't look."

It wouldn't take long. Half a minute, maybe. Just enough time for Poppy to say her goodbyes.

LEO

IT DIDN'T TAKE MUCH to distract him. All he had to do was picture Julien's taillights cutting through the dark—a glowing ribbon of red levitating a few feet off the ground, unspooling along the road until the highway cut right while the crimson band continued straight ahead. There, among a copse of trees, that glowing slash of carmine became a glorious tangle, like party streamers exploding in the air. There, on the outskirts of the woods, midnight was as bright as a blazing bonfire. Too glorious for Leo's father to approach. Too beautiful for him to comprehend. Too transcendent for a coward like Leo's dad to go near, fearing that the red would wrap around him, gag him, steal his breath for what he'd done. He would be afraid of it cinching around his wrists and ankles. Pulling him down, down, down into the earth, down to the place of wailing fire. Down to where he belonged.

Leo believed in forgiveness, but his father's sin was beyond pardon. Had it been an accident, his dad would have called the police and waited for the ambulance to arrive. He would have wept into his hands as the paramedics rushed Julien off to the nearest hospital. Had it been an accident, Leo would have felt differently. His dad would have been deserving of redemption.

But instead, Leo's father had sat stoic at the dinner table a few nights after Julien had wrecked his car while Leo had stared down at his plate, doing his damnedest not to scream or vomit or explode into hysterical tears. After dinner, his father had placed a hand on his shoulder in passing, as if to say *it'll all work itself out, son. These sorts of things always do,* hammering home that age-old adage: everything happens for a reason. As though somehow, somewhere, some good would come from Leo losing his closest friend to a violent end. As though watching Felix snap his sister's neck would make Leo a better person. As though seeing his mother commit patricide would somehow enrich his life.

And Leo's mother? Even if she wasn't convicted of a crime, she'd draw the curtains over the house's every window and waste away inside its gloomy depths. She'd start to drink, or maybe dope herself up with various medications. And then, one day, bad news would reach Leo all the way out in paradise. Somehow, it would find him. Bad news always finds a way.

Leo knew he wasn't responsible for what surrounded him now. He wasn't answerable for Lark or Felix. Not even for his dad. But his mother's death would be on him. It would be his fault, if only for the fact that he was the only one left to shoulder the blame.

His mother had done what she'd done for Lark, for him. But it was also for Julien. It was her attempt to right a wrong, her way of saying, *I did everything I could to vanquish all this pain.* That pain, rooted in a night when Leo's father had undoubtedly hoped Julien had died on impact. That pain, born of arrogant certainty that Julien would be buried not a week later. Unfortunately for Leo's father, he had never taken the time to get to know Julien. If he had, he would have known that he was a tenacious motherfucker. If everything happened for a reason, there was a reason Julien hadn't died that night.

Let's see what the hell else is out there, he had said. *Otherwise, what's the point?*

For Leo to watch his mother spiral into unfathomable depression?

To be confronted with altars of photographs and candles burning in Lark's memory?

To know the father he'd once thought himself lucky to have was a shuddering, shivering, convulsing lie?

That isn't what Julien would have wanted for him. Not in a million years.

What Julien would have wanted was for Leo to pack up his shit, board a plane, and not look back. He'd want Leo to live big, not barely. Like a burst of glowing red streamers slashing across the night sky.

There's a way out, he could hear Julien insist. A way out of this darkness, a way to set Leo and his mother free. Leo just had to find it.

Find it, Leo. Find it...

Find it the way he and Lark had been determined to find Felix and Gemma's boat. Because it had to be out there, and now with no one to avoid, there was nothing to fear. All it would take was skimming the island's perimeter and both he and his mother could be off that rock, gone for good. Gone, away from it all…

His gaze settled upon his sister, and for a flash of a moment he pictured tossing her over his shoulder and hauling her out of that house, pictured them taking her back to a place where she could get the sendoff she deserved. But if Leo knew anything, it was that crematoriums didn't take walk-ins and cemetery groundkeepers weren't keen on accepting undocumented bodies. The police would be called. It would all circle back to where they sat now, to the very moment in time where a choice had been made, a decision that involved leaving his kid sister behind.

"Mom." Leo spoke into the eerie silence, soundless beneath the rain that refused to stop. "We have to go."

For a moment, he wasn't sure whether his mother had heard him. She didn't respond, only sat there with her arms around him, her eyes fixed on a random spot on the blood-splattered floor. She was already starting to fade, becoming a ghost before his very eyes. She was following in his footsteps, losing herself in tragedy, unmoored by emotions that came in drowning waves.

"Mom," he repeated. "Look at me."

He waited a moment, and eventually his mother tipped her chin up and met his eyes.

"We can't stay here," he told her. "This…" He motioned around them. "It won't go away. This will swallow us both."

"That's why you go," Poppy told him, her slick fingers squeezing his forearm. "You were never here."

"What?" Leo shook his head at the suggestion. "Mom, no."

"You're right, Leo," she said. "You're always right. This won't go away. It's too much."

"Which is why we're leaving," Leo said, pausing against the flash of pain radiating from between his ribs before gathering himself up off the ground. "Together."

The hidden gash beneath his shirt shrieked with even the slightest movement. His ankle raged at the weight it suddenly had to support. Leo had no idea what sort of damage Felix had done when he'd stuck him with that knife, but that was of no consequence now. If it was serious, he had to get to a hospital. That, and his mom had injuries, too. He could tell by the way she lurched when she walked. The back of her cardigan was covered in blood. Staying meant dying. All the more reason for them to go as soon as they could.

"Lark and I were going to look for their boat," Leo told her. "It has to be moored out there somewhere, probably on the other side of the trees."

The mention of Lark's name had his mother gazing toward her daughter's body. Leo regretted speaking it immediately, watching his mother cover her face and weep.

"Mom." Crouched beside her, he nearly lost his footing on a floor slick as a frozen lake, Julien's fists pounding the ice beneath his feet. His wounded ankle crackled with agony, every spark of pain biting hard into damaged nerves, his entire leg throbbing like a beating heart.

"Mom, listen." With his hands on her shoulders and his teeth gnashed for composure, he waited for her to look up. It took her a good minute, but she finally did, more than likely forcing her eyes up at him when she realized he wasn't moving, that he'd wait until she gave in. "We both need to go to the hospital," he told her. "We need to make sure we're okay, and we need to do it soon." If she wasn't compelled to leave on account of a murder charge, then maybe self-preservation would do the trick. "We can come back…" he said, convincing himself it wasn't a flat-out lie; assuring himself that he'd talk her out of wanting to return if he could just get her down the pier.

But that wouldn't be necessary. He read the recognition in his mother's eyes. She knew she was being coerced. Of course she did. Leo's gaze shifted, lingering upon his father's corpse.

"I'm not leaving without you," he said, looking back to her, "but I need to leave."

It was then that he lifted up his shirt, afraid to see whatever was hiding beneath the fabric. What he discovered was an angry and oozing wound, too bloody to make out just how severe it truly was. The red trailed down his torso, lessening around the waistband of his jeans, inevitably soaking into his underwear and snaking down his left leg.

"Please, get up," he told her. "We need to go, Mom. Now."

Leo limped away from her, hoping that putting physical distance between them would allow reality to set in. He was sure she understood that they couldn't stay. The life they'd arrived with no longer existed. It had already left the island, gone into the dark.

POPPY

HE'S RIGHT. You know he's right.

She repeated it inside her head like a mantra, praying that if she thought it enough, it would give her strength to gather herself up off the floor and approach the open kitchen door.

But she kept looking back to Lark, her gaze forever snagging on the smallest details. The way a piece of Lark's hair had settled in a perfect 'o' near her face. The way the fingers of her right hand curled up ever-so-delicately as if awaiting a shard of magic, a piece of something beyond the ugliness of the world that would make her eyes flutter open and force air into her lungs.

How was Poppy supposed to leave her lying there? The mere idea of it made her want to beat her fists against her chest, beat them hard enough to crack open her sternum and pluck out her own heart.

He's right, her mind whispered. *You know he's right...*

And yet...

"I can't," she sobbed. "I'm sorry, Leo. I can't leave her. You go. Please."

"Mom—"

She shot a look up at him, determined to chase him off into the rain, to scare him into fleeing without ever looking back.

"Stop arguing and *listen* to me for once!" she shouted past her tears. "I'm your *mother!*"

Leo stiffened, startled by her volume, her insistence.

"It doesn't matter if we both go or if only one goes, Leo. I told you, it's too much. They'll look for us, don't you understand? This is a massacre. They can have me, but not you," she said, her voice dropping to a whisper a moment later. "Thank goodness you stayed behind at home. I begged you to come. Pleaded. But you can't talk sense into some kids. You were never here, Leo. Thank god, you were never here."

Coiling her arms around herself, she let her forehead kiss her knees. She waited for him to protest, but when all she heard was the sound of rain, a glimmer of hope slashed across the dark plane of her metastasizing grief. Perhaps she had gotten through to him. Maybe, as his last act of love for her, he would turn away from that house and step into the night. Each ticking second of quiet assured her he was gone, but it also tempted her to look up, to make sure she was alone among the dead.

"Please be gone," she whispered into her knees. If he was, everything she'd ever loved would be obliterated from her life. The police could come, they could drag her to jail. The state could strap her into an electric chair. Torture her until her final moment on earth. And still, she'd thank them as she died, because no agony could be worse than the pain she knew she'd face in the coming days. Hell, in the next few hours. In the minutes, seconds, fractions of seconds after she looked up and saw an empty doorway, the final half of her heart having gone. *But at least he'll be saved,* she thought. And in her darkest hours, she'd picture him out there somewhere, hiking a jungle trail or swimming in a lagoon. She'd imagine him laughing, basking in the glow of the sun. She'd will him alive. Gloriously alive. Lost to her but out there, taking in the wonders the world had to offer, seeing nothing but beauty because all she could see was despair.

"Please be gone," she repeated, then dared to look up.

Leo wasn't gone. He was exactly where she'd left him, staring back at her, startling her in how he simultaneously appeared older in his determination and heartbreakingly young in his fear. For half an instant, she hardly recognized him, but she was familiar with the expression he wore. She'd witnessed it throughout his life—a look that said, *I have an idea.* A look that assured her that amid the chaos that surrounded them, he'd come up with a plan.

She swallowed against the lump in her throat and took in his posture. Clearly in pain, he still managed to appear resolute in whatever scheme he'd hatched. And then there was the boat paddle held fast in his hands, the one Lark had held only moments before she'd been cut down.

"What—"

Before Poppy could form a coherent question, Leo's eyes flashed, stern and unwavering.

"You're wrong," he told her, "I was here. We both were. And we still are."

She scrambled out of his way as he limped past her, past Lark, past Ezra and Felix. He came to a stop next to Gemma's body. Pulling the paddle back over his shoulder, he choked up on the handle the way a baseball player would on a bat.

Poppy's eyes went wide as realization dawned on her.

She opened her mouth and tried to yell at him, tried to scream in protest at his gruesome solution. But before she could gather enough air to eke out the words, he fired Poppy's own words back at her.

"It's going to be okay. Just don't look."

And then, without a hitch of hesitation, he brought the handle's end down hard against Gemma's skull.

RESURRECTION

LEO

LEO GINGERLY SHIFTED his backpack against his left shoulder, then plucked his coffee cup from the airport's Starbucks counter while struggling with his crutch. His gaze paused upon the name that was written in delicate script—the handiwork of the girl who winked at him from behind the espresso machine.

"What happened to your leg?" she asked, trying to drum up conversation.

"Tripped on a tree root," he told her, then shrugged.

"Running away from something?" she joked.

Leo forced a smile. "Something like that," he said, then looked away, because the longer he stood there, the surer he became that this— the airport, the busy terminal, the backpack hanging off his shoulder, tugging at the stitches beneath his shirt—was little more than an illusion, an impossibility, a dream. In reality, he was back in the coffee shop he and Lark had fled in Raven's Head. He was still in Maine, and his kid sister was still alive.

Except, his nightmares assured him that time had continued on, and his sister's absence was a constant reminder that what he and his mother had lived through was real. Leo had woken in a cold sweat every night for the past week, expecting to see Gemma standing over his motel room bed. His eyes would blink open at the scent of black licorice, at the sound of a bay that wasn't there, at the sight of Felix's leering face.

It's not over. It's not.

But it was about to be. A week of hiding was coming to an end. Leo and his mother had abandoned the family car in the lot just shy of Raven's Head port, hitched a ride down to Portland with a guy driving an old red pickup truck. They'd gone to two separate ERs—one for

239

Leo's injuries, one for Mom's, then traveled to a twenty-four-hour rental car place outside the Portland airport. Driving down the coast straight through, they stopped to use restrooms at gas stations only the most desperate of travelers would consider. They didn't go home, but Leo paid Julien's house a final visit. A much-needed catharsis, but also a necessary risk. Leo meant to be in and out within minutes, but he sat in Julien's room for nearly half an hour, staring at the walls. Then, just before stepping out of Julien's house with the items he'd come for— Julien's driver's license, passports, any legal documents he could find— Leo turned, looked into the dark of the house, and spoke. *If you could see me now,* he said. *You wouldn't believe this shit.*

"Well, I hope you have a good trip," the Starbucks girl said, shaking Leo out of his torpor. "...wherever it is you're going, I mean." She gave him a bashful sort of grin. *See you around,* it said. But Leo knew that wouldn't come to pass. He'd never set foot in the Atlanta international airport, or in the state of Georgia again. It was coming to an end, and it was simultaneously empowering and terrifying, because what if it was a mistake? What if he hated Thailand? What if he got there and all he could think about was coming home?

But home no longer existed.

It was a place to which he could never return.

Coffee in hand, he stepped into the brightness of the airport terminal and limped toward his gate, BANGKOK glowing green on the digital screen. With boarding having started over fifteen minutes before, he was one of the final stragglers to make his way toward the ticketing agent standing at the jetway door.

"Hi there," the agent said, nodding toward the venti coffee held fast in Leo's hand. "A flight like this, I'd have done the same thing." The ticket scanner blipped, clearing Leo for boarding. "Need help? I can call down for a wheelchair..."

Leo shook his head. "I'm late as it is," he reminded the agent.

"Take your time," the agent said, "and have a great flight."

"Thanks," Leo said, then stepped into an echo chamber that vibrated beneath his feet.

A smiling flight attendant greeted him at the door, motioning him to the right rather than the left, away from first class. Coming to terms with the fact that this might be the last flight he'd take in a while, Leo almost regretted not splurging on his one-way trip. Perhaps a first-class flight would have been an appropriate farewell to a life once lived. But it was about pinching pennies, now. There would be no collecting his father's life insurance despite it being there for the taking, no sudden emptying of checking and savings accounts regardless of how much money they held, or running up credit cards that had plenty of runway before they were maxed out. He'd taken all of the cash in his father's wallet when his mom hadn't been looking. He'd checked Felix and Gemma's pockets as well. Not counting Gemma and Felix's cards, Leo made out with a whopping eighty-six bucks.

Taking Julien's money had been different. It had been difficult, had left Leo's hands shaking. Julien had spent over two years squirreling cash away for his after-graduation getaway, and it made Leo sick to fold up those bills and slide them into the back pocket of his jeans. But he couldn't turn away from nearly three grand, and he had to believe that Julien wouldn't have wanted him to.

Shuffling down one of the 747's two aisles, Leo struggled with his crutch and coffee, trying to recheck his assigned seat while not spilling his latte all over the plane.

"Here, let me." The flight attendant, having smartly followed close behind, was now reaching out for his boarding pass. "This is you," she said, motioning one row ahead. "And wouldn't you know it, it's the window seat." She clucked her tongue, eyed Leo's air-casted ankle, and then twisted around to search for open seats on what had to be a packed flight. "I'll ask someone to move," she said. "It'll only take a minute. I'm sure I can find a single to—"

Leo cut her off with a shake of the head. "I'll be okay," he told her, embarrassed by all the eyes that were now on him, the huffs and snorts, the eyerolls he could practically hear. "Thanks, though."

He then gave his seatmate—a rather large man in a track suit—a polite smile and nodded toward the window. "This is me," he said.

The guy rose to let Leo pass. The flight attendant took Leo's crutch, collapsed it, and stashed it in the overhead compartment. Leo winced as he limped to his assigned seat, the sutures beneath his jacket pulling tight. Shoving his backpack beneath the chair ahead of him, he dropped the tray table down and set his coffee cup and boarding pass on top. A moment later, the intercom clicked on and a friendly voice filled the cabin.

"Ladies and gentlemen, it's my pleasure to welcome you aboard flight 237, nonstop to Bangkok. My name is Leigh and I'm your chief flight attendant today, with our fabulous Captain Bowden at the helm."

Leo snapped his seatbelt securely around his waist and leaned back in his seat, then closed his eyes and exhaled a shaky breath. It had been an excruciating week, one where he listened to his mother cry in the motel bathroom every night for hours on end. She had bawled even harder when she had handed Leo the cheap pair of scissors she had procured from the closest pharmacy just a day ago. Leo lobbed off his mother's hair while staring at a box of black hair dye sitting on the bathroom counter, thinking of his sister, of how much it would have tickled Lark to see their mother "going goth."

"At this time, we ask that all passengers take their seats, that all seatbelts are fastened, and that seats and tray tables are in their full and upright position."

If this had been happening in an alternate reality, "all passengers" would have been Julien occupying the empty seat next to him. It would have been he and Leo giddy with anticipation as the jet engines began to growl beneath the soles of their shoes. Just two guys, fresh out of high school, starting off on an adventure of a lifetime—the kind of trip that changed a life, that altered trajectories, that made the pulsing red ribbon of existence veer left when it would have otherwise gone right.

Leo had to keep reassuring himself that Julien would be happy it had worked out this way rather than not at all. Because the alternate options made that red ribbon explode in a tangle of chaos at the end of a burning pier.

"Hi, sorry."

Leo opened his eyes at the hoarse apology, his gaze settling upon his mother. She was unrecognizable with her new hair and dark makeup, but that was the point. His mom was giving the guy in the aisle seat a conciliatory look. Meanwhile, their seatmate was unbuckling his seatbelt and rising for a second time, trying not to look annoyed.

Leo's mother carefully slid into her seat while trying not to wince, and eventually exhaled a deep breath.

"Hope this stuff works," she said, shaking a bottle of Dramamine she'd picked up at one of the airport's convenience stores. "Can I have a sip of that?" she asked, nodding toward his coffee. Leo nodded, and as she plucked it off the tray table to take a drink, the intercom clicked on again.

"Cabin crew, prepare for takeoff."

Leo glanced out the window, their seats situated a few yards behind the airplane's massive wing. He fixed his attention on a ground crewmember out on the tarmac, his orange safety vest and matching batons glowing in the fading daylight beyond the window. It would take them nearly twenty-seven hours of travel to reach their destination. Once they got there, he had no idea what would come next. Empowering and terrifying. Exhilarating and awful.

"Sir?"

Leo blinked away from the window and to a flight attendant's smiling face.

"Hi. Could you please stow that table for me?" she asked.

"Yeah, sorry," Leo said, glancing to the open table before him. But he hesitated, his gaze fixed upon his boarding pass. There, printed as boldly as the Starbucks girl's pretty script decorating the side of his cup, was his new name.

Julien Bellamy.

And beside him, his mother. Gemma.

Their new identities, at least until they reached their destination.

Bludgeoned next to his mother, Leo Parrish was dead. Someone would find them all—Lark, with her head turned at a severe angle;

Ezra, lying in a pool of his own blood. They would identify the bodies quickly—Leo's wallet tucked into Felix's back pocket, Poppy's ID and credit cards all left unattended upon the master bedroom dresser. Meanwhile, all of Felix and Gemma's sources of identification would be missing, taken by phantoms, used by ghosts. The police would flounder long enough for Leo and his mother to erase who they used to be. They would become new but remain haunted. They would turn their backs on what they had lived through, but dream the same nightmares until they, too, were gone.

But for now, they were still here. And as the airplane began to roll away from the terminal, Leo reached over and took his mother's hand, trying, if only for a moment, to forget the darkness that had slithered across that bay.

ACKNOWLEDGMENTS

As I type this, *Dark Across the Bay* is the most difficult book I've worked on to date. I often think it's a miracle it exists at all. That said, I owe endless gratitude to a small girl group that kept me both motivated and determined to finish a manuscript that, at times, seemed as though it would never be complete. Sadie Hartmann, you have been Dark's champion since the beginning, and I can't thank you enough. It seems that I also couldn't have messaged you enough in Dark's early days. Hundreds of messages, I bet. Thank you for not blocking me…though if you had, I'd probably have catfished you like you-know-who. To Ashley Saywers, Johann Trotter, and Kallie Weisgarber, thank you for reading my mess of a manuscript and not insisting I toss it in the garbage, then light a match and set said garbage on fire. All of you have become permanents fixtures on my beta reader list. To Dani Jaeger, my comrade in arms and best friend forever, thanks for listening to me bitch and moan for the sixteen or so months it took me to write this thing. If any other book takes me this long again, please put me out of my misery in any fashion of your choosing so long as it's super-mysterious and good for my dark and spooky author image. Of course, there are a few boys to thank as well. To Paul Miller, I would have never written Dark if it hadn't been for you pushing me to write *something* for Earthling. Let's forget I was expected to write Halloween horror and hit you with this weird thriller instead. You have been fantastic to work with. Perhaps we can do it again someday. To my husband, Will, thank you for not divorcing me during two and a half years of baby chasing plus a full year of pandemic-based solitary confinement. Not ideal conditions for ingenious creativity. Weird, right? To my kiddo, R, you're only two now, but maybe you'll read this someday. Whatever you're stuck on, know that you can push through.

This book is proof that perseverance reaps the rewards, no matter how daunting the task. Also, don't forget to wash your hands and sneeze into your elbow. And as always, to my ever-present readers, thank you all for your continued enthusiasm and support. You guys are the best.

Ania Ahlborn
March 9th, 2021
Greenville, South Carolina

Made in the USA
Columbia, SC
09 August 2023

21438664R00155